PLAYING THE PLAYER

BOOK 2 - THE HARTFORD BROTHERS SERIES

JA LOW

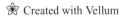 Created with Vellum

Cover Design by Outlined with Love

Editor by Briggs Consulting

Proofreading by More than words

 Created with Vellum

1

NELL

I'm frazzled by the long ass trip from the city to my home in Bridgehampton. *Yes, I recognize it's the end of school, but couldn't you all have delayed till tomorrow to get out of town?* My mood sours by the time I arrive home. I offer my mom a quick hug but don't see Dad anywhere close by; he's probably somewhere down in the stables working.

I shouldn't have had that iced dark chocolate mocha from Starbucks while sitting in traffic because I'm bursting for the toilet. I rush upstairs, taking two at a time, and head down toward my bedroom. During the school year, I live in Manhattan with my mom, while Dad stays up here at the farm training his polo team.

I push through the bedroom door and dash past my bed, through to my en-suite, before twisting the knob and rushing in. "Shit," I curse, looking at an extremely naked Remington Hartford stepping out of the shower.

"What the hell, Nell?" Remi screams at me, snatching his towel from the rail as I dash out the door, stunned.

I've just seen Remington Hartford naked. Oh my god, this cannot be happening to me. My heart beats wildly out of my chest as my cheeks get warm. Tingles flicker across my body. What is wrong with me?

"Nell?" Remi rushes out with a white towel wrapped around his hips. Water droplets fall down his tanned chest. My eyes track the beads as they ripple across his six-pack and melt down into his towel where I now realize lies something I should never have seen.

"What are you doing in my bathroom?" I ask, raising my voice a couple of octaves at him.

"Taking a shower."

"In my shower?" I ask, pointing to my chest. His eyes slip down and seem to notice my newly found cleavage. That's different.

Remi and I have been friends forever. He may be my brother's best friend, but Remi's always been nice to me when he's come over to hang out with him. I've never thought of him as anything more than a second brother until now.

Naked.

In my shower.

And he's never seen me any other way than as Dominic's irritating little sister. Until now, as his eyes wander further south.

"Shit." Remi grabs his crotch and sprints back into the bathroom slamming the door behind him.

What just happened?

My fist bashes against the bathroom door as I call his name repeatedly. "I need the toilet!" I yell as I do a dance, hoping my bladder doesn't explode.

"Hang on," Remi answers sharply. Then, moments later he's dressed again and pushes past me, practically knocking me over.

"Hey," I call out to him, but he's gone.

After finally doing my business, I head over to Dominic's room, where I assume Remi is. This conversation isn't over. I don't even knock as I try my brother's doorknob. I jiggle it twice, but it's locked. I head to the spare bedroom to the right, which shares a bathroom with my brother, and walk right into Remi.

"What the?" I mutter as I bounce off his hard chest.

"Nell?" Remi stares at me in confusion as I take in the spare bedroom and see Remi's things all over the floor.

"Are you staying in here?" I ask, staring up at him with a frown.

"Um, yeah." Remi tilts his head to the side and stares at me.

"For the summer?" I question him.

"No." He shakes his head. "I live here full time."

My entire body stills at his words. Why would Remi be living here full time? Doesn't he have his own family?

"Did your mom not tell you?" he asks softly. I shake my head. "Your dad asked me to join his team full time." Oh. Now I understand. "It was easier. Dom and I will go to school together too."

Wait. He's moved schools too? Why did no one tell me any of this? Why did my brother not tell me?

"I thought you knew," Remi adds.

"I didn't," I reply, shaking my head, hurt that my entire family forgot to mention we have a new houseguest. "Congratulations though," I add, remembering my manners. Remi making my father's polo team is a big deal. He doesn't give spots to anyone just because he's best friends with Remi's dad. Even Dominic had to try out for the team.

"Thanks. I'm looking forward to it. Traveling back and forth from here to the city sucks." He grins, showing off his straight white teeth against his sun-kissed skin. His brown hair flops across his forehead and he gives it a shake, which pushes it back into place. "Look, I'm sorry about before. Your brother has company, so I couldn't use the bathroom, and your room being down the corridor was easier. I didn't think you were getting home till later." He scratches the back of his neck with his hand. "I didn't mean to…"

I wave my hands in front of me, trying to suppress the images of a naked Remi before me. Warmth flushes against my cheeks again as I try to forget all about him. "It's fine."

"Let me guess, Dominic's with Sasha, again?" I ask, changing the subject.

Sasha is my brother's high school girlfriend. She's a mega bitch, whom he's been dating for like a year. Since losing his virginity to her, all they seem to do now is have sex. I don't get what the big deal is about sex. It's not like I haven't done anything with guys before, I have. Just haven't gone all the way. Maybe it's different if you really like the boy. Guess I haven't found anyone I want to lose it to. *Maybe Remi?* Where did that thought come from? Nope. No. I can feel the embarrassment creep up my neck again. I need to get out of here.

"No, not Sasha. It's Claudia."

"Wait, as in Claudia McGee, Sasha's best friend?" My eyes bug out at this bit of gossip.

"Yep." Remi smiles. I know he wasn't a fan of Sasha's either.

"Oh my god, what happened?" I ask, tugging on his arm excitedly.

"Come in and let me give you all the details," Remi states.

I follow and join him on his bed like I have done a million times before, it shouldn't feel weird, but it does now. I'm hoping this weirdness stops.

"Apparently, Sasha has been seeing Danny Grain on the side," Remi explains.

No way! Danny is the captain of the football team, who is Claudia's boyfriend, and one of Dom's friends. This is juicy.

"Understandably, Dom and Claudia were upset, so they hooked up at a party as revenge," Remi fills me in. "But somewhere along the way, they kind of fell for each other."

"No, fricken way." I gasp. Remi just nods in agreement. "Guess Sasha isn't too happy about that?" Remi grins.

"Nope. She's livid and is constantly messaging Dom." What a bitch! "But he's super happy with Claudia and doesn't care."

"Never thought I'd see the day Dom and Sasha broke up." I shake my head in surprise. "Why did he keep this from me?"

"He's a guy. It was hard enough for me to get it out of him," Remi explains.

Still, I'm upset that he didn't text or call me. If Dom kept his socials up to date, then I guess I would have noticed, but he never posts and it's frustrating.

"What about you then? I bet Claudia's friends are excited you're in town." I raise a brow in his direction. Remington Hartford is hot. All the Hartford brothers are, even though they're his older brothers. Remi's only two years older than me; he's turning eighteen later this year, and I'm turning sixteen in a couple of weeks.

"Maybe." He gives me a devilish grin. "But I came here to play polo, not hook up with girls."

Ever since I've known Remi, he's been super focused on his polo career, and now that he has a chance of going professional, I don't think he's going to let some skanky girls distract him.

"And what about you? I bet those city boys are all up in your messages?"

"You know my dad won't let me date till I'm like thirty," I say, rolling my eyes at how overprotective my dad can be.

"He knows what guys are like, that's all."

"Lucky he doesn't live in the city and Mom's cool," I say, grinning at him.

"You better not let some guy pressure you," he warns. Remi's eyes narrow on me as he tries to be all protective. Heat rushes through my cheeks with embarrassment, thinking that he would see me differently than his best friend's little sister. I was wrong.

"It's not any of your business what I do." I rise from his bed, ready to run out of there.

"Nell." Remi stands up and walks over to where I am, his enormous frame dwarfing me. "Boys are assholes, and you're like a sister to me. I don't want any of those fuckers pushing you to do something you don't want to do."

I hate that my stomach sinks at the idea that he sees me as a sister. It's never bothered me before. Why now?

"I'm not talking about this with you." I stare up at him before turning on my heel and disappearing from his room. Thankfully he lets me, and I slam my door shut, locking it for good measure, before flopping down on my bed and screaming into my pillow. This is not how I saw my first day of summer turning out.

After I compose myself, I grab my phone and call my girls, Audrey and Rainn.

"Hey, you made it." Audrey picks up first.

"Yay. You're home." Rainn enters the conversation.

"Girls. I have so much to tell you." The line falls quiet. "I don't even know where to start." I sigh dramatically.

"Spit it out," Rainn states forcefully.

"Fine. I just saw Remington naked." Screams echo down the phone line at my confession.

"How?" Audrey asks.

"Was it big?" Rainn questions.

"Oh my god, Rainn. I don't know," I say, rolling my eyes at my bestie. Not all of us live in a liberal hippie family where sex is talked about healthily.

"Was it long?" She giggles.

"Rainn." Shaking my head at her. "It was… nice."

"Nice?" She seems aghast at my use of word to describe it.

"I don't know, Rainn; I haven't seen many dicks in my life."

"Why was Remi naked?" Audrey asks the burning question.

"He was showering in my bathroom because he lives here now," I tell them.

"He lives with you?" Both girls gasp.

"Yeah. Dad offered him a spot on the team. He's going to go to school with Dom."

"A hundred bucks says Nell gives her virginity to him," Rainn teases.

"What. No. Ew." I scrunch my nose up at that suggestion. "No way, he's like a brother to me."

"But you've seen him naked?" Audrey adds.

"And I bet he looks fine naked." Rainn sighs.

"Oh my god, I called you girls to help me, not complicate things for me." I'm shaking my head at them both.

"You can't tell me that now you've seen him naked that you aren't a little interested?" Rainn pushes the topic.

My mind wanders back to the images of Remi naked, and I don't really remember what we were talking about. "I knew it," Rainn sings happily. "You're thinking about him."

"Am not."

"I think it's going to be an interesting summer." Rainn chuckles.

Gosh, I hate my friends.

2

REMI

There's something seriously wrong with me because I can't stop thinking about my best friend's little sister. The way her brown eyes widened and took me in as I stepped from the shower and her cheeks went a bright red. I liked her not looking away. Hopefully committing it to memory. No. She shouldn't commit anything to memory. What the hell am I saying? She is like a sister to me. *You don't check out your sister the way you do Nell.* I don't even have a sister to check out. Wait. That's not what I mean. This sounds all kinds of wrong.

"Get your head in the game." Dominic clips me over the head with his hand while we train in the arena. This isn't good. I push all thoughts of Nell and her impressive rack that seems to have grown over the school year from my mind while I spend the next couple of hours training.

"Hey, need some help?" Nell catches me off guard as she enters the stalls that I'm mucking out.

"I'm fine," I tell her, gritting my teeth because I don't want to be in close quarters with her while my head is all over the shop. Nell's brows furrow together as she stares at me, probably trying to work out why my tone is short with her.

"What's crawled up your ass?" Nell asks angrily.

I suck in a deep breath, then let it out slowly. "Nothing, just tired and have a heap of work to do before going in for dinner."

"That's why I offered to help." She stands before me with her hands on her hips. She's just come off riding her horse, and she's dressed in a tight-fitting navy polo with tanned jodhpurs that mold to her legs and ass. Lord help me.

"Fine. Just didn't want you to break a nail," I say sarcastically as I shovel the hay into the wheelbarrow.

"You're being a dick; do you know that?" she says with a huff. Then she starts on the stall beside me.

"And I bet you can't stop thinking about mine."

Nell stills beside me; she slowly turns her head and looks over at me. I see pure rage coursing through her body. Her cheeks are bright pink, so maybe there is some merit to my words. Maybe she can't stop thinking about that day like I can't.

"I don't know what's happened to you, Remi, but you've turned into a jerk." She throws down her shovel, and the sound rattles through the stables, startling some ponies while she stomps off. Shit. My attitude isn't Nell's fault. I have flicked some stupid switch in my brain, and now I can't stop thinking about her.

"Nell!" I call after her before she reaches the end of the stables. "Nell!" I call again as I jog after her. She slows her steps before turning around. Her arms are folded across her chest, and I try not to look, but I'm a teenage boy and I just can't help myself.

"What?" Nell asks as she taps her foot in annoyance.

"I'm sorry," I tell her honestly as I run my hand through my hair. "I have some stuff on my mind."

"Are you okay?" Her frown turns from annoyance to concern.

"I will be." I give her a smirk. "I'm not meaning to take it out on you, Nell."

"I thought I did something wrong," she says.

"No," I reply, reassuring her. "It's all me."

"Is it about the shower thing?" she asks. Damn her. She knows me so well.

"No." I shake my head as panic floats over my body.

"Because I was really sorry about that," she starts. "We have to live together, and I don't want things to be weird between us. Especially at the start of summer. I'm looking forward to hanging out with you."

"You are?" I ask, surprised.

"Yeah. Of course. We always hang out during the summer doing horse stuff. Why would this one be any different?"

Of course. What was I thinking? Nothing's changed between us. It's all in my mind. She still sees me as her brother's best friend, nothing more. Obviously seeing my dick had no effect on her, and why would it? It's not magical. I'm letting my hormones cloud my judgment. If Nell Garcia only sees me as a friend, then friends it will be.

"Morning, all," Nell says as she skips into the kitchen, all sunshine and rainbows. Her blonde hair is pulled into a high ponytail, bobbing with each skip she takes. She's wearing nothing but a pink tank top and black shorts that hardly cover her ass. *Do not look, Remi.* Damn it. I look and my dick throbs in appreciation. I need to control him when he's around Nell, especially when her family is present. I'm being a creep and totally disrespecting Mr. and Mrs. Garcia and everything they have done for me, especially opening their home to me. What do I do in return? Lust after their daughter.

"Hey, Remi," Portia, the youngest of the Garcia clan, greets me before elbowing me in the ribs as she passes. I stare down at the little pipsqueak, wondering what she wants. "Close your mouth," she says, giving me a toothy grin.

My mouth automatically shuts, and I glare down at her. Shit. If she noticed my ogling her older sister, then Dom might notice too. I know I will never hear the end of it if he does. Portia skips away delighted with herself, takes a seat at the kitchen table, and starts filling her plate with stacks of pancakes.

"You want a juice?" Dom calls out to me as he stares inside his fridge. His voice pulls me from my thoughts. *Get it together, Remi,* I chastise myself. You have an entire summer with this family; you need to put Nell Garcia back into the best friend's little sister box along with Portia.

"Yeah, man, that'd be great," I say, finally finding my words and walking over to where the buffet of breakfast foods is laid out on the kitchen counter.

"Want some bacon?" Nell asks me as she's waving the crispy strips at me.

"Sure," I answer. My words come out croakily like they used to do when my voice was breaking. Dom gives me a weird look as he hands me a glass of OJ. His brown eyes narrow on me as he looks at me then his sister. Anger flares behind his eyes and I know I'm busted. He's going to rip me a new one when we are alone next.

"I'll see you boys in the stables in twenty," Mr. Garcia warns us as he places his dishes in the sink before walking out the door and leaving us kids alone to eat breakfast.

"Keep your eyes off my sister," Dom erupts, silencing the room. Nell drops her fork on her plate, and the sound echoes through the kitchen. Portia giggles as she keeps shoveling pancakes into her mouth.

"I don't know what you're talking about," I say to him, playing dumb.

"Dom, what the hell?" Nell demands.

"I don't like the way he's looking at you," he says. Those brown eyes narrow on me, and I know he will take it out on me this morning when we practice.

"Dom, you've lost your mind this morning. Remi has done nothing wrong. I think you're the only one seeing something there that isn't," Nell says crisply.

Dom looks between Nell and me and doesn't seem convinced.

"Remi thinks Nell's gross," Portia adds dryly.

"Never touch my fucking sister. You hear me?" Dom warns harshly.

I throw my hands up in the air, promising I won't. He mumbles something before storming out of the kitchen, Portia hot on his tail.

"What has gotten into him this morning?" Nell asks awkwardly.

I shrug my shoulders because, if I'm honest, I'm shell-shocked by what just happened.

"You did nothing."

Other than check her ass out, no, nothing at all.

"I'm sorry my brother was a dick to you," she says, giving me a small smile. "I'll talk to him. Tell him he's being insane, that there is nothing and never will be anything between us. We're just friends, right?" she asks warily.

"Yeah, friends," I say, agreeing quickly. It's for the best, especially with the way Dominic's reacted over me being around Nell. Imagine if he knew I've already flashed her. He would kill me.

"I've lost my appetite, anyway. I might as well sort my brother out." She sighs. "Don't worry, it's all a giant misunderstanding." Nell gives me another small smile and disappears out of the kitchen too, leaving me standing alone, bewildered over how my morning has started.

NELL

"I think Remi is purposefully ignoring me, Sparkles," I say, grumbling to my horse as I brush her down. She gives me a grunt of understanding. "I don't blame him, especially after the way Dom reacted the other day at breakfast," I explain to her. "He got all upset when he thought Remi was checking me out. He wasn't. I mean, I don't think he was. Why would he? Look at me?" I ask Sparkles.

She turns her head and gives me a gentle nudge, making me smile. Remi's going to be eighteen soon. The last thing he is going to be thinking about is hooking up with a sixteen-year-old; he's probably going to go after some college girl or even a MILF. There are plenty of other guys out there for me, closer to my age. Thinking anything will happen between us is stupid. He wouldn't do anything to jeopardize his friendship with my brother or his place on the polo team by starting up something with me.

"I've never seen a naked guy before, Sparkles," I confess to my horse. "I've done things with guys, but that's usually been with our clothes on, never you know… the full show," I tell her. Brushing my horse is therapy for me. Sparkles is used to me coming in and dropping my deepest and darkest secrets to her. She has given me some excellent advice in the past, and at least I know I can trust her not to open her trap to anyone. "Seeing Remi naked shouldn't change things, should it?" I question Sparkles. She gives me a gentle nudge, which makes me laugh. "Now I understand why girls find him attractive." I let out a heavy sigh as I continue the long strokes across Sparkles. "I don't want to find him attractive though, Sparkles. I can't find him attractive. There's no point torturing myself like that. Nothing will ever happen."

"What makes you say that?"

I scream so loud hearing Remi's voice that I spook Sparkles and she rears up and knocks me over.

"Shit, Nell." Remi races toward me where I lay in the hay with Sparkles huffing beside me frantically. Her wet nose nudges me, checking to see if I'm okay after scaring her.

"I'm sorry, sweetheart," I say rubbing her nose, reassuring her it wasn't her fault that I screamed hearing the boy I was talking to my horse about had just heard my entire conversation. I'm mortified. I'd wished Sparkles had knocked me out so I could have amnesia and forget any of this happened.

"Are you okay?" Remi asks. His green eyes looking over me, checking to see if I've broken anything.

"I'm fine. No thanks to you!" I yell at him as I push myself up off the barn floor, shaking off bits of hay stuck to me. "What the hell were you thinking?"

Remi stands there, dumbstruck by my question.

"I'm so sorry, my sweetheart," I whisper into Sparkle's ear. She gives me a quick kiss on the cheek before going back to her feed.

Turning around, I push my way past Remi and out of the stall, away from his imposing presence. I'm waiting for the ground to swallow me up whole because I'm never going to recover from this embarrassment.

"Nell," Remi calls after me. I ignore him. He is the last person I want to see or hear from. "Nell, please," he calls after me again. Nope, not today, Satan. As my feet take off in a run and I head toward the woods, I'm hoping he doesn't follow me. "Nell, come on!" Remi screams, but I push my legs harder, every muscle aching with exertion, and I think at any moment they are going to give out from under me. Then Remi's hand wraps around my arm and halts me. I twirl around, and we both take a moment to gather our breaths. "What the hell, Nell?" Remi asks as he doubles over and catches his breath. "Why did you run?"

"Why do you think?" I ask him. Is he dense? "How much did you hear?"

Remi's hand reaches behind him, and he scratches his neck, a nervous tell, but he doesn't answer me, and his eyes can't meet mine. They seem to have found something interesting in the dirt at his feet. I call his name again.

"Remi?"

"What do you want me to say, Nell? You're already embarrassed." Those green eyes settle on me, turning my insides to liquid. Heat crawls over my skin as I shuffle my feet from side to side nervously.

"Then say nothing!" I yell at him. "Forget everything you heard and leave me alone." Tears prick my eyes, but I refuse to cry in front of him.

"But I can't, Nell, that's the thing," he says, rubbing his chin. "I can't seem to stop thinking about you."

Oh. Everything inside me stills. Did I just hear him correctly?

"I shouldn't be here in the woods alone with you," he tells me. "Your brother would kill me. He already suspects that I have a thing for you."

Did Remi just say he has a thing for me? Heat blossoms inside my chest. "A thing for me?" I ask awkwardly, the words tumbling from my lips before I realize what I am asking.

Remi takes a couple of steps closer to me, those green eyes swirling with flecks of gold, as they never leave me. My mouth is dry as I try to swallow the nerves down my stubborn throat.

"I can't stop thinking about you, Nell."

My mouth forms an O in surprise at his confession. Tingles lace my body as heat pumps through my veins.

"It's wrong, I know, but..." He reaches out and pushes my hair behind my ear. "I can't stop it." I lick my lips nervously as his hungry eyes devour me. "Dom would kill me if he knew I was here."

Oh yes, he would, and so would my father, but I don't care. My insides are doing somersaults as Remi steps closer to me. Is he going to kiss me? Do I want him to kiss me? His hand cups my face and this is it. This is the moment that I feel what it's like to kiss Remington Hartford. My eyes flutter shut for the barest of moments waiting for the pressure of his lips against mine, but it doesn't come. Why is he not kissing me? Opening my eyes, I see Remi is frowning. Oh, did I read this all wrong? Was he just being nice? Humiliation quickly replaces the heat traveling over my body, and I take a step away from him.

"I'm sorry, Nell. I can't."

His words sting like a wasp. "Screw you," I spit back at him. "Screw you, Remington Hartford." I push against his chest, making him stumble back a couple of steps. "Leave me alone!" I scream. The first trickles of tears fall across my cheeks. Remi's face softens, and I can see the anguish my tears are causing him. Well, screw him. "Please, leave me alone," I beg.

"I didn't mean to hurt you, Nell," he says.

"Well, you have." I sob helplessly. He gives me another frown, and I can see he's torn between doing as I ask and trying to make things right. I turn my back to him not wanting to see his handsome face anymore, and wrap my arms around myself tightly and cry. This will be the only time I will ever cry about a boy like him ever again.

4

NELL

"I t's your birthday, bitch!" Rainn says, squealing and hauling me into her arms as she arrives at my home for the weekend to celebrate my sixteenth birthday.

"Happy birthday, boo," Audrey adds as she hugs me too.

"I am so happy to see you both," I tell them, grinning from ear to ear. It feels good to have the girls back together again. I've missed them so much during these holidays, especially since I have seen little of Remi since that fateful day in the woods—not that I want to see him. "We have so much to catch up on. Come on, let's go to my room."

The girls grab their bags and follow me up the grand staircase to the top level where my bedroom is. I flop onto my bed, and the girls throw their bags to the floor, but before Audrey locks the door, Portia is standing there grinning at us all.

"Portia, go away!" I yell at my little sister, who precedes to poke her tongue out at me. She's so annoying. "Portia, I'm telling Mom."

"Whatever. You're just going to moan about Remi not liking you," Portia says, grumbling as she makes gagging sounds at me.

"Get out!" I scream while throwing a pillow at her, which

makes her laugh louder. Thankfully, Audrey shuts the door, locking her out of my room. Doesn't she have friends of her own?

"What was that all about?" Rainn asks while taking a seat on my swing chair and folding her long, tanned legs up underneath her as she sways back and forth. I hadn't told my friends about my humiliation because I wanted to strike it from my mind.

"Remi and I had a moment in the woods…" I say. They both stare at me. "I thought he was going to kiss me, but he didn't. Actually, he said he couldn't, and left me hanging. I've never been so humiliated before, guys," I explain to them.

"Oh, babe, I'm so sorry," Audrey says comfortingly as she takes a seat beside me on the bed.

"You realize there are going to be a ton of hot guys at your party tonight?" Rainn says, smiling. "By the end of the night you are going to forget who Remington Hartford is." Wishful thinking, but maybe she's right.

"I'm surprised you haven't run into anyone up here yet. Everyone from school is here for the summer," Audrey says.

"I've been in a funk and mainly just hung out with my horses for the last couple of weeks," I explain quietly to them.

"This will not do at all." Rainn huffs. "Nell Garcia doesn't pine after a guy. None of us do. They are the ones who are supposed to be pining after us." She jumps up off the swing chair and leaps into action. "What are you wearing tonight?" she asks.

"Um…" I get up from the bed, walk into my closet, and bring out a pink dress Mom picked for me and show them.

"No," Rainn says with disapproval. She shakes her head, looking at the offending garment.

"What's wrong with it?" I ask, wondering what is wrong with the dress. I thought it was cute.

"It looks like something Portia would wear," Rainn says dryly.

"I think it's cute," Audrey adds, always the peacemaker.

"Exactly, *cute*. She's sixteen. She needs something sexy. Something that is going to knock the boys out when they see her arrive at the party."

Rainn comes from a family who is all in touch with their sexuality and bodies. They openly talk about sex and pleasure over dinner—talk about awkward—but that is not my family. As progressive as my dad is, he is still a Latin dad, and his baby girl will not go out dressed like a hoochie momma under his watch. His words not mine.

"You're forgetting one important step in that plan. My dad."

Rainn frowns, then realization kicks in and she nods in understanding. "You did the traditional dress last year for your quinceañera. But I promise we will find something Daddy approved."

"Why did she make that sound sexual?" I say, turning to look at Audrey.

After a quick trip to the shops to get my new sweet sixteen dress, we arrive home to the entire house taken over by the event planners and caterers. People are running here, there, and everywhere through the house.

"Where the hell have you girls been?" Mom snaps irritably. "Hair and make-up have been waiting nearly an hour for you girls to show up. Get upstairs and get ready, please."

Oops, we lost track of time while we were out, but thankfully it looks like Mom went first so we haven't wasted too much of their time.

Hours later, we are done, and all that's left is for me to get dressed and be the belle of the ball. I've been getting tags and messages all day from people following us online. Thankfully, they have all wished me many happy returns, and I have had no hate messages yet. Since my social media profile has started to grow, the trolls and mean girls have increased, especially when I am excited about something they usually like to try and knock me down with their hateful comments. It's hard. I try to ignore them, but sometimes a comment will slip through my defenses.

"Hurry up and get dressed. We need to take photos before you go downstairs," Rainn says impatiently.

"Okay, I'm going." I rush into my walk-in closet, grab the dress hanging up in there, and head on into my bathroom to get dressed. It is a little out there for me, some might say a little pageant-like, but I feel grown up when I put it on. With its pastel pink sequins and feathers on the hem, a deep V showing off my growing assets, and a deep dip in the back. My father is going to die, but I felt beautiful in the dress when I tried it on, and I guess that's all that matters when it comes to clothes. I step back out into my bedroom and look over at my friends' faces to gauge their reactions. Silence fills the room. Oh no. I look like shit, don't I? I look down and smooth out the sequins, wondering if I have time to rush back into my closet and get changed back into the original dress.

"You look breathtaking, Nell." Audrey gasps as her hands press against her lips in awe.

"You're a goddess," Rainn adds.

I give my friends a giggly twirl, and they give me an applause of appreciation. "Are we sure this is it?" I ask.

"Yes," they agree in unison. Okay then, I guess it's time for me to make my arrival.

"Quick, some photos first," Audrey states. We pose for the next ten minutes, filling up our phones with photos we won't post yet, not until I have made my grand entrance into the party.

As I step out of the room, Portia is there waiting for me. Her green eyes widen as she takes in my change of attire.

"Mom and Dad are going to be upset," she says, looking smug.

"Would you stop it?" Rainn says sternly.

I ignore my little sister. I will not let her ruin tonight for me as we head toward the grand staircase where my parents want me to take photos.

"She's ready!" Portia calls out from the top of the stairs before she quickly goes down them, joining my family at the bottom.

"You've got this," Audrey tells me, giving me the strength to go down the stairs. I suck in a deep breath and propel myself forward to the edge of the staircase. I look down the grand staircase to where my family is standing. I see my parents and my brother and sister standing at the bottom of the stairs with enormous smiles on their faces, waiting for me to descend. My parents have their phones ready to capture the moment of prosperity. Gripping the rail beside me tightly as I take the first steps in my heels down the grand staircase, one by one I focus on not falling down them. No one wants broken bones on their special night.

"Sweetheart, you look gorgeous." My mother gasps. Tears well in her eyes as she sees me for the first time.

A frown forms on my father's face. "My love, that is not the dress we bought her for tonight," he questions my mother, not me.

"Hush now. Do not cause a scene. Your daughter looks beautiful, and it's her night," she says strongly. My father nods, looks back up at me, and gives me a blinding smile, his phone ready to take photos.

"Stop right there, sweetheart. We need to take some photos. Smile!" she shouts up at me. I do as I'm told posing for their photos until movement out of the corner of my eyes catches my attention. My face falls and my stomach tightens when I see who has joined the family, Remi. Those green eyes land on me and I swear my legs quake as he unashamedly looks me over. A smirk falls across his luscious lips; how dare he have the gall to shoot me a wink too. He looks handsome dressed in dark denim, with a white button-down shirt. His sleeves are rolled up, showing off his tanned, muscular forearms. I take the next step, but because he's turned me into a flustered mess, I almost miss it and wobble. I can hear gasps from below. *That was close.* Ugh, why did Remi have to come in and spoil everything again?

Why does he have to be here? He's not family.

Eventually I make it down the stairs, and my parents embrace me, wishing me a happy birthday and telling me how beautiful and proud of me they are, which warms my heart. Dominic grumbles with felicitations and Portia pokes a tongue out at me. Remi doesn't say a word; he keeps staring at me intensely, it's a little unnerving.

My father grabs my hand and entwines it with his. "Come, come, ladies. It's time to celebrate Nell," he says as he pulls me through the house and toward the back of our home where I watched the event team set up the massive white tent in the middle of the backyard. Underneath that, scattered across the lawn, are multiple small boho tents which are filled with a heap of cushions scattered all over the floor. I can't wait to relax in one of them with my friends while scoping out the hotties that walk by. They also built a clear dancefloor over our pool and dropped hundreds of LED flowers into the water so that the light can shine through while you dance. I can't wait to see that when it's completely dark.

My father brings me to the back door where a curtain of fairy lights cascades before me, then I hear the tap of a microphone and someone clearing their throat. The outside noise slowly turns down to a dull hum.

"It's time to welcome the birthday girl to her party. Happy sweet sixteen, Nell!" the MC yells through the sound system, practically bursting my eardrums. I can hear everyone outside hollering and calling for me. My father helps me through the curtain of fairy lights out to the back deck area, and I'm blown away by the hundreds of people scattered before me. Wow. People are clapping, they whistle, they're waving. I'm giddy with excitement. My dad holds my hand as we walk down the red carpet toward my party. Flashes are going off all around me as a photographer captures the memories of the family.

"Have fun, sweetheart." My father kisses my cheek and heads on over to where all the adults are congregating. Once the oldies have gone, I'm inundated with congratulations from all my friends. I can't believe so many people made it.

It's a long time until I can sit down in the tent with Rainn and Audrey, but we eventually procure one and I kick off my heels, which are killing me. I had grabbed a donut from the donut wall on my way and am currently shoving it into my mouth. It tastes delicious.

"This party is amazing," Rainn states, leaning back against the cushions, looking like an exotic queen.

"I still can't believe your parents organized for the Sons of Brooklyn guys to come play at your birthday party. That is so freaking amazing." Audrey squeals. Not going to lie, I almost passed out when they walked out on stage. They are our favorite band of all time. I died when they called me on stage and sang to me, then hugged and kissed me. *Le sigh.* I'm so in love with them.

"They were so hot," I say. Taking another bite of my donut. "I wish I wasn't sixteen because I'd happily let any one of them take me home."

"They've all got partners, Nell," Audrey tells me, bursting my bubble.

"Whatever, a girl can dream on her birthday."

"You could have your pick of anyone here tonight, you know," Rainn adds. "Have you noticed anyone tonight or is a certain polo player still on your mind?"

"I told you never to speak of him again," I shoot back at her.

Rainn holds her hands up and gives me a smirk. "He hasn't been able to keep his eyes off you all night," she admits aloud. I hate the tiny thrill of excitement I get over her words that

Remi hasn't been able to stop staring at me. He doesn't deserve it.

"Tad Waltham seems equally impressed with you tonight," Audrey tells me, giving me an alternative to Remi. Tad is one of the most popular guys at our school. He's captain of the lacrosse team, he's on the swim team also, he's rich, good looking, and his parents own some of the hottest bars in Manhattan. He has the connections, but he's a bit of a douche, nothing unusual for the guys we go to school with. Did I mention he's cute? He could be a prospect tonight. I will not end my birthday without a kiss and Tad is perfect for one night. I definitely do not see him as anything more. He's not boyfriend material, not the way he goes through girls, but I've heard he knows how to kiss and that's all I could wish for tonight.

"Hey, sweetheart, it's time for your present." Mom pops her head into the tent, surprising us. Her face lights up in a grin as she holds out her hand for me. Reluctantly I get back up from the mountain of cushions and slip my aching feet into my heels again and head on out to the back driveway where my father is standing next to the MC. Then moments later, the honking of a horn fills the party and I still. Oh, my god. No, they didn't. It was the car that I've been asking for! A Mercedes convertible in silver with a massive pink bow on the front.

"Happy birthday, princess," Dad says while Mom nods in agreement.

Dominic is driving the car and stops it right in front of me. "Happy birthday, Nell," he says happily as he gives me a hug. Tears fall down my cheeks as I'm overcome with excitement. Dom hands me the keys, and I jump in. Rainn and Audrey join in behind me. I honk the horn with excitement, making everyone laugh.

Best birthday ever.

"You looked hot in your car, Nell," Tad says, winking at me. I know that I'm supposed to be swooning over Tad giving me attention because any of the girls here at the party tonight would be interested, but my butterflies are silent. Are they broken?

"Thanks."

"Did you want to dance?" Tad asks. I nod, and he takes my hand and walks me over to the glass floor. He pulls me tight against him, and I can feel every inch of his muscular chest. The same one the girls swoon over when he pulls his shirt off during swim training, showing off his six-pack abs. I know I should feel something, but I don't.

What is going on with my lady bits?

5

REMI

N ell looks stunning tonight, and that dress is sinful. My dick's been hard all night thinking about her. She's still upset with me, and I get it. I overheard a personal conversation between her and Sparkles. Then I confess my attraction to her and told her nothing could ever happen, further humiliating her in my presence. I didn't mean to. I said the words out loud, more for my benefit than hers because I was moments away from pushing her up against the tree and kissing her, thus ruining everything forever. Maybe I should have because I've ended up in the same place I was trying to avoid except without the good memories. Dominic's been riding my ass anytime I look Nell's way, and it's annoying as fuck. Does he not trust me? *You spend every night with your dick in your hand and her name on your lips—of course he can't trust you.*

And now I'm sitting here watching Nell dance with some preppy douche who has wandering hands. Is this what she is in to?

"Hey, you're Dom's friend, aren't you?" a beautiful blonde asks as she sits down beside me on the cushions. "I'm Britney," she says, looking at me with hungry blue eyes.

"Remi." My eyes never leave where Nell is dancing.

"Are you having fun?" she asks cheerfully. The girl's pretty enough, but I'm not interested; another blonde is occupying my thoughts.

"Sure, I guess," I answer.

"Nell looks gorgeous tonight, doesn't she?" Britney asks, following my line of sight. I take a sip of my drink and ignore the turbulence in my stomach over her question. "Tad's always had a crush on her. Guess he's finally going for it." Now she has my attention. I turn and look over at her. She gives me a bright smile before licking her lips.

"Is Tad a good guy?"

"Yeah, I guess," she answers, puzzled, shrugging her shoulders at my abrupt question. "Every girl at this party probably wishes they were Nell at this moment, having Tad's undivided attention." Britney lets out a small sigh. Is she jealous? "If they are still together when we get back to school, those two are going to be the 'it' couple," Britney adds.

If they are still together? Did he ask her out? I thought they were just dancing. No, she can't date him. I won't allow it; he's not good enough for her. *And you are?* Maybe. Dom will kill you if you date her. This is very true he would, but...no, you came here to concentrate on polo, not girls. This is your career. The whole point you packed up your life and moved to Bridgehampton to train with the Garcias. My head is all over the place when it comes to Nell, which means I should probably forget about it. As I turn and look back out to the dance floor, I notice that the two of them have disappeared. Sitting up, I scan the surrounding area to see where they have gone. Shit. I know guys like Tad; he's probably whispered things into her ear and persuaded her to go into the woods with him. He's probably got his slimy hands all over her. No. I won't allow it.

"Sorry, I have to go," I say. Britney just stares at me as if I've lost my mind and maybe I have. I frantically look for Nell and

Tad; they couldn't have gone far. I scan the wooded area off from the dancefloor, but I can't see anyone, then I hear a giggle, and I rush toward the darkness and halt when I see two figures in the moonlight pressed against a tree.

"I want to give you a birthday kiss, Nell." I hear Tad's douchebag voice. I stand in the darkness and watch as he reaches out and caresses her face. Those brown eyes stare up at him, and a small smile falls across her lips.

"Just a kiss, okay?" she warns him softly.

"Anything for the birthday girl," he says breathlessly.

Then I watch in slow motion as the douchebag kisses Nell. My stomach sinks and turns in disgust that she would allow this guy to kiss her. It should be me kissing her, not him. My shoulders slump in defeat.

"Tad, I said no." Nell squeals suddenly.

The sound of her voice has me turning around quickly. My heart thuds against my chest and I'm moments away from ripping this fool in half.

"Get the fuck off her," I snarl viciously as my hand grips his shirt and yanks him backward. He crumples to the ground in a heap.

"What the hell?" he screams, looking up at me standing over him. I'm seconds away from punching him in the face.

"Remi, don't," Nell calls out as her voice breaks. "Leave him."

I turn back to the douche on the ground and glare at him.

"Nell, I'm sorry…" He stumbles over his words. "I got swept up in it all. I didn't mean to push you." Tad looks sick with regret as he stares at a shaken Nell.

"When a girl says no it means no, asshole." I kick him in the ribs, and he lets out a grunt as he cradles his side.

"Remi," Nell warns.

"I'm sorry, Nell. So, sorry," Tad blubbers. "I've learned my lesson. I promise." He looks up at me. My eyes narrow on him, and I really want to do more than a kick in the ribs, but I know that will make Nell more upset with me than she already is.

"It's late. I think it's time you should go. Don't you?" I stare down at Tad.

"Yep. Will do. Um, happy birthday again, Nell." He squirms before jumping up and scurrying away like the cockroach he is.

When I turn around, happy that I got the dick to leave, Nell isn't there anymore. What the hell?

"Nell?" I whisper anxiously into the darkness. Where the hell did she go? Ugh, this girl. I traipse after her into the darkness, calling her name. Until I end up at the stables, where I notice the door is slightly ajar. I hear one of the horses greet the late-night visitor and know exactly who it is. Pushing the barn door further, I stride in and find Nell standing there in her designer dress, whispering to Sparkles.

"If you've come here to give me a lecture, Remi. I don't want to hear it," she says into Sparkles's neck. She gives me an angry huff, clearly noticing the tension between her human and me.

"Why would I be here giving you a lecture?" I ask.

"Dom would. He would say it was my fault for going into the woods with a boy alone, giving him mixed signals," she says, her voice faltering.

Inch by inch, I move closer to her. "I'm pretty sure your brother would have pummeled Tad for pushing your boundaries. He would never blame you for that." She continues stroking Sparkles in silence for a couple of moments.

"Thanks, girl, I needed that cuddle." She kisses the horse and closes the door. She gives herself a shake and walks over to the water trough and washes her hands. I watch in silence, waiting for her to talk. "Thank you for tonight."

"It was nothing," I say, sincerely. I'm no hero in this story.

"It was something to me, Remi," she says. Nell looks up at

me with those doe brown eyes making my chest constrict and my dick throb.

"I'm glad I was there."

Nell gives me a small smile and tilts her head as she stares up at me. "I'm glad it was you too, but…"

But what?

"I'm sorry you had to see me kiss that guy." She scrunches up her nose in disgust at the memory of kissing Tad. "It's not the kind of kiss I was hoping for on my birthday," she adds.

What kind of kiss was she hoping for, and from whom? *Please say me.*

"Was he not the right guy?" I ask. Because if she doesn't say my name, then I'll be crushed.

"Guess you could say that. Maybe I should get back to the party and see who else is out there to erase Tad's lips from mine."

A growl falls from my own lips, surprising me at the thought of her going back out into that party and finding someone else to kiss.

"He won't be out there, Nell. I can guarantee it."

"Really, how so?"

I take a couple more steps closer to her until there is nothing but a hair's breadth between us.

"Because he's standing right here," I say. My expression darkening as my eyes dip down and focus on her pink lips, which fall open with surprise at my words. I reach out and cup her face. A shiver runs down her body as my skin touches hers. Those innocent brown eyes look up at me expectantly, her cheeks have turned a light shade of pink and her lips are still open, inviting me in. "I'm going to kiss you now, Nell. Is that okay?" I ask. After what happened earlier, I want her consent.

"Yes."

Her answer is breathless, which makes me smile,

knowing that she wants this as much as I do. I lean forward and press my lips against hers ever so gently. A shock of electricity rushes over my body as soon as our lips touch, and it's as if a switch turns on between us because the next thing I know she's pulling me against her. Our lips duel, our tongues lash against each other, and soft moans fall from her lips while my entire body feels like it's on fire. My dick is a solid steel rod, and I press it against her softness, and I'm rewarded with teeth nipping my lips. Her hands run down my body and grab my ass, pulling me harder against her.

"I need more, Remi." She groans in frustration as her leg winds around my hip. I feel my dick pressed against her. Shit. I could come in my pants at any moment. Slow it down, Remi.

"I want more too," I say. "I have an idea. Do you trust me?"

"Yes," she answers. I feel elated she does, that she knows I would never hurt her, unlike Tad. My hands fall from her face, and I grab her hand and make my way to the stairs beside the horse stalls, and we head up to the mezzanine area. It's where we store some of the hay and where I sometimes disappear to for a nap, so I know it's perfect for us to make out there and not be disturbed. I grab the blanket hanging up on the side and lay it down for us. I sit first and call her over with my finger, she giggles and joins me on the blanket. What I wasn't expecting was for her to straddle me and push me up against a bale of hay as her lips descend on mine again. We lose ourselves freely this time until things take a turn further than either of us was expecting. Thankfully, I have protection in my wallet because I did not expect for us to lose our virginities tonight. But it feels right. Perfect. There isn't anyone else in the world that I want to experience this with than her. Something that I want to experience repeatedly because it feels so damn good.

6

NELL

ONE YEAR LATER

I t's crazy how much can change in just one year. This time last year, I was celebrating my sixteenth birthday. I lost my virginity to Remington Hartford, and it was the most amazing experience of my life. We were inseparable for the rest of the summer. I fell hard for him and him with me before he blew it up in my face at his eighteenth birthday party that Halloween. We agreed to keep things between us a secret from my brother. We knew the long-distance relationship would be hard, but I attempted to pop back on weekends to see him, and we talked most nights on the phone and texted back and forth. I was excited to get back to Bridgehampton to see him and celebrate his birthday with him, unfortunately things didn't quite turn out the way I had envisaged.

"Nell, can we have a moment?" Remi mumbles solemnly as he enters my room, looking like he would rather be anywhere else than here. My girlfriends' eyes widen at his request, but they jump up and disappear out of the room. He doesn't look as excited to see me as I am him.

"Is everything okay?" I ask, worried. Did someone die?

"Can we talk?" Remi asks again as he stares at the spot

beside me. I pat the space and he sits. My insides do a double flip as he's unable to look at me. What the hell is going on? My anxiety goes into overdrive.

"I don't know how to tell you this, Nell, but..." Remi says softly, "but I've met someone at school." My stomach sinks and my insides give out under me.

"You met someone else?" Moisture tickles my eyes, and I try to suck those tears back as hard as I can because I will not let this boy hurt me like that.

"I didn't mean for anything to happen, but it just did," he explains quietly. "I know we weren't officially dating, but..." he bites his bottom lip nervously and he still can't look at me. I know we never said the words of boyfriend and girlfriend, but I thought we were. No boys at school have caught my attention since being with him. No one could compare to Remi. I thought we would go public at his birthday party, tell my brother that we were in love and that we would be together and now he's telling me we were nothing and he's met someone else. "I'm really sorry, Nell. I didn't mean to hurt you, it just kind of happened," he adds apologetically.

I stand up from my bed because I don't want to be anywhere near him at this moment. It's all lies. What we had was all bullshit. "You didn't mean to hurt me?" I exclaim loudly as I thump my chest. "But you did." Remi looks up at me. His face is pale, his eyes are glassy, and his hands are fidgeting.

"I know, and I'm sorry," he says, pleading.

"You led me on, Remi. You've been calling me every night. You've told me you loved me. I gave you my fucking virginity for god's sake, and you turn around and tell me, oops, sorry, I've been screwing someone else." My own words are like tiny arrows through my heart.

"I'm not screwing anyone else." Yet, I think. "You and I can never be together, Nell. Dominic would never allow it. Your dad *would kick me off the team. I'm sorry but I have too much to lose."*

Wow. He has too much to lose. Basically, what he's saying is I'm not good enough for him to take a chance on.

"Get out. Get the hell out of my room. I never ever want to see you or speak to you ever again!" I scream. He looks a little taken aback by my reaction, which angers me even more. I'd fallen for him, and he's just thrown it back in my face. Tears stream down my cheeks as he scurries out of my room like the cockroach that he is, and my girls rush in and pull me into their arms and hold me while my heart breaks.

The girls insisted I attend Remi's birthday, which was being held back in the city, to show him exactly what he's missing. They made me choose the sexiest dress I could find; they pushed me to get my hair and make-up done, and if it wasn't for them, I wouldn't feel confident walking into the after party of Remi's birthday. As soon as I step into the club, I see Remi, with some brunette in his arms, kissing her. All that confidence that I had earlier vanishes in an instant as I see him with another girl. My besties reassure me it's going to be okay, that I've got this and that I look hot. My anxiety slowly subsides. Remi ignores me all night, partying with his new friends, who I already know because they are Dom's too. They are a bunch of douchebags, so I guess Remi's fitting right in.

"Is that Nell, Audrey, and Rainn?" a deep voice calls out from behind us. The three of us turn around and Remi's older brothers Stirling and Miles are standing there looking as handsome as ever. Remi's brothers are much older than him, but I can appreciate their aesthetics. "You girls look all grown up," Miles adds cheerfully. He's not saying it in a creeper way, he's just being nice. All our families are long-time friends, so we've grown up around each other; these two Hartford guys are more like brothers to us. "Why are you girls not dancing?" Miles asks curiously.

"The boys at this party are not worth our attention," Rainn *answers honestly, which makes Miles break out in a deep chuckle and the ever-stony-faced Stirling even cracks a smile.*

"Well then, I hope two old guys like us are up to par for a dance?" Miles asks Rainn, bemused. She looks him up and down and grins.

"I was always taught to respect my elders, so I guess it should be fine," Rainn quips back, making Miles chuckle again.

We spend the rest of the night having a blast with Miles Hartford. Stirling lasted one song and quickly bowed out, but Miles helped the three of us girls have the best time, and I soon forgot all about his brother.

"I'm going to the bathroom," I tell the girls, who wave me off the dance floor. I head on over to the bathrooms on the other side of the club and do my business. As soon as I step outside to head back to the dance floor, I feel myself being tugged and pushed up against a wall.

"What the hell are you doing with my brother?" Remi explodes angrily as he places his hands on either side of my head, caging me in. Green eyes flare with accusation and jealousy as they stare down at me, his chest heaving with exertion.

"None of your damn business," I stammer, surprised by his reaction.

"Do you want him?" he questions me angrily.

"What if I do? It's none of your damn business." I poke my finger into his hard chest.

"He's too old for you," he growls irritably.

"And you have a girlfriend," I remind him.

"No, I don't," he growls as his eyes dip down to my lips, and the next thing I know, they are on mine. What is happening? Unfortunately, my mouth opens for him, and he pounces at my stupidity. I don't know why I'm not pushing him away. I should have slapped his face for kissing me like this, but I don't. Instead, I reward his bad behavior with a pleading moan. The sound of

metal releasing from the zipper and the crinkling of the foil from a condom wrapper still doesn't stop me from making a poor decision, not even when I wrap my leg around his hip, giving him easier access. Does it stop me? Not even the animalistic grunts that echo in my ear as he takes me in a dark corridor in the middle of his birthday party as if I was his dirty little secret make me push him away. Instead, for some stupid reason the fact that we could get caught and I'm doing something so out of character turns me on. I'm sick. Has to be the reason I let him push me over the edge, and his mouth swallows down my screams. It must be the reason I let him do up his pants in silence without a single complaint. Why, I let him grab my face and kiss me savagely while he growls that I'm his, and no one else's. And why I watch him walk back into his birthday party, back into the arms of another girl.

I'm so stupid.

Never again, I tell myself as I sit in the auditorium of my brother's high school and watch him and Remi graduate. I don't care that Remi has filled out even more since I last saw him, or that his tan has deepened, making him even more handsome than should be allowed. I watch as each student walks up and collects their diploma. Remington Hartford is by far the hottest guy up there, and I know there are a lot of girls thinking the same thing, and probably a lot of moms too. But I've learned my lesson from last summer. Hot guys are bad news, and I've got a new boyfriend anyway, and I'm happy with him. My boyfriend's family is coming up to the Hamptons for the summer, so we are going to spend it together.

I'm ecstatic.

7

REMI

I've finally graduated!

I'm so excited to be standing up here in front of my family and friends collecting my high school diploma. It's been challenging juggling school and polo, but I've done it. Now it's time for me to concentrate on my playing future this summer and trying to move up in the world rankings before I start college. Mr. Garcia explained to Dom and me we needed to choose a college degree before we pursue polo full time, that having a fallback plan if something happens to our careers, like an injury, is a good idea. Especially as it happened to my father, who was involved in a car accident which put an end to his polo career. Dominic will be taking over the family business, but he wants to do more of the animal science side of the business, not the playing part. He's off to Penn State doing equine studies. I chose a bachelor's in economics at Harvard. I thought that might help me when I'm negotiating contracts and stuff. And the best bit is, Dom and I will play against each other on the polo fields in the intercollegiate competition. Can't wait to whip his ass.

I look out into the auditorium and wave to my family, but a beautiful blonde grabs my attention, Nell. She's sitting there with her family smiling and happy for Dom until her eyes fall on me and she turns ice princess. Does she not realize her hate just turns me on even more? It's well deserved, but still hot. I messed up last year. I had Dom riding my ass about flirting with his sister. I had Mr. Garcia training us hard, telling me I needed to focus on polo if I wanted to be the world's best. There was a lot of pressure, and I didn't mean for Reagan to turn my head at school. She was persistent. I tried to hold out for as long as I could, but when she was whispering all the dirty things she wanted to do to me all over school, there was only so much this horny high schooler could take. Nell, being back in the city, it felt like she was on the moon to me. Stupidly, I gave into Reagan but what I thought was going to be our little secret ended up turning into a nightmare once Reagan opened her mouth about how big my dick was and how well I used it. All her friends wanted a ride and who the hell was I to say no to them all, especially when they made it so damn hard to with their come-hither stares and willing mouths. I loved the attention. My ego was being stroked big time, and I fell for it.

That wasn't enough for me, was it? No, jealousy got the best of me that night seeing her dancing with my brother Miles and having fun as if I didn't exist. My ego got the better of me at my birthday party, and I took what I wanted, what I thought I deserved from her. Yeah, not proud of that. Sinking inside Nell was the perfect birthday present. No one compares to her.

"We're free, motherfuckers!" One of my friends wraps their arm around my shoulders and almost crash tackles me as I walk through the door to our graduation party. He then hands Dom and me a red Solo cup of beer before he runs off screaming about freedom or something.

"We did it," Dom declares, triumphantly raising his solo cup into the air.

"Fucking hell we did." I raise my cup, the frothy liquid spilling over the edge and all down my arm, but I don't care. We did it. We finished high school, and this is our last summer together before we must grow the fuck up.

The party is in full swing when I notice Nell walk in with her friends. What the hell is she doing here? I've heard she's got a boyfriend now, some preppy douche she's been dating for months. Her first love or some shit like that Portia sprouted over pancakes one morning. Totally lost my appetite after hearing that news.

So why is she here tonight then? And where is her guy?

Those brown eyes land on me where I'm slumped in the corner with a couple of girls surrounding me. I have one in my lap, her ass doing wicked things to my dick, and I have my arm slung over another's shoulder while she whispers dirty things into my ear. Both girls want me; they've heard the rumors. I guess there could be worse things going around about you other than you fuck like a god. I'd rather that than his dick smells of cottage cheese or something. Nell's lip curls in disgust as she looks over at the two women vying for my attention. I can see behind those innocent eyes how much she wants me still. I'm hoping she can see how much I want her, even if my actions show differently. She throws her hair back behind her and walks off with her two best friends, who both give me the evil eye. It makes me chuckle. If I want something with Nell tonight, I'm going to have to get her away from her two bulldogs. An idea pops into my head exactly how I'm going to do it.

Hours later, the party is still in chaos, and everyone is pairing off or passing out. I've kept my eyes on Nell all night, especially when some dickheads have gone sniffing around. Thankfully, the two friends I sent over to entertain Rainn and Audrey worked, and they are certainly entertaining them with their tongues down their throats. I watch as one by one the guys lead the two girls away to somewhere more private, leaving Nell exposed and ripe for me to slide in. Unhooking myself from the girls currently draped over me, I stand up and head on over to where Nell is sitting on a day bed all by herself, playing with her phone, looking miserable. Luckily, I'm here to cheer her up.

"Nell, you're looking good," I say cheerily as I sit down on the day bed. Her head swiftly looks up, and a frown forms on her face as brown eyes glare at me. She is not happy to see me.

"What do you want, Remi?"

"Haven't seen you in a while, just thought I'd say hello," I say brightly. Her eyes narrow on me, and she shakes her head. Impatience falls across her face as she turns back to her cell, practically dismissing me.

"Don't think your harem of girls would be too happy seeing you over here. You should go back to them," she states coolly as she looks up from her phone.

"Don't worry about them, they will wait till I'm ready," I tell her cockily.

Her eyes widen at my comment and then her face scrunches up angrily. "Who the hell are you?" she asks angrily, "This," she waves her hands at me, "is a douche." Then she swings her legs off the daybed and gets up, gives herself a shake, and walks off.

Oh, baby girl, this conversation isn't done with yet. I get up and chase after her. "What makes you think I'm a douche? I'm far from it. I think if you remember last summer, you were hanging out with a douche called Tad."

Nell shakes her head, ignoring me as her steps quicken along the stone path that leads back inside.

"Nell." I call her name, but she ignores me. She grabs the door handle and pulls the glass door open and stomps inside the house. "Nell." I call her name again, irritation forming across my skin.

"I told you, Remi. I don't want to talk to you. I've been pretty clear in my actions, don't you think?" she yells at me angrily.

Then she stops unexpectedly, and I run into her, nearly knocking her over. My hands come out and wrap around her upper arms and steady her. As soon as our skin meets, a sizzle electrifies and my dick throbs with need. I know she feels it too because her eyes widen with surprise; her cheeks have a pink hue to them as she licks her lips. Her eyes dip to my lips in the briefest of moments, but enough that I felt it in my bones, and by bones, I mean my dick. Everything stops around us as if we are in a transparent bubble that only the two of us can feel. Now is my chance to taste her again. I lean down and press my lips to her. She hesitates before I open my mouth and run my tongue along her lips, which makes her moan. Yes. I've got her. My hands move from her arms and cup her cheeks, pulling her closer to me, which she does willingly. Our tongues meet again, and everything is right in the world.

"Remi, no!" she yells, startled, and puts her hands on my chest and pushes me away from her. Both of us are panting from the kiss. "I have a boyfriend," she breathes, horrified as her hands come up and touch her lips, realizing that she just cheated on her guy.

"He doesn't need to know," I explain to her smugly. Those brown eyes widen and flare with anger.

"Of course, you don't care. I'm a plaything for you, aren't I? You think I'm one of your harem girls who will fall to her knees whenever the mood strikes you. I'm not one of those girls, Remi. You fooled me last year, and finally, I let myself get over the heartbreak you caused me and moved on to someone that means something to me. Who treats me right, and then you come in like some cocky douche and think you can just take and take from me?" she states firmly, her eyes glassing over with emotion.

"You're mine, Nell."

She shakes her head at my comment. "I was yours once. But you messed it all up and now I'm someone else's. You can't keep coming into my life and messing it up!" she screams angrily at me as the first tear slides down her cheek. My heart cracks, seeing the distress my thoughtlessness is causing her.

"I'm sorry," I tell her honestly. They are the only words that need to be spoken. "You're right. It's just…" The words hang there between us. I'm unable to say what I really want to say to her.

Nell looks up at me expectantly, waiting for me to continue with what I was going to say. "Just what?" she asks softly.

"I can't stop thinking about you, Nell," I tell her, confessing my inner thoughts. Nell gasps at my honesty and shakes her head as more tears stream down her face.

"Then why did you mess it all up?" she asks, sounding pained.

"Because no matter how much my heart wants you, right now we can't be together," I explain, feebly.

"Some time soon, Remi, someone is going to come along and sweep me off my feet, and there is nothing you're going to do about it. Because they are going to erase your name from my heart and replace it with theirs," she warns me darkly before turning on her heel and disappearing back into the party. She's probably right.

And I'm going to be the damn fool that will let them.

8

NELL

After Remi's graduation party blow up, he left me alone that summer to spend it with my boyfriend, and it was fantastic. I was moving on from my heartache until I caught my boyfriend in bed with his best friend. Of course, two guys can share a bed and it means nothing, but I'm pretty sure watching my boyfriend fuck his best friend means something else. So, I stumbled home in shock, and the first person I went to see was Sparkles. I wrapped my arms around her neck and nuzzled into her furry side. I told her all about what I witnessed, and she gave me a couple of reassuring neighs for good measure because, in the end, there's not much I can do but laugh about it.

"Wow, what a story," Remi says in disbelief.

I scream upon hearing his voice and spook Sparkles again.

Remi rushes into my stable and gives Sparkles a couple of soothing commands which instantly calm her down. The floozy even gives him a kiss on the cheek. I can't believe this has happened again. I storm out of the horse stalls; he's the last person I want to see, let alone hear my inner thoughts over the breakup. Why is he always there? Like a damn creeper. Why can't he just leave me alone?

"Nell." He calls after me again, and the déjà vu is setting in; we've been here before.

"No!" I yell angrily as I turn around and stop him in his tracks. "I do not want to hear what you have to say. I don't want your brand of sympathy," I state coldly as my eyes drift to his crotch.

"My brand of sympathy?" Remi repeats questioningly before a smirk falls across his face. "What does that entail? I'm curious."

"Oh, you know," I say, flustered, my eyes dipping again to his crotch. Remi's smile broadens as he folds his arms across his broad chest.

"I don't, actually. I think you might have to spell it out for me."

This guy is infuriating. "You know."

Remi scrunches his face up and shakes his head. "No, I don't; that's why I asked."

Is he thick? "Your dick, I'm talking about your dick, Remi!" I yell, annoyed at this entire conversation. Remi bursts out laughing. He's laughing so much that he bends over, cradling his stomach.

"I really just wanted to hear you say 'dick'."

Anger boils beneath my skin, so I shove him hard, annoyed with his teasing. He topples over onto his ass and bursts out laughing even harder.

Oh shoot, I didn't mean to push him that hard. "Are you okay?" I ask, concerned.

"Sure am," he replies happily. "I could use a little help up though."

I take his outstretched hand and pull him up off the ground, except he steps closer to me, our chests almost touching, and he looks down at me, grinning. Those green eyes sparkle with mischief, and I can feel my resolve crumble.

"Let me take your mind off things," he whispers in my ear. "I

can make you forget all about him." I'm sure he could, but...
Remi is bad news, such, such bad news, and I should really keep
my distance from him because all roads lead to heartache. "Use
me, Nell." His words still me.

"Use you?" I question him.

Remi reaches out and tucks a lock of my hair behind
my ear. "I know I'm no good for you, Nell. That I don't deserve
you, but what I can offer is a moment to forget everything he did
to you. Let me make you feel better, Nell?" he pleads.

I shouldn't be thinking about any other answer other
than no. Remington Hartford is bad news for my heart, I know
this as a sound, logical girl but when he is near me all logic falls
right out the window and all I can think about is why I am not
already in his arms and enjoying what he offers.

"One night, Nell," he adds with hope in his voice.

He can't break my heart in one night, can he?

No, it took him another six months to break my heart again.

It was stupid to go back for round two, but I thought it would
be different this time. I thought that now my brother was at one
college and Remi at another, that we didn't need to hide that we
were dating. But once again, Remi's out-of-control ego has
destroyed everything I thought we had.

The girls warned me not to surprise him up at Harvard
because nothing good comes from that. They warned me in
every teen movie that the girl going to her boyfriend's college is
going to end up being the one surprised. Of course, I didn't
believe them, and they were right. I was the one that was
surprised when I knocked on his dorm and he opens the door
rubbing blood-shot eyes, smelling of stale old beer, and wearing
gray sweats with a dick imprint visible.

*"Nell?" He stares at me, confused as to why I would be
standing there. He rubs the back of his neck nervously as he
stares dumbfounded at me. "What are you doing here?" he asks,
groggily closing the door behind him.*

"I knew it," I whispered, defeat written across my face.

"Knew what?"

"That I couldn't trust you."

"Babe," he mumbles.

"Open the door, Remi."

"I can't do that, Nell," he answers tightly.

"Open the fucking door, Remi," I say, gritting my teeth.

"I fucked up, babe," he mutters apologetically. "I got trashed last night and blacked out and woke up this morning with someone in my bed."

Ignoring his words, I push past him and enter his room. A girl squeals when I enter, and she looks as surprised as I do.

"I hate you, Remi. I hate you so fucking much!" I scream angrily as I pummel his bare chest with my fists. "I can't believe you fucked me over again. Why? Am I not good enough for you? Am I not pretty enough? Skinny enough? What am I doing so wrong that you keep fucking me over like this?" Tears stream down my face.

"I was missing you and got drunk. Then things spiraled out of control."

My stomach turns violently at his pathetic excuse. I can't believe he did it to me a second time. I'm an idiot to have fallen for his bullshit again. This is the last time Remi that I will ever let you fuck me over ever again.

"I'm done, Remi. You and I are through," I tell him seriously. "Come near me again, and I will make sure that I tell my father you broke my heart and then let's see how long you last on his team."

Remi's face pales at my threat. Good, because one phone call from me and his dreams will go up in smoke. And with that, I turn on my heel and disappear out of Remi's life for good.

9

NELL

I t's my eighteenth birthday today! And I plan on celebrating it to the fullest. Firstly, I graduated from high school. I got into Columbia with my girls. We are all doing a Bachelor of Arts majoring in Business Management. Maybe one day my mom might believe I'm good enough to join her company. She's an ex-model turned fashion designer, primarily designing equestrian-inspired clothing which works well for around the farm, but I would love for her to get into more upmarket designs. Mom told me to come back to that idea once I got an education and experience in business before she would look at any of my suggestions. It stings how Mom won't take me seriously. But I will not worry about that because it's my birthday and I'm going to have the best day ever. Rainn and Audrey arrived last night, and this morning I've taken them out on the horses for a celebratory ride.

"Can I ask the elephant in the room question?" Rainn asks cautiously as we trot along the beach on the horses.

"Sure."

"How come Remi's not here training? I thought he would have been?"

I still as Audrey's eyes widen at our best friend's question.

"He's in Hong Kong with the Harvard polo team for the summer," I say. My father mentioned it to me the other day in passing. "Why would you ask me about him?" I ask, questioning my friend.

"Because I wanted to know how wild you were going to get tonight," Rainn says. Turning her head and grinning at me. "I didn't want Remi's presence to put a dampener on your night."

"Have you spoken to him?" Audrey asks softly.

"Nope. Not once in eight months," I tell them proudly.

"That's good; his socials are nothing but thirst traps. And there are a lot of thirsty women out there," Rainn tells me.

"The guy goes to Harvard and looks like a Ralph Lauren model; of course he's going to get attention," Audrey adds dryly.

"Good for him then," I say, annoyed.

My two best friends look at each other, knowing the topic of Remi gets to me.

"Now that you're eighteen, maybe you need to start posting sexy photos of your own," Rainn suggests.

"Yes. We can do a photoshoot when we get home. Really rub it in his face what he gave up when he cheated on you," Audrey says excitedly. This is very true.

The three of us over the past couple of years have built up quite a following on our social media, sharing our extravagant life. And I did get a heap of presents sent to me for my birthday from companies who want me to test them out and post about them to my following. I think that makes us influencers, which is crazy because we only share our life; it's not like it's our job or anything. But if people want to send us things, that's kind of awesome. Maybe now that I'm eighteen I should consider this a little more seriously, that I could do something with all that influence, maybe even make money from it. That would show Mom I'm serious about business making my money instead of relying on her and dad. And if I can make Remi jealous in the process, seems like a win-win situation.

"Okay, I'm in," I tell them excitedly.

"We have to do this quick before my parents come home. My dad will flip if he sees me half naked on the back of my horse," I tell the girls nervously.

"Just making sure there aren't any nip slips anywhere for the camera," Rainn says to me while Audrey helps to style my hair. This company sent me some gorgeous statement jewelry, and we thought it would be a good idea to look like I'm naked on the back of my horse draped in nothing but the jewels. In reality, I have a flesh-colored G-string on and bandeau bra over my boobs, well, barely covering my boobs.

"We might need to hurry it up. Sparkles is getting moody. We have a diva on the set," I tell the girls while I snort-laugh at my joke.

"Okay, I'm ready for you to make love to the camera," Rainn tells me.

We get a couple of good shots and I'm finding my groove. I don't know how Mom did it for all those years it's kind of exhausting.

"Hey, happy birthday, Nell," a stranger's deep voice calls out, which spooks Sparkles, and she decides she's had enough and tries to buck me off. As I'm positioned laying on her back, the sudden movement jolts me off, and I tumble hard onto the earth as Sparkles gallops off. "Shit, Nell. Fuck," Miles swears loudly. He drops whatever he is holding and rushes over to my side. "Are you okay?" he asks, turning into doctor mode, and oh my, is that sexy. "Where does it hurt?" Strong hands work their way over my near-naked body, examining all the places that could be broken. "I didn't think." Miles looks up at me with familiar green eyes and I know I shouldn't melt, but I do. Something deep inside of me flips, and my stomach turns over Miles

Hartford. The same way it used to over…doesn't matter, he lost his chance a long time ago. "Can you stand up?"

"I don't know."

"Here," Miles says, holding out his arms to me to cling onto, and the moment I wrap my arms around him and feel the hard, tight muscles under his shirt sends my body on fire. He picks me up as if I weigh only a feather and holds me tightly against him. My nipples pebble and in the bra that leaves nothing to the imagination. As soon as I place my foot on the ground and put some pressure on it, I wince. Oh, that stings. "What hurts?" Miles asks, concerned, as he feels me tense.

"I think it's my foot," I tell him.

"When she fell off the horse, I think she hit her foot first," Rainn explains to Miles.

He nods in understanding before dropping to my feet and examining. He turns my ankle around, back and forth, and I tense again. Miles stares up at me seriously. "I think you've sprained your ankle. You're going to need to put an ice pack on it and rest." His eyes glance ever so briefly to my breasts before he stands up.

"Oh no, your party. We're going to have to rethink your outfit now that you can't wear those cute heels," Audrey whispers to me.

"I'm sure Nell will look beautiful in whatever she wears," Miles adds, and my heart swoons at his compliment. "Come on, I'll carry you inside." He holds out his arms again for me and I shift into place, and he picks me up and carries me all the way back to the house. I can't help but take a deep inhale of his cologne because he smells amazing.

"What were you doing on the horse in your underwear?" Miles asks as we walk.

You know, just some revenge photos for my ex, who's your brother. Yeah, don't think so.

"Don't laugh, but someone sent me all these jewels. Apparently, I'm an influencer. I thought now that I'm eighteen that maybe I would make the photos a little sexier," I explain to him, my teeth sinking into my bottom lip nervously.

"You don't need to take your clothes off to be sexy, Nell. It comes naturally to you." He compliments me and the butterflies in my stomach do an excited little dance. Maybe my eighteenth birthday is going to be okay after all.

Miles places me on the sofa in the living room, and I feel awfully exposed suddenly. "I'll go grab you some ice. Which way to the kitchen?" Miles asks, confused.

"I'll show you," Rainn tells him.

I watch as the two of them walk off together. "Oh my god, Aud. Miles is so hot," I exclaim, excitedly fanning myself.

Audrey gives me a small frown. "What about Remi?"

"What about him?"

"Miles is his brother."

"So?"

Audrey frowns again but doesn't push the subject. "I'm going to go upstairs and grab you some clothes. The last thing you need is your dad to see you naked on the couch with Miles." She's right. I've already slightly ruined my night with this stupid ankle. If Dad sees me like this, he's likely to call off my entire party. Audrey rushes off to get me some clothes as Rainn and Miles walk back into the living room with a cold pack.

"Here," Miles says, placing the pack around my ankle. "Keep this on for the next hour. Take some Advil, and you should be ready to go for tonight."

"Are you staying? You're more than welcome to stay," I say, trying not to sound hopeful.

"Um, well. I need to head back to the city, as I have an early shift in the morning. I was here dropping off your birthday present from Remi which I just realized I dropped in the yard."

Oh, my stomach sinks at the mention of Remi's name.

"Remi got Nell a present?" Rainn asks, sounding skeptical about this. I am too.

"My brother can be thoughtful. Shocking, I know." Miles grins at his joke.

Rainn looks between Miles and me. "I might go out and look for that present," Rainn says, awkwardly excusing herself from the conversation.

"I heard what my brother did to you last summer, and I can't apologize enough for his stupidity," Miles states sincerely. I'm not sure what to say to that. "He's young and dumb."

"Guess so was I."

10

NELL

FOUR YEARS LATER

F reedom! College is done.

There was a point there when I didn't know if we would make it. Especially when we accidentally lit our apartment on fire with a candle and a strong breeze. Yeah, fun times. But outside of that incident that shall never be talked about, we made it, we've graduated. My besties and I are in Europe to celebrate the summer and the end of school and becoming fully functioning adults. Now the three of us are making bank from being influencers, we have put a pause on a career path for the moment. Getting paid for being you is fun. It seems shallow on the outside, but I enjoy it. We're young, we have our entire lives ahead of us to worry about a job.

The more followers we have online, the more companies want to work with us. At first, it was a little brand here and there, but now its multinational companies and the contracts they are offering are serious. Totally over our heads. Thankfully, Rainn's oldest sister Meadow is COO of The Rose Agency, a PR and Influencer Agency. We signed with her agency, and they have been looking after our careers ever since.

Dom tagged along on part of our journey to Europe, we've

dropped him off in Brighton, England. He's just graduated from Penn State with honors and is now studying his master's in animal science over here. He also got asked to join the prestigious Cowdray Polo team when they found out he would be studying in the same area. Dad was super excited about the offer. Apparently, it's a big deal, something to do with royalty and whatnot. But in all fairness, it is a great opportunity for him, and as disappointed as my father is that he won't be joining his own team, he's super proud of my brother. My brother jokes Remi is the son our father wishes he had. I know Dom is joking, but I feel like there is some truth to it. It sucks that Dad has more in common with Remi. They are carbon copies of each other. Remi is more into the playing, whereas Dom is more into the breeding of the ponies. Both are equally important, except my father was one of the world's best players, so that is his passion. Not that Dom isn't good at polo, he is, he's just not as passionate.

And that's why I find myself in England with my brother, attending a stuffy black-tie affair for his new polo club.

"Lucky we like your brother because this party blows," Rainn says.

Dominic invited us for the opening of the polo season event, and as he doesn't know anyone in his new home yet, I volunteered us to attend. The beaches of Mykonos will still be there waiting for us in a couple of days.

"Least there are cute polo players to look at. Not everyone is the same age as my grandfather," Audrey whispers beside me, making me giggle.

"Now, can we welcome to the stage the game's newest rising star, Remington Hartford?" the MC says excitedly as the crowd goes wild for the last person I thought I would see tonight.

The girls look as surprised as I do, with their mouths hanging open.

"You didn't tell me he was going to be here," I say to my brother. Dom gives me a frown, wondering why I would care so much that Remi is here and why he would have to tell me. Remi's his friend.

"Of course, he's here," Dom explains. He's annoyed by my question, judging by the look he's giving me. He doesn't know the history between Remi and me. I feel Audrey's hand under the table, giving me a reassuring squeeze. At least I look good tonight and chose something sexy, thinking we were going to an exciting black-tie event, otherwise this dress would have been wasted. Not that I want Remi to appreciate it, just...I don't know, I'm a little frazzled that Remi is here in London when I thought he was halfway across the world. I hate that hearing his voice over the microphone gives my skin goosebumps and makes my body tingle. I haven't seen Remi in years thanks to college and his jet-setting around the globe with polo. It was great out of sight out of mind, but now he's standing up on that stage mere feet away and confusion swirls in my stomach, on the one hand I'm happy to see an old friend, and on the other I don't want to see the guy that broke my heart—twice.

I excuse myself and go to the bathroom to get it together. My brother is excited to see his best friend and I know he's going to want to go out tonight with him. It would be weird for us to turn down the invite, but maybe I can pretend we have another party to go to instead, but I know them, and they will want to tag along. I don't think I'm going to escape Remi tonight. Might need to pull my big girl panties up and just deal with it. *Try to remember what it was like before you stupidly slept with him.* Try to remember that guy who you grew up with; he's still there underneath all that um...handsomeness. Damn him for getting even hotter after all these years. I had hoped that maybe something happened and scarred his perfect face. Of course, the universe wouldn't be so cruel, and instead they have him shed his teenage self and now put before me a man. A handsome fricken man, with a square jaw, speckled with light stubble, and chocolate hair that is a little longer than he normally wears it.

The style just elevates him so much more. It looks like he's been working out a lot, his chest has grown wider, his thighs appear thicker, and his tan deeper. The boy who broke my heart has turned into a man that will shred it if I give him a chance.

"You're looking well, Nell," Remi whispers, surprising me as I step out of the bathrooms.

"Do you always hang out around the women's toilets like a creeper?" I ask him.

"No. Kind of seems like that's our thing, don't you think?" he says, grinning.

Do not smile, Nell. Dammit. My lips twitch at his words.

"You look as beautiful as ever," he declares flirtatiously. No. Don't do it, girl.

Do not fall for that handsome face.

Be strong, Nell. You can resist his charms.

11

REMI

Didn't realize how much I missed Nell until the moment I saw her sitting at the table with her brother at the polo event. She looked breathtaking in her red evening dress that dipped low as it crossed over the front, and then when she turned around, it was completely backless. I watched as she walked through the ballroom, exposing her long legs via an indecent split. It should have been illegal. Every single man in the room was impressed by her outfit too. I wanted to rip their eyeballs out of their creepy old eye sockets. All they see is the beautiful packaging on the outside, not the wonderful woman on the inside.

Unfortunately, I've fucked up so many times with Nell that there is no way in hell she will ever give me another chance, nor do I deserve one. But I miss her friendship all the same. If she could give me a second chance at being her friend, I wouldn't mind that.

Since graduating from Harvard a couple of years ago, my life has become a whirlwind. Nell's dad, Nacho, took me on full-time with his polo team. I can never repay him for the knowledge and experience he has given me these past years. As my polo star has risen, so has my public profile, and that has been the strangest side of this business that I wasn't expecting. I know I'm not an ugly guy, but the amount of sponsorship and ambassador deals I've gained since going professional has shocked me. Somehow, I've become a model with photoshoots all around the world. Working with some of the most beautiful women, being paid an enormous amount of money to do what I love is a blessing for someone my age.

Now, here I am being honored with an award in London in front of royalty and the richest people in England and all I can see is Nell when I stand up on stage and collect my award. My stomach sinks as I notice her reaction upon hearing my name being called. How she sinks down in her chair, and a look of panic crosses her face as her friends reassure her she's going to be fine. Not going to lie, it hurts me to my core watching the visceral reaction she has over me. I'm sad that I've messed up so badly that all these years later she still hates me, that my mere presence irritates her. I guess I have a long way to go to get any kind of relationship going again with her.

My eyes never leave her location no matter who I am talking to, it's as if there is an invisible string between us. Whenever she moves, I know exactly where she is always.

"Congrats, man," Dominic says, finally able to pull me away from some guys wanting to chat about the old days. It's so good to see him, it's been a long time since we have been in the same room together.

"Congrats to you too. I heard that you've signed with Cowdray, that is big, man," I tell him excitedly.

Dom likes polo, he's grown up with it, it's a part of him, and I know he never wanted to let his father down because he knows he's always wanted Dom to follow in his footsteps, but Dom enjoys working with the animals more than playing the game. He always told me how happy he was that I could fill the shoes that he couldn't for his father, that I took the pressure off him and let him pursue the things he's always wanted to do. It makes me happy I could do that for him.

"I can't believe we are finally in the same place at the same time," Dom says, grinning.

"It's been too long. Hey, I have this after-party thing I have to go to. Did you want to come?"

"Sure. But I'm here with the girls. Is it an open invitation to them too?" he asks.

"I thought I saw them. They should come along too. If it means you and I will have time to catch up without people wanting to talk shop, then the more the merrier," I say, giving him a slap on his shoulder.

"Must be hard being the famous Remington Hartford, world's best polo player." Dom chuckles, teasing me. Just as I am about to refute his claims, someone interrupts our conversation.

"Sorry," I say, annoyed that I'm being pulled away from my friend. "I'll text you the address. And we'll catch up then," I tell him. He gives me a nod in agreement as I'm being ushered away and introduced to someone else.

Eventually I'm able to excuse myself from the hundredth person wanting to chat with me to go to the bathroom. Ouch, my cheeks hurt from smiling so much and I feel like I've got a crick in my neck from nodding politely all night. As I step out of the bathrooms, a vision in red captures my attention as she walks into the ladies' room. Now's my chance before anyone else demands my attention. I stand outside playing on my phone with my back to the ballroom while I wait for Nell to reappear from the bathrooms.

"You're looking well, Nell," I say, glancing down at her. She looks so beautiful and my hand itches wanting to touch her. A gasp falls from her lips as I surprise her.

"Do you always hang out around the women's toilets like a creeper?" she asks, annoyed.

"No. Kind of seems like that's our thing, don't you think?" I say, reminding her of the time that I found her in a dark corridor and had my way with her. I don't mean to flirt with Nell, but it just comes so easily. She's trying not to smile, but her lip twitches and that tiniest of movements lights a fire in my belly. Maybe there is hope for me, that she may not hate me, just dislikes me. "You look as beautiful as ever."

"I know," Nell states confidently before flicking her hair over her shoulder.

"Every man in this room wants you tonight," I state matter-of-factly. "It did not impress their wives."

"Unlike you, Remi, I'm not a cheater," she replies tersely.

That little barb stings. I took her for granted, let my ego get the better of me, and hurt the one person I never, ever wanted to hurt.

"You're right, Nell. And I probably have never told you this, but I'm truly sorry for the way I treated you all those years ago. I was young and stupid, still am. You deserved better, and I knew better, but I wanted you. Still do," I confess to her. "But I know I don't deserve a third chance." Nell's doe brown eyes widen at my honesty. I watch as she takes in my truthful words and her eyes become glassy with emotion. "Hey, I'm sorry. I didn't mean to upset you."

Nell holds up her hand, shaking her head at me. "No. I'm... surprised, that's all. I never thought you would ever apologize, Remi," she tells me softly. She then looks up at me through dark, long lashes. One tiny tear escapes and cascades down her cheek. Without thinking, I reach out and swipe it away with my thumb as I cup her face.

"I hate that I hurt you. And I hate you hate me for it."

"I don't hate you, Remi," she whispers, holding my gaze. "Not now anyway."

A shaky breath leaves my chest at her words. "I want us to go back to being friends, Nell. I miss you."

"Friends?" she asks, surprised by my request.

My thumb caresses her cheek subconsciously. I realize what I'm doing, and I let my hand fall back beside me. "Yes, friends. That's all. Polo is my life, and everything is a whirlwind at the moment. It's all I can give to you," I tell her honestly.

"Does that mean no flirting?" Nell asks curiously as her tongue sweeps across her bottom lip and my dick notices.

"Not sure if I'll be able to stop that with you," I say, giving her a flirtatious wink, which makes her giggle.

"Guess that was too much to ask from you." Nell smiles widely. It's the first one she's giving to me in years, I'll take it.

"I spoke to Dom earlier, and I told him about this after-party. I wanted to invite you all there, too. Will you come?"

"Will there be free booze?" she asks happily.

"Yes."

"Then we'll be there," she answers lightly before turning around and heading back to her table. "Oh, and, Remi."

I look up at where she is standing with a smile still on her face.

"You're looking good too."

12

NELL

"How are you feeling?" Audrey whispers softly as we take a taxi to the club that Remi has invited us to. Rainn and Dom are having a loud conversation about something and aren't paying attention to our conversation.

"He apologized and asked to be friends."

"And how do you feel about that?" she asks.

How do I feel about that? I'm not sure. It surprised me that Remi was so open with me tonight about all the ways he majorly fucked up in the past. Never did I ever expect that, and now I don't know how that makes me feel. A guy being mature about his feelings and owning his shit. It shouldn't be hot, but it kind of is. Maybe I'm defective if I am thinking anything Remington Hartford does is hot. Even if he wore the shit out of his tuxedo tonight. And touched my cheek, capturing my tear or the way he so easily flirts with me.

No.

Stop.

Do not pass go, Nell.

Back away from those thoughts slowly. Nothing good will ever come from them.

Can I be friends with Remi, then? *Sure.* I think so.

"I don't know, Aud," I say honestly to my best friend.

"Sometimes you can't rationalize the way you feel about someone," Audrey explains carefully. "If you slip up, don't be hard on yourself," she tells me, with a smile on her face. "Enjoy it for what it is."

"Nothing will happen," I tell her, shaking my head.

She just nods and smiles.

It's not long till we arrive at the club. Dom walks up to the door woman manning the VIP entrance and drops Remi's name. She looks down at the list on her clipboard and then nods to the bouncer to let us all in. We follow Dom, who seems to know where he is going, and as soon as the doors open, loud music thumps against our eardrums as we make our way through the VIP section. We turn the corner and there, sitting in the booth, is Remi taking center stage while a gaggle of women surrounds him. Of course he does. My stomach sinks at the realization that Remi's womanizing ways are not behind him. I was foolish to think he had changed.

"You made it," Remi says excitedly, his face lighting up. He jumps up from his booth and pulls Dom into his arms and gives him a hard bro hug. Then he waves at us girls. "Come, come," he suggests eagerly, with his arm around my brother's shoulder. "Guys, make room for my friends," he tells everyone in the booth who start shuffling down, making room for us on Remi's command. Dom takes a seat beside Remi in the booth, where someone hands my brother a drink. He takes a large gulp. Remi looks up at the three of us girls and a frown forms on his face as he sees we didn't follow him like his other minions.

"We're just going to head to the bar," Rainn says politely, pointing past the booth to where a silver mirrored bar is set up. She didn't even wait for Remi to answer before walking off. Audrey and I follow her. "I'm sorry, babe. But I will not subject you to all that male testosterone," Rainn tells me angrily. I love my girl. "We know how this story is going to end tonight," Rainn grumbles, annoyed as she rolls her eyes. "Six tequilas please," Rainn asks the bartender. Moments later, he brings back a tray of shots. "Bottoms up, girlies," Rainn squeals with delight as we all throw back our shots.

My head hurts. Why? I roll over and hit something hard. What the...? As I force my eyes to open. A tanned back comes into focus. On white sheets. I roll onto my back and stare at the white ceiling as my heart runs a million miles inside my chest, so much so that I swear I'm having a heart attack. Then my eyes move down lower, and the further down my eyes travel, the faster my heart beats. I lift the white sheet that is covering me, and that's when I realize I'm naked.

No. No. No.

Who the hell did I go home with last night? My mind draws a blank. Shit. Where the hell are Audrey and Rainn? They must be worried sick about me going home with some random. Carefully, I roll over and search for my belongings. Thank God my phone is on the bedside table. Easing myself over, I grab it off the glass table and turn it to silent so as not to wake Mr. One-Night Stand until I'm ready.

I open the group chat with my friends which is filled with messages from them.

Rainn: I can't believe you went home with him.

Audrey: Please, like you haven't gone back to one of your exes.

Rainn: Good D is hard to find.

Rainn: He better have made you come, Nell. Otherwise, what a wasted walk down memory lane.

Audrey: Have fun. We love you.

Audrey: Message us when you're up. We are staying at the same hotel as you.

Rainn: Don't hate us. We took Remi's bribe so he could spend the night with you.

Audrey: That makes us sound like her pimps.

Audrey: It wasn't like that, babe. You wanted to go, actually your lips weren't separated for long. So we probably didn't really have time to talk about it.

Rainn: Don't worry, we ran block with Dom. We wing womaned the shit out of him, so the coast is clear.

Oh no. No. No. No.

Turning, I look over my shoulder at the tanned body beside me. Fuck. I lay back against the silky sheets, trying to stave off a panic attack. How the hell did this happen?

Then a memory hits me.

Tequila. It's always fricken tequila.

I've sat here all night watching these groupies sit there giggling at anything and everything these guys say. Making them think they are the funniest guys on earth. They aren't. The hair flips, the titty bounces, the bending over in front of them while pouring drinks. I think I have RSI from the number of eye rolls I did all night. Are these the type of women Remi is into now?

"Remi hasn't stopped staring at you all night," Audrey tells me. I turn my head and true to her word, there he is, staring at me over his glass with those intense green eyes. His arm slung around the shoulders of some groupie who is stroking her hand down his chest while her overinflated lips whisper something into his ear.

"He can stare all night, but I'm not interested," I tell her, exhausted by his antics. I throw back another shot of tequila,

hoping to scrub any memories of Remi from my mind. "I need another shot."

"Are you ignoring me, Nell?" Remi asks seductively as he joins me by the bar where I just ordered myself more drinks.

"No," I answer absently. "You look like you've had your hands full all night," I reply, stirring my cocktail with my straw.

"Jealous?" he asks with a chuckle.

I take a sip of my cocktail before answering him. "Of them, no." I shake my head.

"Good, because I couldn't keep my eyes off you," he whispers in my ear, sending shivers down my spine.

"That's nice," I answer, avoiding his eyes while I sip my cocktail. Remi moves closer to me, and I can feel his heat radiating against me.

"Wanna get out of here?" he asks flirtatiously.

My mouth falls open, and I stare at him in shock. "Oh my god, you're a dick. That line may work on that harem of groupies of yours waiting back at your table. But I'm not one of them," I say angrily poking him in the chest as I turn on my heel and walk away from him before my drink ends up all over him.

"Everything okay?" Audrey asks as I take a seat beside her, huffing and puffing because my blood is boiling by his audacity.

"Remi just asked me to get out of here with him. Can you believe that?" I ask her in disbelief, shaking my head. "Like as if the last couple of years never happened?"

"He's a player, you know what they're like. Plus, like I said, he hasn't been able to keep his eyes off you all night. So, I'm not surprised," Audrey tells me. I sip on my cocktail, still feeling annoyed by him.

"My work here is done," Rainn says, smugly taking a seat on my other side. Audrey and I look at her, confused. She stares back at us in silence for a couple of beats, wondering why we are staring at her strangely. "Oh, your brother has picked up and is going home with someone. You can thank me later."

Hang on, what did she say? "Dom did what?" I ask.

"I wing womaned for him, and now he's off to get laid by some hot chick. Now we don't have to worry about your brother being overbearingly protective of you tonight. You can thank me later," she says with a wink.

This is awesome news. I love my brother, I truly do, but sometimes he thinks he's an extension of my father and becomes the fun police. "Then why the hell are we sitting down? Let's hit the dance floor."

13

NELL

I lose myself in the music and try to dance off all the calories from my alcohol. My hips sway to the beats, my Latin roots kicking in when the beat drops and I let it. The music takes away all my cares, anxiety, and stress from tonight and my body becomes warm and loose. Next thing I feel is hands on my hips, but I'm so lost in the music that I don't care, plus whoever is touching me must be hot otherwise my girls would have shooed him away. Strong fingers dig into my hips as he sways to the beat easily. Oh, this man has rhythm. You know what they say about a man who can move like that, he's good in bed so maybe my night is looking up. I put all thoughts of Remi from my mind and enjoy the attention of the stranger behind me. His powerful body pressed against mine, moving with me as if we were one.

"I want you, Nell," a deep voice whispers a confession against my ear, then he's turning me around. His hand is around my neck as his thumb runs along my bottom lip, teasing me. A shiver runs down my spine at Remi's bold move, but the music has hypnotized me as I don't object. I can't move. I just let Remi rub his thumb along my lips as he stares down at me intensely.

Opening my mouth when he runs his thumb along my lips again, I capture in between my teeth. The groan Remi releases has me melting all over. I look up at him through dark lashes as I suck seductively on his thumb.

"Fuck, Nell."

Seeing Remi on the verge of losing control is the biggest aphrodisiac.

"You are so beautiful," he says in awe. Staring down at me through hungry eyes. I let go of his thumb with a pop and grab his shirt and pull him to me. Fuck it. Just one kiss, that's all I want. I can stop after that.

Then our lips meet, and sparks fly between us again, the entire dancefloor melts away. Thick fingers tangle in my hair as he holds my lips to his. A moan falls from my mouth as his tongue slides against mine and my hands grip his shirt even tighter. My body is alight with hunger, with every nerve ending electrified. As we pull away from the kiss, it equally stunned both of us by the intensity of it.

"I need you, Nell," he states hungrily, those green eyes swirling with desire. I can feel his need resting against my stomach, the tequila fueling my desire for more of Remi. You're not wanting forever with him, Nell. Remi isn't Mr. Right, he is and will always be Mr. Right now. The good time guy who knows exactly how to blow your mind, but he won't be there in the morning cuddling you or making your breakfast. He'll be gone like a thief in the night.

"One night only," I say with certainty. This way, I can protect my heart. I know what I am getting into bed with this time around. My eyes are wide open, and I understand Remi isn't looking for anything more than a roll in the hay. Like he said earlier, he doesn't have time for more, not with all the opportunities coming his way now, especially when they include some of the most beautiful women in the world falling at your feet. What guy is going to give that up?

"One night?" he questions me curiously.

"Yes. One night. That's what this is. If you want anything more than that, forget it," I say seriously to him. Remi's eyes widen in understanding that I will gladly walk away from that kiss and go home, alone.

He grabs my face intensely. "If one night is all I have, then I better make it good," he states hungrily as his lips capture mine in a feverish kiss. "Come on, let's get out of here."

"What about my friends?" I ask, concerned about them.

"They can come too."

"Um, I love my girls but not that much."

Remi bursts out laughing as he realizes I've misunderstood his comment. "I mean, they can come to the hotel too. I'll get them a room to hang out in. They can order all the room service they want," he states eagerly as his thumb drags along my bottom lip. Right, well, that's settled then, as he grabs my hand and hauls me from the dance floor to where my friends are seated drinking cocktails.

"So um, I'm like…"

"You're going home with him," Rainn answers with a smile. I nod in agreement. "Have fun then. Stay safe," Rainn adds cheekily.

"I was going to organize a room for you both at the same hotel as I know you weren't expecting to be in London this long and missed the last train back to Dom's place," Remi explains helpfully to them both.

They both look at each other with raised brows, then look back at Remi with enormous smiles.

Next thing I know, we are stumbling out of the nightclub and into Remi's limousine that is waiting out the front for us.

"Wow, Rem. You really are moving up in the world," Rainn states dryly as she settles into the luxurious car before opening the minibar and pulling out a bottle of champagne. The sound of a champagne cork popping echoes in the car's interior and my friend's giggles follow.

"I can't wait to get you alone," Remi whispers into my ear as his fingers grip my hair and his tongue slides along my skin, sending goosebumps all over my body. "It's been too long since my tongue has tasted you. But know that I haven't forgotten what your sweetness tastes like. The memory helps my hand when it's wrapped around my dick." Heat pools between my thighs, hearing Remi's dirty words. "I haven't forgotten the sounds you make as my dick slides between your folds either, Nell. It's seared into my soul." An unsteady breath releases from my mouth as I try to stave off this insatiable need to straddle him. If only we were alone. "I can feel you squirming in your seat, Nell. Your pussy is eager to be filled, isn't it?" Is he trying to kill me with his words? Because he is. I feel as if I'm about to combust at any moment.

Thankfully, it's not long till we are pulling up out the front of Remi's hotel. He holds open the door for us all to get out of the limousine; Remi takes my hand while escorting my friends into the foyer of the hotel. He strides confidently toward the reception desk, and the woman behind it jumps to attention when she sees him, her eyes widening, taking him in, as a flush falls across her cheeks. I'm used to that reaction; most women have it when they encounter Remi for the first time.

Looking at the woman's name tag, Remi addresses her. "Lisa, could you add a room for these lovely ladies to my account please and anything they want from room service? They can put it on my tab." Lisa nods and types furiously on the computer. "You all good, ladies?" Remi asks my friends.

"Yes. We're fine. Go, have fun," Rainn states happily, shooing us away.

Remi nods and tugs my hand to show we are on the move. I turn around and give my friends a smile and see them both giving me the *thumbs up as Remi hauls me toward the elevators. Thankfully, one is there, ready and waiting for us. He pulls out his wallet and taps it against the wall, which makes a beep as he presses the button for the penthouse and the doors close. Of course, he's staying in the penthouse, it's not like Remi wasn't rich before, but that money was his family's, and now he's making real money on his own which makes me extremely proud of him. As soon as the doors shut to the outside world Remi is on me, pushing me up against the mirrored wall of the elevator, one large hand is resting at the base of my breast, and his thumb is rubbing over my nipple, while his other hand is pressed against the wall of the elevator, caging me in.*

"If there weren't cameras in here, I'd be on my knees with my head up your dress."

I close my eyes and suck in an unsteady breath. There have been a couple of guys since Remi, but none that turns me on as much as he does. The man is sex on legs. He's pushed me so far past the point of no return with his dirty words that I don't even care that the hotel's security team could see us getting down and dirty in the elevator.

"I can see that look on your face, Nell, and as much as I want to be on my knees in front of you, your pussy is for my eyes only." I hate he knows me so well that he can read my innermost thoughts. The doors open to the elevator and Remi moves away from me. He lets me exit first, and as I pass him, he gives my ass a hard slap on the way past which makes me squeal.

14

REMI

I wake up with a feeling of pure satisfaction and happiness because Nell and I spent the night together. Never thought I would ever get a third chance with her, but somehow the gods up above granted me my wish that I could have her in my bed again. Just thinking about Nell being in my bed has my dick hard and aching to sink inside of her. No woman has ever left me wanting more than Nell does. Eagerly, I roll over to continue another round of what we did last night, but when I reach for her, there's nothing. Sitting up, I stare at the space beside me. I reach out and the sheets are cold. Is she in the bathroom?

"Nell?" I call out curiously. Nothing but silence greets me. I kick off my sheets and grab a pair of shorts from the ground and slip them on. I stomp out of the bedroom and into the living room to see if she is out there. Nothing. Even though I'm in the penthouse, the suite isn't that large, and I scan the room one last time. Nothing. She's not here, she's gone. I run my fingers through my hair, confused by her disappearance as I stare out over the rooftops of London through the floor-to-ceiling windows and replay what happened last night.

We walk into my penthouse suite, where a bottle of cham-

pagne is waiting for us, and some chocolate-dipped strawberries too, compliments of the hotel. I hadn't gotten around to sampling yet, but now that I see them, my mind races with a multitude of ideas about how I can use them on Nell. She spots them as soon as she enters and gives me a delighted squeal as she rushes over and grabs a strawberry, popping it in her mouth, where she moans as the juices run down her chin. My dick can't take it anymore as I slowly stalk toward her, placing a hand on the counter behind her. Those molten brown eyes widen as she realizes how close I am to her. I lean forward and press my lips against her mouth and use my tongue to lick up the strawberry's juices. Nell's eyes stay wide. She takes another bite and I do it again. We play this game until the strawberry is gone. Unable to control myself with this foreplay anymore, I grab and spin her around, pressing her up against the suite's bar, making sure she knows how much I want, no need her. My dick is like a steel rod in my pants and honestly it's painful as fuck.

"Open those legs for me, Nell," I whisper in her ear. She does as she's told and widens her stance for me. My lips meet the back of her neck, and I can feel the goosebumps under my skin. My fingers unzip her evening dress ever so slowly, watching her skin ripple with goosebumps in the cool air of the hotel room. I slide the dress off her shoulders, and it falls to the floor. I bend down and move her feet one at a time out of the designer gown before picking it up and laying it on a chair for her. She looks like a vision standing there in nothing but the tiniest of G-strings, with her back to me. Her perfect peach of an ass is on display, long toned legs down to a pair of killer heels.

"You're so fucking gorgeous," I tell her softly, admiring her in my own time. She turns her head ever so slightly and looks over her shoulder at me, the smallest hint of a smile falling against her lips.

"I'm waiting, Remi. Don't make me wait," she tells me flirtatiously, and she's right, we have been dancing this foreplay

dance for hours now and I can't wait any longer to hear her moan my name while I'm nestled deep inside of her. I take a couple of strides toward her and push myself up against her near-naked body, my hands running down her familiar curves, and a sense of home grips my chest. One of my hands grips her peachy ass, giving it a hard squeeze.

"Get up on the bar," I command Nell as my hands move to her hips and pick her up and place her on the edge of the bar. I reach over and grab the bottle of champagne and pop it. Nell's eyes widen in curiosity at my movements. I place the bottle back down beside me and move between her legs. My fingers grab the tiniest scraps of fabric of her G-string and roll them down her long legs. All the while, Nell watches me with bemusement.

"Widen those legs for me, sweetheart," I suggest to her. She does so willingly. I raise my hand to my lips and bite down against my fist on a moan as I take in her glistening pussy spread out before me. Nell lays back, resting on her hands against the bar in a relaxed pose with a knowing smirk on her face as she takes in my reaction. "Pick up the bottle of champagne," I tell her. "Then slowly drizzle the liquid down between your thighs because I'm thirsty."

Nell bites her bottom lip and hesitates at my command for a couple of moments before she does what she's told and pours the champagne between her legs. My mouth is there in an instant as my tongue laps at the bubbles as they cascade between her creamy thighs.

"Fuck, Rem." Nell hisses as I continuously lap at her. I think this might be my new favorite drink, one I could drink every single day of my life. Nothing tastes sweeter than Nell's perfect little cunt dipped in bubbles. But I need more, want more, until my hands reach out and I pick Nell up, still keeping per pussy pressed against my mouth she squeals as I lift her high on my shoulders, but my tongue doesn't stop. Her thighs stay wrapped around my ears, anchoring her to me. She can't get away from

my tongue. Her fingers dig into my hair as she holds on for dear
life, but there is no way in this world I would ever let her fall, not
when I have perfection wrapped around my ears. I don't walk far
as I stumble into a couple of armchairs and bruise a knee, but
it's all worth it. I bend down to my knees and turn around so that
my back is to the lounge. I set her down, stomach first, over the
edge of the couch, and stand up quickly.

"Stay there, Nell," I command strongly before my hand
comes down and slaps her ass hard again, anchoring her into
the position that I want her to be. I unzip my trousers and pull
out a condom and sheath myself before I position my dick back
between her thighs. "Open wide," I ask her, nudging her legs
wider as I slide myself through her folds. She hisses at the
contact and arches her back toward me, her hands gripping the
edge of the couch as I push myself into her, finally sinking home.
Her head falls back against my shoulder, and my fingers dig into
her hip as I stay deep inside of her, both of us unable to move.

"I've missed being this deep inside of you," I whisper into
her ear. I'm rewarded with a hearty hum from her lips as her arm
locks around my neck. My other hand reaches around her front
and finds her clit. The first strums of my finger against her sensitive bud has her moaning in my ear. That's my sign to fuck her. I
pull myself almost all the way out before slamming back into her
again, which makes her scream all the while as my fingers dance
across her skin.

"Yes!" she screams wildly as I continue to thrust inside of
her.

"Miss this, baby girl?" I growl savagely into her ear.

"Yes."

"Say my name, Nell. Tell me how much you missed my dick
being the only one that can fuck you right."

She shakes her head, not wanting to give me the satisfaction
of knowing that no matter how many guys have come before me
or after me, I'm the only one that knows what her needs are and

can deliver them to her. I pull her back against me, deepening my fucking, which has her pussy clamping down against me.

"Say it," I demand against her skin. "Say my name."

She hesitates for the briefest of moments until I can feel her legs quake as my fingers continue to circle around her. "Remi. Fuck. Yes. It's always been you." She curses on a scream as her pussy convulses around my dick and she dissolves into a liquid mess of an orgasm. My dick swells hearing her words and I hasten my fucking as I chase the orgasm that is floating over my body, pushing me closer and closer to the edge until I'm unable to hold on any longer and I come on a roar emptying myself inside of her. I slump against her, unable to stand myself, breathless over what we had done. Slowly, I pull myself out of her, tie off the condom, and shove it back into my pocket.

"Come, let's get you cleaned up." I pick up her sated body in my arms and walk her into the en-suite. I place her down onto the cool tiles and turn the shower on for her. I test the water and get it to the right temperature, which is scolding. She gets in, and I quickly undress and get rid of the condom before joining her. I pull her to me and kiss her, unable to stop myself because she looks so beautiful after being thoroughly fucked.

"Fuck, I've missed you," I tell her honestly. As I brush her wet hair from her face, she gives me a warm smile, and that smile is like an arrow to my chest. "I still love you, Nell." The words fall from my lips, and maybe it's too soon to say them, but it's the truth it doesn't matter how many people we are with. She still holds my heart.

"Remi."

"I know it doesn't change things between us, but I need you to know that you own me, Nell," I tell her truthfully.

"You broke my heart, Rem. You smashed it to smithereens."

"I know, baby." I run my hand through her hair. "And I'm so sorry about that. I was young and dumb. I was scared because I

know what we have together I'll never find with someone else. And I'm not ready yet for that."

Nell gives me a frown. "You can't say these things to me, Remi. I put you in a box, a box clearly marked one-night stand. I don't want you declaring your love for me." She pulls away from me and automatically I feel the distance creeping in between us again.

"I know I will only ever have tonight with you, Nell. Just needed you to know how I felt," I tell her honestly.

"Don't make me the bad guy here giving me those puppy dog eyes." Her voice softens. "We agreed one night."

"What happens if I want more?" I ask seriously.

"No," she answers flatly, shaking her head at me. "I can't let you in."

"You let me in between your legs," I state, annoyed. Her hands come out and push me away from her, my back hitting the shower's glass wall. I deserved that, letting my ego and pride get in the way. "I'm sorry, Nell. I didn't mean that. Fuck, I'm a dick to you." I swear furiously, disappointed with myself again.

"It's easier to have you between my legs than in my heart." The words slip from her lips quickly before she turns around and reaches for the soap to wash herself. I close my eyes and suck in a deep breath as I take a step forward and press a kiss against her shoulder.

I wrap my arms around her and grip her tightly. "If that is all I will ever get from you, I'll take it. I'd rather have some part of you than none."

She stops lathering herself and turns around in my arms, then in silence she lathers me up with the bubbles from her own body. My dick twitches back to life.

"Do you mean that?" she asks seriously.

"What, that I'll happily be a friend with benefits over no benefits at all? Yeah, one hundred percent." Those brown *eyes look at me as she wraps her arms around my neck, and she gives me a smile.*

"I think I can handle that."

Wait, she's serious? She's saying that this won't be the last time I get to sink deep inside of her.

"You can?" I ask, double-checking I'm hearing her correctly.

"As long as we keep our relationship strictly sex then you can't break my heart again."

Her comment makes me frown and my stomach sinks, but it's a start. We can rebuild the other parts of our relationship at another time, but for now, the fact she will let me stay inside of her is all I could ask for. "I think we might need to christen our new relationship, don't you think?"

And we did all night long.

So why did she disappear on me?

15

NELL

"**Y**ou dirty bitch." Rainn jokes, answering the door to their hotel room. I push my way through, dump my stuff on the floor, and slump on the bed where Audrey is sitting, playing on her phone.

"Are you okay?" she asks softly, looking at me with concern. I nod my head, answering her.

"Please don't tell me it wasn't as good as you remembered?" Rainn asks with a laugh. I lift my hands from my face and glare at her, which makes her laugh harder. "Damn, the D is still that good." I nod and cover my face again, burying it into the sheets. "What's the problem then?"

"He broke her heart, that's what the problem is," Audrey comments, shaking her head.

"Nell isn't looking to be in a relationship again with him, is she?"

I uncover my face and see Rainn staring at me intensely, waiting for me to answer.

"No. No way in the world. But he told me last night he still loves me."

"Oh my god." Audrey squeals excitedly.

"Did he say that during post-coital bliss?" Rainn asks, unconvinced.

"Not the point. I told him too bad, that it was one night only, and…" memories of our conversations filter back through my mind. "Oh, no."

"What?" Rainn and Audrey reply.

"I agreed to be friends with benefits with him."

"Of course, you did," Rainn adds, rolling her eyes.

"Do you think that's a good idea?" Audrey asks, concerned.

"No, I don't, but at that moment, I thought it was a great idea. Thinking I could guard my heart against him ever breaking it again."

"I think that's sound logic, Nell," Rainn states simply.

"Can you really sleep with Remi and keep your feelings in check?" Audrey asks sympathetically.

"I don't know." Pressing my face back into the sheets. This is why tequila is never a good idea, poor decisions happen. They sound great, but upon reflection, probably not so good. Why the hell did I do this to myself? My phone rings, pulling me from my self-loathing, but Rainn grabs it out of my bag before I have a chance.

"It's Remi," Rainn states with a grin.

"Hang up," I scream at her wildly.

"He's probably worried that you disappeared from his bed. He might think someone has kidnapped you. I should answer it just to let him know you're okay. Hey, Remi, it's Rainn. How are you?" I'm going to kill her. "She's just got back to the room. Which, by the way, thank you. Audrey and I had such a splendid night's sleep. We may have ordered one too many bowls of truffle fries, but no hangover this morning, so I think they did the trick. Sorry, Nell's in the shower. I'll let her know you called, though. Want me to pass on a message or anything? No. Okay. Again, thanks for hooking us up. See ya, around." She then hangs up and throws the phone at me. I catch it before it hits me in the head.

"What did he say?" Audrey asks. Yes, I want to know too.

"He's worried that you weren't in his room. That he wanted to make sure you were okay and if you could call him back," Rainn states, smirking.

"That's nice of him," Audrey adds.

"I guess."

"Just text him back saying thanks and have a nice life," Rainn insists.

Maybe she's right. It was nice of him to worry about me once he discovered me gone. I shouldn't ghost him just because I'm embarrassed over what happened.

"Right, I'm going to go have a shower," Rainn explains, leaving the room.

"Just text him," Audrey urges me before putting her air pods back into her ears, leaving me to it.

I stare down at my phone and type in my passcode to open it. I see Remi's phone number on the call list and create a message from that.

Nell: Hey, sorry I left. You were passed out. Didn't want to disturb you.

The three little bubbles immediately pop up, and my anxiety skyrockets.

Remi: Was looking forward to round 2 or is it round 4 or 5?

Remi: Was also looking forward to us having breakfast together.

He's right, it was four, but that's not the point.

Nell: As we established last night, we were just friends with benefits. Didn't think I needed to stick around for wifey duties.

Remi: Having breakfast after a night full of sex is wifey duty? Didn't realize this.

Nell: Didn't think having breakfast with your conquests was in the player handbook.

Remi: So now I'm a player. This keeps getting better and better. Tell me more.

Nell: Please you know you're a player. That ego of yours needs to be stroked constantly.

Remi: It's not the only thing that needs to be stroked constantly.

Nell: I walked into that.

Nell: Anyway, thanks for last night. It was fun. And thanks for putting my friends up, that was kind. Good luck and see you around.

Remi: That's it?

Nell: Yep,

Remi: When will I see you again?

Nell: Not sure, but good luck with everything. You're killing it.

And with that, I throw my phone onto the bed and sigh.

"All good?" Audrey asks, curious.

"Yep, all good."

"I still can't believe Dominic got invited to the private after party of Duo, the biggest DJs in the world, in Ibiza," Rainn states excitedly.

I like music, but I'm not as up to date with who is who like Rainn is. She surrounds herself with creative types of people. We changed our itinerary to come to Ibiza a couple of days earlier because of these tickets Dom was able to get for us. I haven't been to Ibiza for a while. Dom's letting us crash at his holiday home before we can check into ours. The island is fully booked this week, so we couldn't get the extra couple of days before-hand at our place.

"You made it," Dom says happily as he opens the door for us. I give my brother a kiss on the cheek and bypass him, enchanted by the view. The luxury home is bathed in a neutral stone palate which doesn't take away from the floor to ceiling glass doors that are pulled open, blurring the lines between indoor and outdoor space that takes you out to the infinity pool which juts out over the edge of the ravine and meets the azure of the ocean behind it. I think I've died and gone to paradise this; is gorgeous.

"The view is unbelievable, isn't it?" Dom states smugly, joining me by the railing.

Turning my head to look at my brother, "How the hell can you afford this?" I ask curiously.

Dom gives me a smug smile. "Oh, I didn't. It's one of Remi's MILF admirers that's letting us stay here," he tells me, chuckling.

Everything inside of me stills at the mention of Remi. "Remi's here?" I ask. My brother sure as hell forgot to tell me that bit of information when he invited us down here.

"Yeah, he's probably thanking the woman as we speak." Dom bursts out laughing, not realizing the knife he's just twisted into my chest.

"Dom, can you get us some drinks? We're parched from the flight," Audrey asks him in her sweetest voice.

He gives her a grin and walks back inside.

"Fuck, Nell. We can turn around and go straight back to the airport," Rainn suggests.

"What about Duo?" I ask her, knowing how excited she was to come here and see them.

"It's no biggy. I'll see them again," she adds, shrugging her shoulders.

"I can't believe Dom didn't mention this was Remi's place," Audrey adds, unimpressed.

"Remi's booty call's home," Rainn corrects her.

"We're here now, there's nothing we can do. I mean, look at this place it's gorgeous," I say, waving my hands at the gorgeous view.

"But what about Remi?" Audrey asks.

"What about him? We hooked up in London a couple of weeks ago. So what? We're in Ibiza. Do you have any idea how many hot guys there are here?" I ask them, raising my brows.

"Guys with Spanish accents too," Rainn adds with a grin, but Audrey doesn't look as convinced.

"I'll be fine. Remember, there's a wall around this," I tell her, tapping my heart with my hand.

"Drinks, ladies," Dom states, interrupting our conversation. We all take the cold drink because the Spanish sun has us all overheated.

Moments later, Remi emerges from a room with a towel wrapped dangerously low around his hips, water droplets cascade down his toned body, and I hate that seeing him like that makes me tingle.

"Nell?" Remi says my name like a question. His brows crinkle as those green eyes narrow on me. He shakes his head twice as if he can't quite believe I'm standing here in front of him. I'm guessing Dom didn't give him a heads up either. "What are you guys doing here?"

"Dom invited us," I answer for the girls.

Remi turns and stares at his best friend in surprise.

"I said I was inviting the girls," Dom states, shrugging his shoulders as if our being here is no big deal.

"I thought you meant different girls."

Then, behind Remi, a gorgeous brunette slides out of the door he exited moments before and stands beside him. She's a lot older than him. I'd even say double his age, but she's flawless. She's wearing a white dress that molds to her toned body, her chocolate brown hair is pulled up into a high ponytail, and she is dripping in gold and diamonds. Then I watch in horror as she grabs Remi's face and kisses him passionately. My fingers grip the glass that I'm holding. I'm worried it will shatter. She then pats his face and whispers something into his ear before turning around and looking at us.

"Welcome to my home," she says warmly. "I'm off, back to work. Have fun. Make yourselves at home." That's nice of her, damn it. She then gives Dom a heated kiss and gropes his ass before she strides out of the home like a goddess.

"I want to be her when I grow up," Rainn says quietly beside me.

"I'm just going to get changed," Remi says. He looks over at me with a frown, then disappears into his room. I will not let him ruin this holiday for my girls and me, plus there are plenty of other men to have fun with while we are here.

I don't need him.

16

REMI

I could kill Dom for that bullshit in the living room. But I can't because he does not know that anything's happened between Nell and me. Watching Nell's face as Leonora came out after our morning session, giving me a kiss before exiting, killed me. I could see the hurt that washed over her face and then the stubbornness of trying to hide it, but I saw it. Why did I think when Dom said girls, he meant someone different? Of course it was going to be his sister and her friends? I'm an idiot.

I've known Leonora for a couple of years now from the polo scene. She's known for her penchant for young, good-looking polo players. She likes to wine and dine them, have a little fun, and move on to the next. So, when she suggested I stay at her villa for some R&R and to bring my friends, I jumped at the chance. As soon as I introduced Dom to her when he arrived, she was thrilled over new meat. Dom was a little unsure at first when Leonora was hitting on him, but when I explained what the deal was with her, he stopped saying no to her advances. I could hear her screams throughout the villa most nights. It didn't bother me in the slightest. Lenora is all about fun. She isn't a jealous woman, and she expects the same back from you.

But Nell doesn't know that; all she's seen is me emerging from Leonora's bedroom, practically naked.

The sun is shining, and it's hot already. The pool is calling me as I walk out into the living room. I notice the girls and Dom lazing by the pool with cocktails in their hands, laughing. They haven't noticed me yet, and I take the uninterrupted moment to take Nell in. She's dressed in a barely-there white bikini that leaves nothing to the imagination at all. Her pert little ass is on display beneath the tiniest bikini bottoms, and her breasts are almost falling out of the tiny triangle top. All I can think about is what I would give to push that fabric to the side and sink deep inside of her. My dick twitches and I tell it to behave because walking out to the pool with a semi is going to look a little suspicious.

"Oh my god, Nell. You, in this light, is everything. Quick, throw me your phone and I'll get a picture of you in that bikini for the brand," Rainn exclaims eagerly. Nell throws it to her, and she opens it, then tells Nell to get into various poses by the pool's edge, turning it into an instant photoshoot.

"If you girls are going to do this all afternoon, I'm out." Dom moans before standing up out of the lounge chair and heading back inside. "They are going to be awhile." He groans, passing me.

I don't care, I'm happy watching Nell model in various seductive poses for the camera. Walking outside, I take a seat beside the girls. Nell turns her head before rolling her eyes at me and going back to her various poses. I can see why the girls get paid to model the clothing; the three of them are stunning. I can imagine how many creepers they get. And yes, I'm one of them. This photoshoot goes on for thirty minutes, and I understand now why Dominic bounced, it's hot, and the pool is looking rather inviting. Fuck it. I've stayed out of their way long enough. The pool is to be used. Placing my phone and glasses down beside me. I take a couple of steps before bomb diving into the pool and spraying the girls with the water. When I emerge, I hear screams and curses as water drips down all over them, which makes me smile.

"You're such a dick, Remi!" Nell screams angrily at me, shaking off the water droplets from her skin.

"I was hot and needed to cool down," I say, smiling up at her as I backstroke across the pool. Nell just sends daggers my way, which makes me smile even wider. "Why don't you come in. It's nice?"

"I'd rather be anywhere else," Nell says, mumbling to herself.

I will not let her negative words affect me, she's angry because she caught me with another woman. I get it. But I know the fact that it bothers her so much makes me hard. I'll bide my time for now, before I try to push the boundaries to our friendship again, but I will, mark my words.

Ibiza is the party capital of the world, and no one really starts heading out until one in the morning. Most clubs continue through the morning till lunchtime. I can't go too crazy because next week I'll be back down the south of France playing again. I took some time off to hang out with Dom and relax for a little because I've been working hard and now thanks to my rising star, I'm allowed to take a couple of weeks off to enjoy the fruits of my labor. It's late or early depending on which side of the coin you're on by the time we head out from our villa and into town where all the major clubs are. The girls, of course, are dressed like sin, with Nell wearing a vintage t-shirt that stops just under her ass and knee-high boots that have my dick hard. She's looking rock chick sex kitten and I'm here for it. We're escorted from the car directly through to the VIP section, which is up on the balcony overlooking the mega club, where thousands of people are dancing beneath us. The DJ booth is to the right of us, and we get an up-close look at them working their magic. The gorgeous bottle girls arrive with sparklers attach to champagne bottles. They dance around a bit to hype up the crowd. The girls squeal with delight, pulling their phones out, capturing the moment. Once the sparklers have died down, the girls get about pouring us glasses and handing them out to us.

One girl taps me on the shoulder and asks if I need anything else. I shake my head, showing that I'm fine, but she doesn't move. She then leans in again and tells me she is at my service and her job is to make sure I'm having a good time. I look across our table and see Nell's eyes narrow in on the girl who has her hands on me. Is that a flare of jealousy I see behind those brown eyes? I let the girl keep talking to me, telling me all the things that she would like to help me with while my eyes never leave Nell. She looks like she is moments away from jumping the table and clawing the girl's eyes out and I'm here for it, as is my dick that begins a hard throb in my pants.

"Seriously, can you not go anywhere and not have women hitting on you?" Dom questions me.

"Jealous, buddy?"

"Damn right I'm jealous," he tells me honestly, which makes me chuckle. "Teach me your ways." He grins.

If only he knew I don't care about all these other women. Yes, it's fun to have fun with them, but I know this life isn't forever that the shine of being used for a convenient fuck gets lonely after a while. I also know that I'm not ready to settle down yet which creates a conundrum in my head. Let's be serious, it's only a conundrum when Nell is around. Nell glares at me over her champagne glass, and I give her a flirtatious wink, which has her shaking her head at me.

"You really love annoying my sister, don't you?" Dom asks, raising a questioning brow in my direction. Panic flows through my veins because this is the first time he's ever questioned me about her.

"She makes it so easy."

"You don't annoy her because you like her, do you?" he asks inquisitively.

"What, no." My answer comes out a little louder and higher-pitched than I was going for. Dom's eyes narrow on me, sensing my discomfort over his question.

"You two have always been close. I was always too busy to notice it, but I do now." Dom turns his full attention on me. "Has anything happened between the two of you?"

This is the moment I die. I knew it would happen one day, but I didn't think it would be today. "No." Yeah, I'm chicken shit. Dom rolls his eyes at me, not believing the bullshit that fell from my lips. "Fine, we've kissed twice, that's all." Dom stares at me for a couple of beats and nods as he takes a gulp of his champagne.

"Thought so," he says as he continues taking a sip of his drink.

No raising of his voice. No telling me I'm a piece of shit. I'm still alive.

"That's it?" I ask him, wondering why he hasn't lost his mind. Dom shrugs his shoulders. I stare at him for a couple of moments, wondering if it's a delayed reaction or something?

"Am I happy about it? No. That's my sister. But we were kids and I get it. You two hung out a lot, so I assumed something may have accidentally happened. I mean, I hooked up with Rainn before."

I literally choke on my drink at his comment because this is the first I've heard about it.

"Um, when?"

"One holiday when she stayed with us. I think Nell was dating some douchebag and left Rainn on her own. We hung out and one thing led to another, and it just happened," Dom states as if it's no big deal.

"Does Nell know?"

"No. And she will not know. Rainn and I swore we would never tell her. You know what she'd be like, either weirded out or trying to set us up. So, don't fucking tell her." Dom points his finger at me. I throw my hands up in the air in defense and tell him she will not hear it from me.

The night continues in a blur of drinks, music, and dancing. Now that the DJs have finished their set, they have started the after-party in the VIP section. I can see the excitement on the girls' faces when they're introduced to the DJs. I don't understand what the appeal is. I especially don't understand what Nell sees in one of them when he comes over and wraps his arm around her shoulder and starts whispering into her ear, making her laugh. Not sure what's so funny.

Dom's left me for a hot blonde in the corner, and I'm sitting here with a scowl on my face while Nell flirts with someone else. It sucks. The cushion beside me dips, and I turn to see who's taking a seat beside me. I'm surprised by the gorgeous redhead.

"I think you and I might be kindred spirits," she suggests with a purr.

"How so?" I ask, intrigued.

"You can't seem to keep your eyes off those two either."

I follow her line of sight and realize she is looking at Nell and one of the DJs looking cozy on the couch together. "I'm going to assume you have a history with the beautiful girl?"

"Shall I assume you have a history with the guy she's flirting with too?" Looking back over at the redhead.

"You'd be right." A smirk falls across her lips. "Unfortunately, I fucked it up and I guess this is my penance watching him fawn over every groupie that falls into his lap."

"She's not a groupie," I tell her.

The redhead raises a manicured brow in my direction and gives me a warm smile.

"Let me guess, you fucked up?" Her green eyes dip and take me in. They flare with attraction as if she's just noticed who she's sat beside. A chuckle falls from her ruby red lips. "Oh yeah, you most definitely fucked up, pretty boy."

"You don't know me," I tell her, annoyed at her assumptions.

She just gives me a shoulder shrug of indifference.

"What did you do then? That causes you to be sitting here with me and not over there?"

"I slept with the other guy in his band," she tells me.

A low whistle falls from my lips. "That would probably do it."

"It was an unfortunate mistake and one that cost me him," she states sadly.

"So how do you know them?" I ask her, intrigued suddenly.

"Known them all my life, we were friends." She lets out a sigh before shaking her head. "Then sex messed it all up." Always does, as I look back over to where Nell is now sucking face with the DJ. "Guess they are both trying to prove a point." The redhead explains, taking a sip of her drink while we watch the two people we both want, be together.

"I'm assuming you're sitting here, wondering if I'm up for a bit of mind fuckery?" I ask, turning my head back toward the beautiful redhead.

"That's exactly why I'm sitting here, pretty boy," she explains to me with a grin. I raise a questioning brow at her before I lean in and capture her lips with my own.

17

REMI

"W"hat the hell do you think you're doing?" Nell asks angrily as she grabs my arm as I exit the bathrooms.

"Taking a piss."

Nell rolls her eyes at me, looking rather annoyed. "No, I mean with that redhead," she sneers at me.

"Same thing I'm assuming you're doing with your DJ friend, having some fun."

"Are you going to take her back to the villa tonight?" Nell questions me.

"Not sure. Are you taking your friend back to the villa to fuck him?"

Those brown eyes narrow on me, and a fiery anger rages behind them. "What's saying I haven't already fucked him?" she hisses angrily.

"I'm assuming it wasn't that good then. Because you've come to find me," I say confidently before spinning her around and pushing her up against the brick wall, crowding her personal space. Nell lets out a surprised gasp and a grunt as her back hits the wall. "You know I can finish the job properly," I whisper into her ear.

"You think you're the biggest player, Remi, don't you?" Nell asks me angrily. "Women drop to their knees anytime Remington Hartford asks them to. I'm not one of those girls."

"And yet here you are accosting me in the hallway."

"I was trying to warn you," Nell exclaims.

"Warn me?"

"Yeah, that girl you're with is only using you to make her ex jealous," Nell tells me honestly.

"And you don't think I'm doing the same thing?" I ask her, arching a questioning brow at her. Nell is a little stunned by my comment, her mouth falls open and those brown doe eyes blink slowly at me computing what I just confessed. "That's right, little one. I wanted to make you jealous. Did it work?" I ask with a smirk as my thumb rubs against her cheek.

"No," she answers softly, as her teeth sink into her bottom lip.

"You sure about that?" I ask her again.

"Yes, I'm sure." She answers breathlessly. "I was just being a good friend in case…"

"In case what, sweetheart?" I ask, finishing her sentence.

"That you wanted to date her," she mumbles beneath her breath. Her comment catches me off guard and I burst out laughing, which makes her frown at me, and I can see she is getting upset by my laughter as her eyes narrow on me. "Stop being a dick, Remi," Nell snaps back at me.

"I think it's cute that you're worried about my heart getting broken, Nell," I tell her, as my eyes drip down to her mouth, it's been too long since I last tasted her. "The only woman that could ever break my heart is standing right in front of me." Nell gasps and those brown eyes widen at my honesty. "I've never cared about another like I have you."

"Remi," she says my name softly as her hand rests on my chest. I think she is going to push me away, but she pulls me to her as her lips meet mine. The kiss starts off softly, as she accepts that I still have feelings for her. I don't want to rush Nell when she is the one that made the first move this time, so I let her set the pace. Her tongue runs along the seam of my lips, begging me to open fully for her, and I do. As soon as our tongues collide, it's game over as sparks fly. Hunger takes over the two of us, and we consume each other as if we're starving and we probably are because it's been weeks since we were last together. I need more of her because once I've started tasting Nell, I must finish. Unhappily, I pull myself away from her lips and grab her hand and head into the disabled toilet cubical in the club. I shut and lock the door behind me, and unfortunately, stark fluorescent light fills the room, but I don't care. My lips are hungry on her again, and I shove her up against the white-tiled wall and push one of her legs up so that I can get myself closer to her. I run my hardening dick against the seam of her panties, which pulls a moan from her lips. I don't dare let my lips move from hers while she's letting me put her in this position, not when she could change her mind at any moment, and I would have to let her leave. My hand slides down her smooth thigh before slipping between us. My fingers find her damp underwear, which makes my dick throb with greedy need that she's turned on. My knuckles press against her underwear, teasing her. Breathless moans fall from her lips the harder my knuckle runs along her dampening slit. With a careful flick of my wrist, I move her flimsy underwear to the side and my knuckle is sliding between her sweet folds. Nell moans louder at the contact, which sends shivers of excitement over my primed body. It doesn't take long till I sink one than a second finger inside her heated cunt.

"Fuck, Remi!" Nell screams, throwing her head back against the tiles, her eyes sliding close as her chest heaves with each delicious thrust of my fingers inside of her. I don't let up on my rhythm, curling my fingers inside of her, knowing exactly the spot that sends her flying higher, then when it's time I add my thumb and caress her clit, which has her thighs shaking moments later. "Don't stop." She hisses and pants as I give her exactly what she asks for and don't stop moving until I can feel her quake and her pussy clenches around my fingers until she screams my name as I push her over the edge. I don't let her come down from the orgasm because my other hand has already unbuttoned my pants and pulled my dick out. With experienced fingers, I pull the condom from my back pocket, and in a well-practiced move, I roll it onto my dick one-handed and seconds later I am sinking deep inside of her. "Fuck, Rem," she hisses on contact.

"That's exactly what I'm going to do to you," I growl into her ear.

"Yes. Harder. Make me forget you!" Nell screams in my ear.

I'm so far gone that I don't have time to understand what she means by *"make me forget you."* I'm lost in the moment, unable to make a coherent thought, so I file it away for another time. I grab Nell's leg and hoist her up higher, letting me sink deeper inside of her. "I'll always know what makes you feel good, Nell."

"I know." She moans as her nails dig into my shoulders.

Tingles race up my spine, and my balls throb as I continue to fuck her.

"I know." She screams again as I hit her deep inside and her legs shake as I feel her walls tighten around me, squeezing the life out of my dick, making my eyes roll back inside my head at how delicious it feels to be wrapped tightly by her cunt.

It doesn't take me long until we are both coming against each other after a couple of deeper thrusts, each of us moaning our release against the other. My head falls forward onto Nell's shoulder as I try to catch my breath because this woman literally takes my breath away each time I fuck her. I gently ease myself out of her and toss away the condom before tucking myself back into my pants. I grab some toilet paper and hand it to Nell to clean herself up with and she does before throwing the paper away in the toilet. Once Nell's pulled herself back together again, I register the frown on her face.

"Everything okay?"

"I'm annoyed with myself," she says, straightening herself up.

"Why? Did I not make you come?" I ask, genuinely worried that the screams I pulled from her were fake.

"Oh, no, you did. You always do," she tells me, shaking her head, but she still doesn't sound happy about that.

"Then did I hurt you?" I ask, worried that in my frenzy that I may have done something that bruised her.

"No. You didn't hurt me, this time," she adds. "I'm annoyed that I've fallen into…" She starts but stops herself as if realizing where she is for the first time "… a nightclub bathroom with you again." Her lip curls sourly as she shakes her head in disgust.

"You're upset because it was with me, aren't you?" I ask her angrily.

"Of course, I am!" she yells at me, pushing me away from her. "Because you think you're God's gift to women, and I stupidly keep falling for it."

"Is that why you screamed *'make me forget you'*?" I ask.

"Yes."

Dammit, I curse internally as I rake my hand through my hair. "Nell, I'm sorry for the shit that I did years ago. I truly am. Are you going to punish me forever over it?"

"Yes. Because you broke me, Remi. You broke my heart into a million miserable pieces. You were the first boy I ever loved, and you destroyed it. You threw my heart back into my face as if it meant nothing to you. You ruined me. You left me with trust issues." My heart thunders in my chest at hearing her words. That the stupidity of my youth created a permanent scar on her heart. Nell wraps her arms around herself as if she feels exposed now toward me. "And the stupid thing is, I keep coming back for more, even though I know the consequences of my actions will be another dent in my heart, thanks to you, Remington Hartford. But you're like a drug that I need even though I know you're no good for me."

"Nell." I say her name softly as I reach my hand out to cup her face. "I hate being your regret."

"I'm not trying to hurt you," she says, letting out a heavy sigh.

"I know, sweetheart. I'm a big boy I can handle it," I whisper in reply as my thumb continues to stroke my cheek.

"I don't think I can, Rem." My stomach sinks at her words. "I don't think we can be friends either," she whispers gently.

"Why?"

"I'm just going to keep falling into bed with you at every moment."

"And what's wrong with that?"

"Because I'll never get over you if I do," she tells me sternly.

"I don't want you to get over me."

"But I do," she states firmly, tapping her chest. "You're this polo playing playboy. Your star is rising and what comes with that is more women, more attention, and more money."

"So, I've worked fucking hard to achieve all that I have," I tell her, annoyed by her comment.

"And I'm your biggest fan, Rem. Please never doubt that," she tells me, reaching out and touching my chest, my skin lighting up under her fingers. "But I still love you."

"What's wrong with that? I still love you too," I tell her honestly, placing my hand over hers on my chest. Her eyes look down at where our hands meet, and she stares at them for a couple of moments before she pulls them away. I feel their loss immediately.

"I have to go," she says impatiently as she pushes me to the side and tries to pull the locked bathroom door open without unlocking it first. She shakes the handle in frustration twice, even banging on the door with her fist. I walk over and press my front against her back, making her gasp. I place the barest of kisses on her neck and her skin breaks out in goosebumps under my lips. I reach out and turn the lock on the door, making it click, before turning the knob and pushing it open for her and moments later, she disappears into the club. The thought of not having her in my life feels like my entire being is being ripped from my soul, but seeing how upset I made her, maybe I should give her some space.

Reluctantly, I walk back out into the club, the deafening thumps of the club track throb in my ears as I find my seat back in the VIP section beside the redhead, who gives me a what the fuck look over with her eyes. She hands me a drink, and I throw it back in one large gulp.

"Something happen?" she asks curiously, arching a manicured brow in my direction before her eyes drift over to where Nell is sitting and chatting with the DJ. His arm slung around her shoulders as if she were his. She's not. She will always be mine. It's going to take time I understand it, because we are both not ready, but there will come a time in the future when the stars align and that will be it.

"Nothing I can't handle."

18

NELL

"Let's party!" Dior screams as we enter the club. Dior is a new friend to our group. I met her on a photoshoot a couple of months ago, she's this gorgeous blonde bombshell who absolutely kills it in a bikini. We met on a shoot in the Bahamas and just became fast friends, she's also a total party animal. She's wild. Dior has dragged us to the opening of some new club that she knows the owners of, and they have asked her to bring some influencers to the opening to create a buzz. My girls and I are always up for a good time, so we are happy to party for free for some photos.

"This place is amazing," I declare in surprise. It's as if we have stepped into a tropical rainforest in the middle of downtown. They filled the walls with vertical gardens. The sound of water trickling is in stark contrast to the thundering beats of the DJ, but the club feels serene nonetheless. We follow Dior toward the VIP section. She speaks to the bouncer to tick off our names and lets us enter through the velvet rope. Dior squeals when she sees her friends and air kisses them. She pulls us toward the group of extremely good-looking guys, introducing them to us all. Tonight is going to be fun.

"Tequila for the table!" Dior screams into the darkness, and moments later bottle girls arrive with tequila and they begin pouring shots out for us all.

Bottoms up.

Okay, I now realize tequila, high heels, and dancing on tables do not mix. Nothing is going to end well for anyone who tries this, and when I say anyone, I mean me. I'm currently splayed out on the floor of the club in a twisted mess as I laugh, and cry at the pain radiating through my leg. This is not good.

"Shit, Nell. Are you okay?" Audrey asks, alarmed by my current predicament.

"Um, no not really," I say through clenched teeth. "I think I might need to go to the emergency room. Something doesn't feel right."

"You can say that again your ankle has blown up double the size," Rainn adds anxiously.

Moments later, security rushes over to me and glares down at me.

"Think it might be best that you girls leave now. You've had enough for tonight," one of the large security guards grumbles at me. I'm mortified.

"She kind of can't move, otherwise we would be out of here," Rainn answers angrily, almost standing toe to toe to him. The security guy looks down at my ballooned ankle and his jaw ticks. Then he bends down and picks me up from the floor as if I weigh nothing and storms out of the VIP section.

"Nellie, what the hell?" Dior squeals when I pass her.

"I'm okay, just off to hospital, I'll be fine," I tell my friend, reassuring her.

"Right, okay. Well, I'll call you tomorrow. Look after yourself," she tells me before joining her friends back in her booth. Rainn's eyes narrow on my friend, but I'm not in the mood to worry about Dior. The guard continues storming through the crowd until we are outside, where he unceremoniously dumps me on the street.

"Hey, watch it, dickhead," Rainn sneers at him.

"Don't come back," he growls before shutting the club's door in our faces.

"Wow, that was excessive," I say through gritted teeth. Thank goodness the tequila is still in my system, otherwise this would hurt like a bitch.

"I can't believe they kicked us out," Audrey exclaims, bewildered.

"It was a sucky club, anyway," Rainn answers, rolling her eyes.

Moments later, a taxi pulls up, and I hobble inside. Rainn gives the driver directions to the nearest hospital, but I interrupt and ask to be taken to the one uptown instead.

"That's going to take us ages to get there," Rainn questions me.

"I know, but Miles works there, and he should be on call at that hospital," I explain to her.

"Are you flipping serious, Nell?" Rainn yells, irritated by my logic.

"How do you know he works there tonight?" Audrey asks.

"I just know his schedule, all right," I answer irritably.

Rainn shakes her head at me.

It's a long silent journey to Miles's hospital, but we finally make it. Audrey helps me from the taxi while Rainn pays the driver. I awkwardly hop into the emergency waiting room and take a seat while my friends check me in. I look around and see the other poor souls who're stuck in an emergency waiting room at two in the morning. There are some grizzly kids with sleep-deprived adults, a frat boy with what looks to be a nasty gash to his head, a homeless man asleep on a bench, and me.

"They said the wait shouldn't be long," Audrey explains to

me as she takes a seat beside me, her eyes falling on the interesting group of people settled in around us. We distract ourselves with our phones and an hour later, I'm being wheeled into a room where the doctor will see me. So many scenarios run through my mind about what Miles will do when he sees me. Will he stare up at me from my foot before our eyes meet and he declares he has always had a crush on me, and fuck it, he wants to take me out on a date? Is this my meet-cute moment?

"Nell Garcia, hi, I'm Dr. Olga Renner. Let me have a look at this foot." An older woman greets me.

"Oh, I thought Dr. Hartford would be here tonight?" I ask her. She stills and looks up at me through thick, dark lashes, her ice-blue eyes narrow on me. "Our dads are best friends. I've known him since I was born. Just thought it would be nice to see a friendly face." I stammer, "I mean, not like you're not friendly, just that…"

"Stop talking," Rainn whispers into my ear, and I shut my mouth immediately.

The doctor gives me a questioning look before looking back at my ankle. "I swapped shifts with Dr. Hartford, otherwise he would have been here," she states while moving my foot around, which is causing pain. "He's quite popular in our hospital, so you wouldn't have been the first ladies to come in hoping to see him."

"Oh no, Miles is like a brother to me. Ew," I add quickly. My face feels like it's on fire with embarrassment.

"You have a badly twisted ankle. Judging by these heels, I understand why." The doctor gives me a smile.

"Probably the fall off the table added to it too," Rainn adds unhelpfully.

The doctor looks up at my friends and smiles. "Yes, that would be a problem too. I'll get one of my students to come in and wrap your ankle up. Take some Advil and keep off it for forty-eight hours. If you feel like it's not getting better, pop back in or give Dr. Hartford a call," she suggests dryly.

Well, that was embarrassing.

"All is not lost, Nell. You can still call Miles and ask him to do home visits," Rainn teases.

19

NELL

Not being able to walk sucks. But thankfully I'm all set up in bed. I have my phone, TV, and snacks, thanks to our housekeeper, Rhonda. Since I've graduated, Mom has moved up to the farm full time, leaving me on my own in our Manhattan apartment. Portia's at college, but she's decided to live with her friends instead of sharing an apartment with me. Which is fine. I like the solitude, and it's not like I'm home all the time anyway. It's somewhere for me to sleep and get my clothes washed.

There's a knock on my door, and a couple of moments later, Rhonda is popping her head through.

"You have a visitor, miss," she tells me. Must be the girls. I tell her to send them through.

"Please tell me it's not true. That you fell off a table and twisted your ankle?" Miles asks playfully.

Wait, Miles Hartford is walking into my bedroom like he owns the space.

Miles freaking Hartford is in my bedroom.

Am I having another dirty dream?

"What are you doing in here?" I question him, not that I'm complaining.

"Your mom called my mom and asked me to check on you," he explains. He takes a seat at the end of my bed, a wide smile falling on his face. Thanks Mom, a warning would have been great. I have no make-up on, and I'm dressed in a thin T-shirt, no bra, and booty shorts.

"You didn't have to do that. I'm fine," I tell him.

"I know, but my mom would have killed me if I hadn't. You know what they're like," he explains. "Plus, I ran into Olga yesterday at shift change, and she told me all about a very cute friend of mine that came in after falling off a table. I thought she was having a laugh, then Mom called, and all the pieces fell together."

I want to die of embarrassment as I bury my face in my hands.

"Hey," Miles says, pulling my hands from my face while chuckling. "I've done some pretty stupid shit in my days, too. I remember a time in college when I was at some frat party. I knocked myself out after doing a keg stand. I'm going to blame my friends for that one, they didn't hold me properly. Then I woke up with a cock and balls drawn on my face, but I did not know all night and didn't understand why people were looking at me funny. Until a girl eventually took pity on me and took me to the bathroom and rubbed it off." I raise my brow at this story. It sounded dirty, and I bet that's not all she did. "I didn't mean for that to sound the way it did," Miles explains, laughing at his innuendo.

"I'm sure she still thought you were cute with the drawing on your face, anyway," I tell him, rolling my eyes with a smile.

"Well, yeah, we dated for a couple of months after, so I guess there's a happy ending to that story." We both stare at each other and burst out laughing at his use of happy ending. "Would you stop it? Why is everything sounding wrong coming out of my mouth?" he says, shaking his head smiling.

This is exactly what I needed to pick me up today. "I sure hope this isn't your normal bedside manner, Dr. Hartford," I joke with him.

"Depends on the person in bed," he states seriously. Those familiar green eyes stare at me intensely. Is he flirting with me? No. It must be the painkillers because there is no way in hell Miles Hartford is flirting with me. "Anyway, let's have a look at this foot," he says quickly, changing the subject and breaking the tension between us. His hand touches my skin and instantly goosebumps run up my leg and I'm thankful that Miles says nothing. I know my cheeks are probably a bright shade of pink as I feel the heat pump through my veins as his soft fingers touch my ankle, moving it around, assessing it thoroughly.

"It's a nasty sprain but nothing a couple of days' bed rest can't fix," Miles tells me happily.

"Thanks."

We then both sit there in awkward silence for a couple of moments. "You're more than welcome to stay. I'm just going to watch a movie and chill. Not that I can go anywhere," I say, shrugging my shoulders.

"You'd want to hang out with an oldie like me?" he asks, teasing me.

"You're not old," I say, rolling my eyes at him. Yes, he is eight years older than me, but I don't notice it. "When was the last time you sat and did nothing? I can't imagine you've ever done that."

"Don't think I have. Not in a long time. Usually, it's about catching as much shut-eye as I can before I do a double shift," he explains.

"That's sad, Miles. It does wonders for the soul sitting and doing nothing. Plus, Rhonda is an amazing chef so she can whip us up some nachos or something."

"Okay, now I'm sold. You said nachos I'm in," he says, giving me a grin. Then he looks around the room and grabs one of my armchairs and pulls it up to the side of the bed.

"That will not be comfortable for someone your size. Look, I can move over," I tell him, shuffling over in my bed. He gives the bed a strange look, and I can see he is having a slight freak out. "Miles, we're practically family. It's not weird," I reassure him. All lies because I've dreamed of the moment Miles Hartford was in my bed. Did I think it was to watch a movie? No, but I'll take the start of my dirty fantasies anyway they come. He hesitates for a moment before kicking off his shoes and sliding in beside me, over the covers, of course. "Now, shall I text Rhonda to make us her famous nachos?"

"Yes, please. I'm starved," he says, rubbing his taut stomach, the action drawing my attention to a region I shouldn't be looking at.

"Right, um. I'll get her to grab us some sodas unless you want something stronger?" I ask.

"No, soda is fine," he tells me. The woodsy smell of his aftershave hits my nose, and my lady bits tingle. Easy girl, he's like a wild horse he could bolt at any moment. Forget that he is there until he relaxes and whatever you do, stop thinking about jumping him. It will not end well.

We settle into an action movie of his choice, and I'm surprised at how well the conversation flows between us. Because of our age difference, we've never really spoken one-on-one much and this is nice.

"Did you see Remi's billboard in Times Square?" Miles asks.

I choke on my drink as the surprise conversation turn. "Um, no," I splutter.

"Let me show you," he says eagerly, pulling out his phone and scrolling through to the photos. "So fricken proud of him."

I stare at the half-naked image of Remi in his underwear, his large package fully on display as well as his tanned and well defined six-pack, that flirtatious grin plastered on his face, and I hate that my body reacts to seeing him like that.

Yes, he is gorgeous.

Yes, his body is to die for.

Yes, he knows how to use that large package.

But he still broke my heart.

"Good on him," I say, handing Miles back his phone. He gives me a curious frown and I can tell he wants to ask me more but doesn't.

"Have you spoken to him recently? I know you guys were close," he asks.

"Nope, it's been months. He's pretty busy," I add.

"He shouldn't be too busy for friends though?" Miles questions.

"We've grown apart. Plus, he's more Dom's friend than mine," I explain to him, hoping the Remi questions will stop because if I'm honest, all I want to do is lean over and kiss those perfect lips and I will not let Remi cockblock me.

"Fair enough, shall we watch another movie?" Miles asks, changing the subject to my relief.

"Oh, wow. I'm sorry to interrupt." Rainn's voice echoes through my consciousness.

Why am I dreaming of Rainn? Especially when I feel nice and warm.

"Shit," a male's voice curses, and I'm shoved to the side, the hard warmth leaving me. "We must have fallen asleep," Miles explains.

"I can see that," Rainn adds, amused.

Finally, the last fog of my sleep clears my mind, and I realize that Miles and I have fallen asleep in each other's arms. He is up and out of my bed so quickly I almost have whiplash.

"I came over to check on Nell's foot and I guess we watched a couple of movies and passed out," Miles explains to Rainn as he runs his hand through his hair. He's acting as if she just busted us making out. I wish. Nothing happened between us. Nothing.

"Rhonda made her famous nachos, and you know how good they are. Next thing you are in a food coma," I tell Rainn.

"Rhonda makes the best nachos." My best friend grins, but I can see it in her eyes she has so many questions.

"Well, I better go," Miles suggests as he looks between the two of us. "Rest up, Nell." And with that, he's gone like a shot.

"What the fuck did I walk into?" Rainn questions me.

"Nothing," I say, flopping dramatically to my side, rubbing my face into the warm sheets he just occupied. They still smell of his woodsy scent. I'm never washing my sheets.

"You two looked pretty cozy when I walked in. His arm around you, and you were snoring," Rainn states, smiling. Oh my god, how embarrassing.

"His mom made him come over to check on me," I explain to Rainn. "Then I asked him to hang out, and he did, and now he's bolted."

"Maybe it's for the best."

"Why?" I question her.

"Because of Remi," she explains.

"Remi has nothing to do with what happens between Miles and me," I tell her angrily.

"They're brothers. Of course, there is going to be drama if you hook up with Miles."

"Well, I didn't, so there's nothing to worry about is there."

"Not yet, anyway," she adds solemnly.

"Forget Remi, he always seems to sour the mood even when he's not here," I grumble miserably.

"Fine. I just came to check up on you and hang out, but if you need a couple of moments to relieve yourself from being that close to Miles, then let me know," Rainn suggests jokingly.

I throw a pillow at her, which has her laughing.

20

NELL

"This wedding sucks," Audrey states, taking a seat beside me at the table. We are at her brother Rhys's wedding to a woman that his family hates. How do I put this nicely…because she's a gold digger.

"Not much you can do about it now, they're married, and your brother looks happy," I add.

"I know. I just heard her yelling at the staff because they didn't bring her the right champagne. She's horrible," Audrey grumbles as her shoulders fold in on herself.

"Your brother seems happy though."

"I know that's the killer, he truly is, but I know that in the not-too-distant future she's going to mess up and break his heart." Audrey sighs heavily.

"He's a big boy, Aud. He has to work it out for himself," I tell her, hoping to help her unease.

"I know. Better get back to the wedding table. Have fun. Chat soon." Audrey gives me a kiss and disappears into the crowd.

Moments later, I feel someone behind me.

"Looks like we're seat buddies," Remi whispers into my ear.

Turning my head at the sound of his voice, our lips almost touch as he is invading my space. "You have to be shitting me."

I haven't seen Remi since Ibiza, and I've kind of liked the distance between us. Seeing him tonight, I realize the distance has been good because my heart doesn't skip a beat at seeing him again. It feels kind of liberating to not have to worry about succumbing to his advances, which I know will be coming.

"I've missed you too, Nell." Remi grins, taking his seat beside me. I'm going to kill Rhys for this table assignment, especially as his brother Miles is sitting right across from me next to Rainn, who looks like she's flirting with him. I hate the unease simmering underneath the surface, overseeing the two of them together. She knows how much of a crush I have on Miles. I can feel Remi's eyes on me, but I dare not look at him. "Seems like Rainn and Miles are getting along rather well, don't you think?" Remi asks teasingly. I turn my head and give him a glare, which makes him smirk and raise his glass at me. "Guess you're stuck with the wrong brother, then?"

Ignoring him, I pull out my phone and text Rainn, asking her to swap seats because I will not sit here all night listening to Remi's play-by-play of them. I watch as her phone lights up and she looks down at my message subtly, then she looks over at me, then to Remi. Her eyes widen as she takes in the stone statue I've become and finishes up her conversation with Miles. Then she stands and walks over to where I'm seated.

"I think there must have been a mistake with the names because I thought this was my seat, Nell?" Rainn says seriously as she looks down at me, giving me a reassuring smile.

"I'll think you and I will have more fun anyway, Rainn," Remi adds with a chuckle.

Is he serious? He's flirting with my best friend. My eyes glare at him as my spine bristles at his statement.

"Don't think you could handle me, Rem. I'm so far out of

your league," Rainn warns him. This just has Remi laughing even harder as he sips on his drink.

Right, well I've had enough of his childish games. Standing up from my seat, I grab my name tag and purse before giving Rainn a thankful kiss on the cheek and heading on over to the other side of the table where I take my rightful seat beside Miles. All the while, I can feel Remi's eyes on me, but I dare not look over at him because I don't care. I mean, I shouldn't care. Dammit, five minutes around him and my defenses are crumbling.

"Hey, Nell. Long time no see." Miles greets me warmly with a kiss on the cheek, which lights up my entire body. It has been a while. Last time he saw me, I was in bed with a bad ankle. Miles looks delicious tonight, dressed in a navy-blue suit, and a white shirt with a silver tie. He's freshly shaven as he always is, his chocolate-colored hair styled simply, but it works for him. He doesn't need that designer just rolled out of bed hair that Remi sports. "Guessing my brother was annoying you?" Miles asks with a playful grin.

"Everything about him is annoying," I explain to Miles, who cracks up about my barb.

"You two have always annoyed each other, even as kids. He would pull your pigtails. Then you would punch him in the balls. It was great." Miles chuckles, reminiscing about my childhood.

"Guess I've grown up," I explain to Miles. I reach out and grab the champagne glass to take a nervous sip because being this close to Miles Hartford has my body on fire.

"Yes, you have," Miles states flirtatiously.

Wait, did I hear that right? I turn my head slowly and stare at him. Those familiar green eyes dip ever so slightly to my lips before looking back up into my eyes.

"I better behave because I'm fairly sure my brother is sending daggers into my back," Miles whispers as he grabs his drink and takes a generous gulp.

I do the same and take an uneasy sip of my drink and look over at where Remi is sitting and see a deep scowl on his face as he stares at Miles and me.

"I think my brother might still have a thing for you?" Miles grins as he places his arm on the back of my chair, moving himself closer to me.

"He doesn't," I assure Miles.

"I highly doubt that."

Miles has never been this overtly flirtatious with me before. I'm surprised. I thought that maybe this was all one-sided.

"I think his white knuckles around his glass say differently."

"You see, I'm upset with my little brother at the moment," Miles confesses to me.

"Why?" I ask curiously, turning my head in Miles's direction, which brings us almost nose to nose. My breath hitches and my chest tightens at how close we are. I can smell his expensive aftershave as the exotic scent tickles my nose.

"If I tell you, it might make you think less of him."

"Believe me, I already have a low assessment of him." Miles raises a brow at me, then smirks. "What did he do?" I ask, curious. What could Remi have done to Miles to have upset him so much? Remi idolizes his two older brothers. So, I'm confused over what he could have possibly done to hurt Miles so much. Hurt him enough to flirt with me, that is.

"He slept with my girlfriend," Miles explains angrily.

He did what? No. I know Remi is a player, but I can't imagine him doing something so...despicable. "Are you sure?"

"Of course. I caught them in bed together. They thought I was at work. Guess that's what I get for letting him crash at my place for a couple of days," Miles says frowning before throwing the rest of his drink back and pouring himself another.

"Why would he do that to you?"

"He's Remington Hartford, a famous polo player," Miles answers tightly. "Women love that shit."

I frown at Miles's comment. Look, I know Remi is a dick, and that dick seems to find it hard to stay in his pants most of the time, but I could never imagine him sleeping with his brother's girlfriend.

"Please, you're a doctor. Women love *that*," I tell him, placing a reassuring hand on his arm. His very hard, thick arm. How does he have time to work out on his schedule? Miles looks down at my hand on him, then tilts his head and gives me a blinding smile.

"Excuse me, miss, here is your starter." The server interrupts the intense conversation by placing the salad down in front of me, giving me a moment to collect myself because this champagne is going to my head.

Thankfully, the table distracts us from our one-on-one conversation, as the group chit chats about this and that. Occasionally, I catch myself looking up at Remi and imagining his thought process while sleeping with Miles's girlfriend. Every single time I look in his direction, those same green eyes stare back at me, daring me to flinch my attention away from him. And as much as I want to, my body won't let me look away from him, as if caught in his web, which I probably am, as he seems to weave it around me easily enough. Stupidly, I keep falling for it. Maybe a lobotomy is my next course of action or hypnotherapy.

Once we made it through the main course, then the speeches, cutting of the cake, then bride and groom's first dance, the party was in full swing. What I wasn't expecting was for Miles to grab my hand and whisk me onto the dance floor. Strong arms pulled me close to his chest as we slow danced to some romantic ballads. This is what I have dreamed about, isn't it? Being in Miles's arms, feeling his prickly cheek against my own, firm hands running all over my body as he sang the words to the song into my ear, his soft lips touching my skin every so often, raising goosebumps.

"Thank you for tonight, Nell," Miles whispers into my ear.

"You've been a great friend to me," he tells me before swinging me around the dancefloor. "Listening to me complain about my brother." He did that a lot. Not that I don't mind a good Remi rant session, but in that moment, I kind of felt disloyal to him. Don't know why, I'm still unsure why Remi would be that much of a douche to do what Miles said he did. Remi is no saint, but he loves his brothers. He looks up to them because he is so much younger than them. Maybe his newfound fame has changed the guy since the last time I saw him. What's saying his personality hasn't done a full 180 in that time. Next thing I feel is Miles's lips against my neck, and I freeze, unsure of what to do next.

"I've had enough of this," I hear behind me, just before I'm ripped from Miles's arms by a furious Remi who's staring down at his brother as if he is moments away from punching him in the face. We are in the middle of the dancefloor with all these couples around us at his brother's best friend's wedding. I will not allow these two to throw fists at each other and ruin the happy couple's day. Grabbing both of their arms, I pull them from the dancefloor and into a quiet corner where we can talk this out like fucking adults.

"What the hell is going on between the two of you?" I hiss as I narrow my eyes on them both. They stand there in silence, each with folded arms and narrow eyes. Right, so not only are they idiots, but they are stubborn, too. "Come on, you two, you're family. Let's squash this right here, right now."

"Yeah, Remi. Why don't you tell Nell how you fucked my girlfriend in my living room while I was asleep in my bedroom," Miles grunts angrily.

My attention swings to Remi, curious about what he's going to say to his brother's accusation.

"I told you, I did not know you and she were a thing when I brought her home." My stomach sinks at hearing Remi's words. So it is true he slept with Miles's girlfriend. "She didn't act like she had a boyfriend when we were at the club. She came on to me," he explains. "She was the one asking me to take her home. I mean, she didn't even know it was your fucking apartment until you walked out and saw us."

"Yeah, when I saw my brother's dick fucking my girl," Miles sneers at him. Remi sighs and runs his hand through his disheveled hair, looking exhausted by the conversation. "Fuck this, I'm done listening to my brother's pathetic excuses!" Miles says angrily before exiting the wedding venue.

21

REMI

My brother is upset and drunk. I have to remember that. I'm not proud that by some blimp in the fucking matrix, I brought home the woman that he's been sleeping with. Like what the hell, Universe? From what she said after Miles found us on the couch together, she and Miles were fuck buddies, nothing more. Hence the reason she had never been to his apartment. They work together, and because their schedules are so full, when they need a fuck, they call each other. Miles is acting like I'm the biggest asshole on the planet. How the fuck would I know any of this? She was some random woman I met at the club who I got on well with. Brought her home, yes, to his apartment. We had fun, and then Miles walked in on us. How could any of this have been premeditated?

But what has pissed me off the most is that he's used my fuck up to turn Nell against me. I had to sit here all night watching him flirt up a storm with her, rubbing the crush she has on him in my face. He has no interest in her. He was trying to hurt me, and he knows she's my kryptonite. The way his hands slid over her body on the dance floor. Getting lower and lower the drunker he became had my blood boiling until I couldn't take it any longer and had to break them up.

What I wasn't expecting was the pure rage and hatred thrown my way. Miles doesn't like to share, he never has, and I'm guessing that means he doesn't enjoy sharing his women, either. That man has a revolving door of nurses. Why is he upset about this one? Unless he started developing feelings for her and was too chickenshit to say anything about it? I mean, stranger things have happened, I guess.

"He's drunk, we can't let him leave like that. Let me go grab my bag and I'll come with you," she tells me.

"It's between him and me. I'll sort it out," I assure her. As I look down at her beautiful face, an ache that has been present since she left me in Ibiza slowly subsides now that I'm in her company again. But I'm sure Miles's words will have added some damage to the already fractured relationship we have. Probably severed it for good. "I didn't know he was seeing her."

"I know, Rem," Nell whispers softly. "You're a lot of things but screwing over family is not something you'd do. I tried to tell Miles that, but he won't listen."

Did she really confess to having my back with my brother? Reaching out, I cup her face, and as soon as my hand touches her skin, electricity runs through my veins, and I feel alive. My heart beats uncontrollably in my chest as if she's revived it from its slumber, then it sinks when she removes my hand from her face.

"Now's not the time, Remi. Go find your brother."

I'm torn. Now I have her attention. I don't want to leave because I know I won't get this moment back, but I need to sort things out with Miles. I hate the fact that I hurt him.

"Don't leave without me tonight, okay?" I ask her desperately.

"Okay," she answers reluctantly, but it's something.

I turn on my heel and rush outside of the venue and into the dark courtyard garden of the hotel. I see my brother slumped against the wall, with his head in his hands, looking worse for wear. "Miles!" I shout out into the darkness as I jog over to where he is standing. My brother's head lifts, and he gives me a defeated look as his shoulders sag against the brick wall. "Hey, what the hell happened in there?"

Miles just scrubs his face and shakes his head at me. "I'm sorry about all that. I'm not normally that dramatic." He groans awkwardly.

"I'd expect it from Stirling, but not you." This makes Miles chuckle. Can always count on ribbing on your other brother to bring a smile to your sibling's face. "Look, I'm really sorry about Tracey. I did not know you and she were a thing."

"Nah, man. I'm sorry. I overreacted. I know you didn't mess around with her on purpose, just was a shock at seeing the two of you together. You caught me at a bad time, and I took my shit out on you," Miles explains exhaustedly to me. I was not expecting that, not after what just happened earlier.

"Sounds like there is more to the story then?" I ask my brother.

"You have no idea," he states, turning and looking at me and for the first time in my life. I see my big brother looking lost.

"I know we may not be as close as you and Stirling are, but I'm here for you," I tell him sincerely.

"It's fucking embarrassing that's all," Miles explains.

"Do you have any idea of the amount of embarrassing shit I've done in my life?"

This makes him laugh. "Tracey and I were fuck buddies; that part was true, but what she forgot to mention was that we were both going for the same promotion at work." He lets out a heavy sigh. "A couple of the nurses I'm friends with warned me about Tracey, that she liked to use her assets to her advantage. I thought they were just being catty, because well, you know..."

"You might have fucked them?" I answer for him.

"Yeah. That," he agrees, rolling his eyes at me. "That they might have been jealous of my budding relationship with her. I mean, Tracey and I were spending so much time together outside of work that I stopped sleeping with other people and she told me she had too. Neither one of us was looking for a relationship."

I nod in understanding, I think I'm putting the dots together.

"The day before I found the two of you in my apartment is when I found out that Tracey had gotten the promotion and was now my new boss. Which is fine, I thought she deserved it, and she's a good doctor. Until the nurses pulled me aside again and told me that Tracey had been sleeping with the head of the department for months even though he had a wife, and they believed she did that to secure the promotion."

I remember how hard he had been working for that promotion, and shit, I've just poured salt into his wound by hooking up with the one girl that fucked him over.

"The nurses didn't like Tracey. She used to treat them like shit, but again I thought that was them being petty." Miles chuckles. "Fuck, I thought I was god's gift that these women were jealous of me fucking someone else. Such an idiot." He shakes his head at himself. "They were trying to warn me so many times, but I didn't listen until they played me a recorded conversation after I found out I didn't get the promotion. Apparently, the nurses had enough evidence of the department head and his sleazebag behavior, that they set up a sting in his office after their complaints had gone unheard. What they recorded was my boss offering Tracey the promotion if she agreed to keep sleeping with him." Well, shit, damn. That is crazy. "You can imagine the next morning after finding all this out, seeing her in my apartment fucking my brother. I sort of lost it." Honestly, I don't blame him. "I'm sorry about all that. None of this was your fault. It was a fucked-up situation, and I took my anger out on you because I couldn't take it out on her."

"What's happened now?" I ask, curious.

"They started an internal investigation this week. They have called me in to give evidence. It doesn't look good that I was having relations with her as it's frowned upon at the hospital, but as we were at the same level, it's not as bad." He lets out a shaky breath. "Fuck, I'm sorry that I flirted with Nell. That poor girl probably thinks I'm the biggest creep, but I just..." he states honestly. "I wanted to hurt you for no good reason."

I reach out and cup his shoulder, giving it a squeeze. "You don't have to apologize to me."

"Yes, I do. I know that you have a crush on Nell. And I still did what I did."

"Actually, she has a crush on you," I tell him honestly.

He stares at me in surprise before shaking his head. "I don't know what to say." He looks genuinely confused. I shrug my shoulders because there isn't anything I can do about it. It is what it is. "I always thought you and Nell had something together?" he says, turning his head in my direction.

"Once a very long time ago, but now I'm friend-zoned."

"Probably for the best. Can't imagine Dom would be too happy about that." He chuckles to himself. "Again, I'm sorry for this messed up situation. Are we good?" he asks sincerely.

"Yeah, we're good, bro." I reach out and give him a brotherly hug, which he receives warmly.

"Right, well. I think that's enough excitement for me tonight. I'm going to head on out." I give him a nod and a wave goodbye and watch him disappear into the darkness. Shit, what a night.

"Everything good?" Nell's voice surprises me in the darkness.

"Yeah, it's all good. One giant misunderstanding," I explain to her as I shove my hands into my pockets because all they want to do is reach out and pull her to me and I can't. Nell walks over and stands against the brick wall with me.

"I knew you wouldn't have done it on purpose," she whispers.

"How?"

"You are loyal to your family and friends, Rem," she tells me honestly.

"And yet I fucked it up with you," I confess in the darkness.

"Yeah, you did," she answers solemnly.

We both stand there in silence, letting those honest words swirl around us.

22

NELL

Why, after everything, am I still drawn to Remi? Why, after all these years, I still can't flush him from my system. No matter how much time we spend apart, I still want to climb him like a tree and have my way with him?

"I saw your billboard the other day in Times Square," I tell him, breaking the awkward silence between us. Remi chuckles as he leans back against the brick wall. "Why do you look so embarrassed about it? It's a great shot," I tell him sincerely.

Remi turns his head and looks down at me through his thick lashes, green eyes glowing in the moonlight. "Because my dick's been blown up to the size of the moon."

"I don't think anyone's complaining."

"Really?" Remi questions me.

Dammit, I didn't mean to pay him a compliment. "Oh, how I've missed your ego, Remi," I joke with him.

"Is that the only thing you've missed?" he asks flirtatiously.

And here we are back in the same spot I find myself in again and again. Remi flirting with me, me unable to say no. Next thing, we will roll around in the garden with my dress hiked up while I ride Remi on the bench. *Not like that doesn't sound like such a bad idea.* Stop it. You have been doing so well on your Remi cleanse, don't fall off the wagon now. *But he looks so hot in his suit. The black fabric cut to perfection over his muscular body, the palest of pink shirts on underneath with the red tie.* What kind of man can pull that combination off? *Damn supermodel, that's who.* Which is kind of what he is now, based on all the fanfare over his billboard. He is literally stopping traffic with his billboard. There have been news reports on the increased traffic accidents around his billboard. His dick is distracting drivers. I get it. He's dickmatizing. And here I am about to refuse his advances when any woman on this plant would give their left arm to be in this situation. It's been a couple of months since I've slept with someone and suddenly, my lady bits have woken up and are screaming, *"Do it, do it, do it."* She needs to slow her roll because nothing is going to happen, not with him, anyway.

"Remi," I say his name in warning.

"Nell."

This man is exhausting. "Right well, this conversation has taken a turn for the worse," I say, pushing off the brick wall. "It's been great catching up again. Like old times, but I'm going to get going back inside," I tell him before I turn around and leave him in the garden.

"Or you could stay, and I could give you multiple orgasms," he suggests seriously.

I'm so shocked by Remi's words that I turn around quickly and stare at him in surprise. The cocky bastard gives me a grin like he's just told me it's going to be nothing but sunshine tomorrow, not that he's just declared he wants to give me multiple orgasms.

"Hear me out." Remi holds his hands up in the air to halt me, knowing I'm moments away from hauling my ass back into that wedding. "The way I treated you when we were teenagers, I broke your trust in me forever. I get it now. I keep doing stupid shit and messing things up between us." This is true, but it's not all him, I've done some stupid shit too. "Which just proves your point of never being able to trust me."

"Rem," I say his name, but he holds up his hand to pause whatever I want to say so he can continue, which I do.

"These past couple of months of you having me blocked everywhere has driven me crazy. But it has made me reflect on things between us."

Well, that's good for him even though I feel as confused as ever.

"We still have this unexplainable pull between us, Nell. You can deny it all you want, but I know you feel it too," he explains confidently.

"I will not deny it, Remi. I'm sick of denying it. I agree every time we are around each other, I want to rip your clothes off. There I said it. I put it out there. The stupid elephant in the room," I tell him honestly. Remi's green eyes widen in surprise at my candor. He wasn't expecting me to be so honest about our situation.

"I knew it," he says with a confident smirk.

"Don't be a dick." I groan as I playfully swat at him, which makes him chuckle.

"In all seriousness, Nell. There isn't anyone I want more than you. Hands down, you're stuck beneath my skin." Damn him and his heartfelt words. He knows just what to say to pull me back toward him. "But I know I'm not boyfriend material yet, a long way from it. Maybe that's what growing up teaches you, to dig deep and be honest with yourself," he tells me honestly. Wow. Wasn't expecting this turn of events.

"You have the world at your feet at the moment, Rem. You're on billboards. You're the number three polo player in the world, soon to be number one. And I know your new rising star brings a lot of benefits. Enjoy everything life offers you in this moment because this life can be fleeting."

"You mean that, Nell?" he asks sincerely.

"I may not say it often, but I am so fricken proud of you and everything you have achieved in your life. I remember you and Dom talking about your dreams growing up and being the best in the world was your dream. As far as I'm concerned, you are." Remi's face softens, and he looks emotional at my words, but it's the truth. As much as I hate his guts sometimes, I can't hate on his achievements, his hard work, and dedication to polo.

"That means a lot, thank you." Remi rubs the back of his neck nervously, not used to my compliments. He caught me in a good mood he better not get used to it. "What about you, Nell? I thought you wanted to work for your mom's fashion line, not just model for it," he asks the one question I've been too afraid to ask myself.

"It's complicated, you know that. Mom still doesn't take me seriously even though I have a degree," I say, looking down at the stone ground, uneasy about the topic.

"Hey." Remi places a finger under my chin and makes me look up at him. "Your mom loves you, but she's a control freak over her business. If this is what you want to do, show her it is. Unless you're happy being a model?"

"What's that supposed to mean?" I question him defensively.

"Babe, nothing. I meant nothing bad by my comment at all. It's okay if you want to continue modeling for your mom. It's the family business." He tries to backtrack. I know he meant nothing by his comments, but Mom and her business are a sensitive subject for me. I thought after graduating Columbia, that maybe she would take my ideas seriously, but she's still not interested. So, I fill my time being an influencer, at least there I'm appreciated.

"I know, Rem," I whisper softly, letting out a long sigh.

"Hey, I get it. Remember, I used to live with your family," he says, trying to soothe me as his hand cups my face. His thumb slides ever so slowly across my cheek as if trying to help erase my insecurities. "Just know I believe in you."

Hearing him say *"I believe in you"* was something I wasn't expecting but needed to hear. Reaching out, I wrap my arms around him and pull him into a cuddle.

"Hey, baby girl, you okay?" he asks, chuckling at my sudden neediness. I nod as I bury my face in his chest. "I know I don't show my feelings cause I'm a dick. But you know that no matter what, I will always have your back, Nell." I nod again because I truly believe him. I stay wrapped around him for longer than is appropriate, but he says nothing. We stand there together in the moonlight in silence. "I didn't mean for our talk to get so serious. But I'm glad it did," he mumbles against the top of my head. I inhale deeply, committing his scent to my memory again. "Guessing you really needed this cuddle?"

"Yes," I mumble into his chest. My body vibrates against his chest as he laughs.

"You can cuddle me anytime you want, sweetheart."

I let my hands fall from him. I knew it wouldn't take long till it turned sexual again with him. "You couldn't let me have that?"

"Not when you have my dick coming to life. Just needed to warn you, otherwise I'm sure I would have ended up with a knee in my dick. And that is not how I envision ending my night." He gives me a wide grin.

"How did you envision your night ending?"

"You really want to know?" he asks seriously, raising a brow in my direction.

"Yes." I whimper breathlessly.

"I was hoping it would end with my mouth between your legs to start with," Remi whispers. His gaze is like a laser directly set on me. I'm finding it hard to swallow after that declaration. What am I meant to say to that? *Yes. You're meant to say yes, please.*

"Oh," is the only sound I can make. The two of us stare at one another, neither one of us daring to break the spell that is weaving between us.

"Fuck it." Remi curses and grabs my hand in his and starts pulling me deeper into the gardens. Thankfully, it's a full moon tonight, so there is enough light streaming through that I don't fall and break an ankle as we make our way across the gravel. Remi stops when he spots a park bench and heads toward it.

"Take a seat, Nell," he commands sternly. "Then I want to see your dress pulled up around your thighs." His dirty words send shivers down my spine, and I quickly do as I am told. I'm over fighting this pull between us; it's exhausting. I just want to enjoy the delicious orgasms that Remington Hartford pulls from my core like he is some pussy whisper. I can't change the fact he knows exactly how to play my body to perfection. It doesn't matter how many times I fight it, I always end up the same way on my back screaming his name. Maybe I should just give in more and enjoy the satisfaction that no strings attached sex can give me. What I should say is what no strings attached sex with Remi feels like, because no other man delivers like he does. It's rather inconvenient.

As my ass hits the cool park bench, Remi is on his knees helping me lift my dress. His large shoulders push my legs wide for him, and I don't even have a moment to prepare myself before Remi is diving between my thighs and his tongue is running along my slit. He makes a deep guttural growl as soon as his tongue tastes my wetness, and the vibrations send sparks all over my body.

"Oh, God," I groan as his tongue delves deeper inside of me. Thank goodness there is a back on this park bench, otherwise I would have fallen onto the ground. I've missed this so fricken much. I'm done. Remi can take me any way he wants, any time he wants if he keeps doing what he's doing with that magic tongue. My fingers entwine in his hair as I hold his head in the spot that makes my legs quake. "Yes, there. Right there, don't move." I urge with a rough pull of his hair, which makes him chuckle against my lips. My eyes roll back in my head as I rock against the roughness of his stubble, giving me delicious friction against my thighs until he gives my clit a hard suck just as he inserts a thick finger inside of me, which makes me splinter. Not knowing if we are alone in this garden, I clamp my teeth down hard against my lips, drawing blood as I stifle the insane orgasm that he just drew from me. Of course, Remi doesn't stop he keeps pushing and pushing, trying to pull as much pleasure from me as he can, he loves turning me into a liquid mess of goo. And I'm here for it. Moments later, his thick fingers are hitting their spot, and I explode a second time, clenching hard around his finger. *Oh, how I have missed Remi's orgasms.*

The crinkle sound of a condom wrap fills the night air, and when I eventually look up, all I see is Remi sliding the condom along his thick length. I lick my lips as I see my wetness on his fingers as he rolls the latex down along himself.

"Get up, Nell," Remi states roughly. "And ride me."

Yes, please. I quickly jump off the park bench and change positions with Remi. Holding up my evening dress, I straddle his thick thighs, reach between us, and wrap my hand around his dick. He hisses at my touch, which makes me grin. I line myself up before slamming down hard against his length, making both of us groan at the connection.

"Fuck, how I've missed your little cunt, Nell." Remi grabs my face with his hands and glares at me intensely. "Nothing feels better than your pussy lips wrapped around my dick." Dammit, dirty talking Remi has come out to play, and I can feel myself getting wetter with each filthy word. "No one compares to you, Nell," he confesses before his lips crash against mine in a blistering kiss. As soon as his tongue touches mine, he moves inside of me. I'm his to do with as he pleases, and he does. He takes every ounce of pleasure from my bones until neither one of us can take it any longer and we both scream our climax against each other's lips.

"Wow. Right. Give me a moment," Remi asks, panting. Seeing him so spent makes me so happy. "Remind me again why we don't do this more often?" Remi quips.

"There was a reason, but I'm finding it hard to think of it at the moment," I answer lightly. He nuzzles his face into the crook of my neck, and it feels right, and I know I shouldn't let it feel right, but I do. We stay there for a moment, enjoying the silence between each other.

"I'm going to ask something, and please don't hate me for asking," Remi states as he looks up at me. His hand moves my hair from my face gently. "I want us to be friends with benefits again," he says the last bit in a rush and squishes his face up, waiting for me to lose my mind because normally I would.

"We tried the friends with benefits thing ages ago. Didn't work out so well," I remind him.

"I know. But I think this time it might be different. We've had space, time to work on ourselves and I hope enough to put the past behind us?" he asks. Do I forgive him for breaking my heart all those years ago? I have to, I can't keep harboring this resentment toward Remi for shit he did when we were teenagers. Doesn't mean I want a relationship with him again, but I need to let it go.

"Yes. The past is in the past," I tell him. He looks relieved.

"Good start. Now we both know we can't keep our hands off each other," he states, raising a questioning brow in my direction. I nod in agreement, it's true, especially as his dick is still inside of me for this conversation. "Right and to be honest, I don't want to stop fucking you," he adds with a grin.

"Okay, I agree," I tell him reluctantly. He seems surprised by my words then, as his green eyes widen.

"So we agree we continue having sex with each other, but that's it?" he asks cautiously.

"Correct. No emotions. No feelings. No jealousy," I add.

"That's fair. And we can see other people as well."

"Yes. But you must be safe. Condoms all the time. Sexual health tests updated; you know all that stuff." Remi nods in agreement.

"You sure about this, Nell?" he asks.

"Sure am. Are you?" I question him.

"Oh, hell yeah," he replies excitedly.

23

REMI

The Garcia family have their annual polo day in the Hamptons during the height of summer. I'm excited because I get to see Nell today. I haven't seen her since the wedding. And I know I said that we should be friends with benefits and that whatever we have between each other is super casual. I know I said all that, but in reality, I have been stalking her socials like a creeper all summer. Enjoying her photos in her next-to-nothing bikini on some yacht in Greece with some billionaire shipping heir. Of course, I was jealous seeing his hands all over her, but I knew the next time I would see her she would let my hands do the wandering and I couldn't wait. I was buzzing with need over the expectation of seeing her again, and I know I shouldn't be, but I am.

"It looks like an enormous crowd out there today. Let's give them a show." Nacho slaps me on the back while we are preparing the ponies for the event. I better get my mind together to concentrate on the exhibition and then, once that's done, I'll try to find Nell.

I ride back into the stables on a high—we won, which is always good for the ego, and the crowd was ecstatic.

"Another cracking game, Rem," Dom states, thumping me on the back. I have spent little time with Dom since he lives in the UK, but it sure is nice to see my old friend.

"It was good playing with you again," I tell him sincerely.

"Not sure if my body is up to the same level as you are now. Fuck, I'm done. I need a beer and a beautiful woman on my lap to ease my sore muscles."

"Come on, let's get cleaned up because you fucking stink. Don't think the ladies will appreciate our stank as much as the ponies do," I tease.

Once we are fresh and ready from our showers, we head over to the large white tents set up around the field where everyone is partying. As soon as we step inside the bustling tents, you can tell everyone has had one too many drinks, but the atmosphere is jolly. We're stopped constantly, Dom and I, as we maneuver our way through the crowd toward the bar area.

"How do you stand there with a smile on your face entertaining these rich assholes while they suck up your ass?" Dom asks as we order our beers.

"Part of the job," I tell him, clapping him on his shoulder.

"Is part of your job eye-fucking the rich guy's young wife too?" Dom quips with a grin.

"Not my fault if her husband wants to arrange private polo lessons for his wife. I always offer a full-service lesson."

"You're such a dick." Dom groans at my comments. "One of these days, some woman is going to have you by the balls, and you are going to be powerless to stop it. And I'm going to sit back, watch, and laugh," Dom teases me. Little does he know some woman already has me in knots.

"There's more chance of you settling down before I do," I tell him as we rough house around with each other at the bar.

"You're probably right. And if I do, I ain't bringing her around anywhere near you. I don't want my bride to be giving you come fuck me eyes like all these other women do," he jokes with me, but I feel the sting of truth peppered beneath his words.

"Hey, come on, I'm not that bad," I say, grabbing our beers from the barman. Dom glares at me as if to say *"I'm that bad"* before taking a gulp of his beer. Whatever, he's just jealous. We run into some of our old polo friends as we continue through the party. I haven't seen Nell anywhere. There is no way in the world she is missing her family's event; she has to be somewhere.

An hour later, I notice a gorgeous blonde dressed in a blue and white sundress, and I know exactly who it is. It's as if my body can sense that she is near as tingles race through me.

"Oh, there's my sister." Dom reacts first, pointing to the blonde across the tent. "Do you mind if we go over and say hi?" he asks.

"Of course. I haven't seen Nell in ages," I explain to him as if we are old friends catching up.

"Do not touch my sister. There are a million other women here tonight that you can have. Leave her alone," Dom warns me.

"I'm not interested in your sister, Dom," I tell him. Yes, I feel like a dick lying to my best friend, but if I say otherwise, he is going to watch Nell and me like a hawk all night, and if he does, it means I can't whisk her away and fuck her in the stables again like old times. Dom's eyes narrow on me for a couple of beats, and when he sees that I'm being honest with him, he drops it. We head on over to where the girls are standing, talking, and taking selfies.

"Ladies, long time," Dom greets the girls happily. They are all so happy to see him and welcome him warmly. When it's my turn to say hi they are not as equally excited to see me. I get it, they are loyal to Nell, and they still remember me as the idiot that cheated on her years ago.

"Congrats on your win. You guys played really well today," Nell compliments us both.

"Please, it was all this guy. He's the star of it all," Dom says, slapping me in the stomach with his hand. I wave his compliments away.

"Don't be modest, Remi. That's not like you," Nell teases me.

"It was a team effort," I tell her. She just raises a manicured brow in my direction but gives me a warm smile. This is good, she's happy to see me, it's a start.

"Says the world's number three," Nell jokes.

"Number two, actually. He's just gone up in the rankings," Dom answers for me.

"No way. That is amazing," Nell exclaims warmly, and it feels nice that she's acknowledging my accomplishments. She makes me feel invincible. "Next season you'll be number one."

"Hell, yeah, he will be." Dom grabs me around my neck and tries to ruffle my hair, but I have a good inch or two on him and we rough around a little, laughing amongst ourselves.

"Right, well, all this testosterone is making me thirsty, so I'm going to go grab a drink from the bar. Dom, you want to come?" Rainn asks through long, thick lashes. Dom releases me quickly and trails after Rainn as she heads toward the bar. Is there still something going on between them?

"Um. Yeah. I'm going to go grab a drink too," Audrey adds, not wanting to stay with Nell and me.

Now we are alone together. "You're looking good," I say as I rake my eyes down her sundress, admiring her subtle curves.

"I know that face, Mr. Hartford, and it means trouble," Nell warns, crossing her arms in front of her.

I take a step forward and lean in toward her ear. "You do not know the amount of trouble I want to cause with you," I whisper, letting my lips touch her skin ever so gently. When I stand back,

I can see her nipples are hard, pressed against her dress and her cheeks have the faintest of color set across them.

"Fine. Meet me in my bedroom in five. And make sure no one sees you. Okay?" Those doe eyes are warning me. I nod in understanding and watch her pert little ass sway as she walks away from me before I turn in the other direction, knowing another way to get to her bedroom so that no one notices us missing.

I take the long way around the Garcia manor and make my way through the staff entrance, which is filled with staff running around madly with empty plates and glasses. No one pays much attention to me as I dash through the kitchen. I give Chef Liam a high five as I pass through; thankfully, he's busy and can't stop to chat.

"Keep killing it, Remi," he calls out after me.

"Will do, boss," I call back, chuckling to myself. He looked after me well when I lived here, always having an extra bowl of his famous chili waiting for me after training. I swear it was the only thing that got me through Mr. Garcia's insane workouts. I slip right out of the kitchen and into the main corridor of the home. Thankfully, it's empty with everyone outside at the event. I take the stairs of the grand staircase two at a time, reaching the top with little effort. I make a right at the top of the stairs and head on down toward Nell's wing.

"Remington Hartford." I still upon hearing my name. Oh shit. I turn around and there standing before me is little Portia Garcia, or should I say grown up into a gorgeous bombshell, Portia Garcia. Wow. I barely recognize her.

"Portia?" Those familiar brown eyes narrow on me, and I know she's seen Nell come this way and now I am too. Think quick, Remi. "Oh, my goodness, you're all grown up."

"Oh, my goodness, you're still sneaking around with my sister," she says sarcastically, with her hands on her hips.

"No, I'm not," I answer quickly. She's not buying my bullshit, judging by the arch of her brow. "Fine. I just wanted to talk to her. It's been a while."

"Whatever. I don't care. But my silence is going to cost you."

That sneaky little shit. "How much?"

My question makes her smile. "Two bottles, no five bottles, of champagne for my friends and me," she states matter-of-factly.

"You're underage. Your father would kill me."

"I just graduated from high school. I'm eighteen. I'm an adult now," she states, giving me sass.

"Two bottles," I tell her, hating negotiating with tiny terrorists.

"Three."

"Fine. I'll go grab you some but give me a moment I need to talk to your sister," I tell her, eventually giving in because I don't have time to waste out here talking to her when I could be in Nell's room, balls deep.

"Only a moment, Rem? That's not what the rumors say." She chuckles.

"Fuck you, Portia. I'll get you your shit, now fuck off and annoy someone else, will ya." I glare at her, which makes her laugh as she skips her way happily downstairs. Damn her for ruining my vibe. I continue down the corridor toward Nell's room. I open the door and close it behind me, turning the lock. The click echoes through the room. Nell is staring out her window, her back is to me.

"Did anyone see you?" she asks, turning her head and looking at me over her shoulder.

"No. Coast was clear," I tell her. I know that was a lie, but it's just a white one, she doesn't need to know her sister just extorted me.

"Good." She smiles before looking back out the window.

I reach her in a couple of steps. My lips press against the curve of her neck, and she falls back against my chest. My hand is underneath her dress in a matter of seconds, and I hiss when I feel nothing but bare skin. Dammit, Nell, as my dick throbs with excitement. I kick her legs out, widening her stance for me as I slip my fingers between her soft thighs, it's been too long. She's already wet and ready for me. "We have to be quick, Remi. Before anyone notices we're missing," Nell states, looking over her shoulder at me. I wanted to take my time with her as it's been a while since the last time I saw her, but if the woman is saying be quick, then I'll have to be.

"You know going quick is against everything I believe in," I growl into her ear.

"Yes, Remi, I get it. We will keep your reputation for being a player intact I promise I won't breathe a word of your quickness to anyone," Nell says with a laugh.

"You fucking tease," I curse as my hand comes down on her ass with a hard whack. Nell squeals as my hand connects with her skin and the delicious sound reverberates around the room. I watch in fascination as she wiggles her ass again for me, asking for more.

"Does my handprint across your ass turn you on, Nell?" I ask before my teeth sink into her shoulder, giving her a tender nip.

"Yes," she answers breathlessly. Naughty little Nellie, she's never told me about this little kink for spanking before, maybe I should have tested it more often.

"As we suggested, I need to be quick. We might have to come back to this recent development another time," I tell her, as my hand runs down the curve of her ass and my fingers slip between her thighs, finding her wet and wanting. I quickly undo my trousers and sheath myself before I run my dick between her thighs again, coating myself in her juices before teasing her entrance with the tip of my dick.

"Please, Remi," Nell begs as I continue to tease her, never giving her what she wants, which is my dick deep inside of her.

"You better put on a show for the good people down below, Nell." I hiss as I push forward inside of her. Nell releases a frustrated moan, and I don't give her time to adjust to me before I slam back into her again. My fingers dig into her hip as she tries to maintain a normalcy as she stands at her bedroom window. "You like the fact that anyone could look up and see you being pleasured, don't you, Nell?" I ask her hoarsely through gritted teeth.

"Yes," she answers in a moan.

"It makes you wet the thought of being caught." Another heated moan falls from her lips. "Who knew Nell Garcia was an exhibitionist," I grunt as I thrust into her.

"You love it too. You love the fact that no one knows that you're my dirty little secret, don't you?" She curses. "That you can fuck me in my childhood bedroom or in a nightclub bathroom then walk right out as if you didn't just do the filthiest things to me." Dammit, she's right. I love it. Just thinking about it has my dick painfully hard and my thrusts lose their rhythm as the dirty thoughts of fucking Nell right in the middle of her family's party where anyone could find us has me so fucking hard there's no chance of me being able to stop even if I wanted to.

"I'm addicted to you, Nell." I curse as I thrust harder into her.

"I know, me too."

"It's fucked up I know, but I can't help it," I answer on a groan as I continue to fuck her. A couple more thrusts, and we are both coming. I need a moment to collect myself before slipping out of Nell.

"Why is it always so good with you?" Nell queries on a hiss as I drag myself from her. I pull off the condom and tie it off, then grab some tissues and wrap them around it before placing it back into my pocket, last thing I need to do is leave any evidence of what's happened in her bedroom because I know the cleaner will say something to Mrs. Garcia.

"I'm just that good."

Nell turns around playfully, gives me a shove, which pushes me back a couple of steps, but she is smiling, so that's good. Nell straightens herself up before heading over to her drawer, pulling a fresh pair of underwear out, and slipping into it. All the while, I can't take my eyes off her.

"What?" she asks with a frown, wondering why I'm staring at her the way I am. Instead of answering her, I walk over and grab her face and kiss her passionately. "Wow, um, what was that for?"

"Just 'cause," I tell her. She gives me a little frown but says nothing more about it.

"Right, well, I should get going because Rainn and Audrey are probably looking for me," she says awkwardly, running her hands down her dress trying to smooth it down. I say nothing and watch her disappear out the door. There's a sense of emptiness that fills the void that she has left inside of me, but I push it away, hoping to bury it beneath me. I suck in a breath, steadying myself before opening the door. I pray no one is in the corridor to see me leave her room. I thought I was in the clear until I get down the stairs and run right into the glare of a teen, Portia.

"Don't forget our promise, Remi." She glares at me icily. This chick is crazy.

"I won't. I'll send the bottles to your room. Give me twenty, okay?" I explain to her impatiently. She gives me a nod and disappears.

Later that day, once the sun sets and most of the polo crowd have left, the after-party begins. Which is wild, the Garcia family really knows how to throw a party, all their friends turn up, even my parents show up which is great as I haven't seen them in ages, so I spend a lot of the night catching up with them. Stirling is there with friends, and it turns out to be a great night. I've been so caught up in catching up with my family that I haven't seen Nell all night, not until I stumble upon her and some guy making out in a corner of the tent away from her family. There's a gut punch I wasn't expecting. When they eventually pull away from each other, I see it's the douche from her holiday in Greece, the shipping heir. I hate the way she is looking up at him as if he could deliver the moon to her. I hate how she hangs on every paltry word he is saying as if it's interesting. I hate she is laughing at his pathetic jokes. I hate that while one of her friends distracts her, he's checking out other girls at the party. I hate him.

"Rem, there you are," Dom greets me happily. "You need to come meet these girls; they are so hot, and they have accents. Double whammy." He taps me on the shoulder as he tries to pull me toward his newfound friends. I give Nell one last look and shake my head. You wanted this, you asked for this, now deal with it.

"Okay, man, let's go have some fun," I tell my best friend.

24

NELL

Ugh, I feel so sick.

I should have stayed with my family in the Maldives, but no, I had to come back to snowy Manhattan to go hang at some star-studded New Year's Eve party when really, I should be laying in the sun with a mimosa in my hand, not a hot water bottle. I'm miserable and feeling sorry for myself because I had a cute outfit planned and now nowhere to wear it. Plus, I'm home alone as my parents gave Rhonda, our housekeeper, the holidays off so that she could be with her family.

My phone rings beside me, and I answer it. "Hello."

"You sound like shit, babe," Rainn tells me honestly.

"I think I'm dying," I say dramatically, which makes Rainn chuckle.

"Aud and I are canceling New Year's and coming to stay with you."

"No. Don't do that. I can't let you girls get sick. Plus, you both have to go to the event; your sponsors are hosting it," I remind her.

"Dammit." She curses angrily. "We will be there first thing in the morning as soon as our obligation is up." I love my girls. "What about Dior? Can't she come over?" she asks. I love my friend Dior, but she really isn't the most reliable out of our friend group. She would rather be at a celebrity-filled party than stay in on the year's biggest night looking after me. "I think she has a photoshoot next week in the Bahamas for a campaign. I can't get her sick for that." Silence stretches between Rainn and me.

"If you need anything, just text Audrey or me and we will be right over no matter what, okay?" she says to me sternly.

"I know you will, but I'm going to be in and out of consciousness, so it would be a waste of time coming over. I love you both, but please enjoy New Year's for me. Go find some hotties and take them home and ring in the new year with orgasms." Someone should have fun tonight if it's not me.

"Fine, if we must," Rainn jokes. "But call us any time day or night if you need us."

"I think I'll be calling Miles Hartford first if I need anything medical," I tell her with a chuckle that turns into a cough.

Ugh. I hate being sick.

"Very true. Could be the start of something. Miles comes over and tends to you while you're sick. You look across at each other, and he finds your bloodshot eyes and snotty nose adorable, and then you fall into bed together and live happily ever after," Rainn teases me.

"Hey, I like the sound of that. Great way to start the new year," I tell her.

"I think you're delirious, Nell, but I'll let you live in hope."

"Whatever, go have fun. Think of me. I'll be following your socials all night so make them good."

"Will do," Rainn says before hanging up the phone. The phone call must have exhausted me because moments later I am snoring happily, wrapped in my blanket cocoon.

The sound of banging wakes me, and I sit up too quickly, and my head spins. But I hear a crash and a deep-throated curse from the kitchen. There is someone in my apartment. I shake my head to clear the sleep fog from my brain. Who the hell would be in here? There is no way the bellman would let anyone up to our floor that isn't on the list, so it must be someone safe. My family is halfway across the world unless…my dream of Miles coming to look after me is really coming true. Of course, my parents would call Miles to ask him to check up on me like they did when I hurt my ankle. Oh my god, this is it. This is the moment he falls head over heels in love with me. Then I look down and realize what a mess I must look like. I have stains on my shirt from wiping my running nose on it. I've scattered balls of tissues around my bed like confetti. My hair is a bird's nest of knots tied up in a messy bun. No make-up on. On shaky legs, I jump up and head to the bathroom, I almost scream when I glimpse myself in the mirror. Wow, you look disgusting. I don't have time for a shower, but I can splash my face, put a comb through my hair, clean my teeth, put deodorant on, and change my clothes. That's all the energy I have.

I'm dressed and cleaned to some sort of normalcy. I chose a long-sleeve white tracksuit top, even put a bra on, black leggings, and my UGG boots. My hair is pulled up in a high ponytail, and I put some lip gloss on then spray some perfume; it's all I can do without collapsing. I walk out of my stuffy bedroom and into the corridor and down toward the kitchen, where more grumbling and cursing are coming from. When I turn the corner, I let out a squeal because that is not at all who I thought would be standing in my kitchen dressed in a tux looking like a damn GQ model while he fumbles with the stove.

"Remi?"

"Oh shit, did I wake you?" he says as a frown forms on his face, looking at me with concern.

"Yeah, kind of."

"Sorry. I was trying to cook up some chicken soup I picked up from Rhonda's place. But I realize I don't have the best culinary skills." He stares at me, looking helpless and I don't think he's ever looked cuter. I must be sick because seeing Remi in my kitchen trying to cook me up some chicken soup has my heart beating wildly. I don't think it's him doing it. Must be my cold. "How the hell do you look so good when you're so sick?" Remi asks, catching me off guard with his question. *Because I thought you were your brother, no, I was hoping you were your brother.* You're such a bitch, Nell, look at him helping you like he is, he doesn't have to.

"I don't get why you are here?" I ask him.

"Your mom called my mom who called Miles, but he's working, so couldn't help. So, he called me because Stirling is out of the country, to go to Rhonda's place in Queens to pick you up a batch of her flu busting chicken soup and bring it to you as I had an event to go to in the city and was the closest," he explains, as if this was a normal request. "You look pale, Nell." He stares at me with concern before rushing toward me as I stumble to the side a little as the room spins. "Hey, you, okay?" he asks, holding me by my arms. I shake my head weakly as I don't feel great suddenly as my temp skyrockets.

"I've got you," Remi says before he picks me up in his arms. I feel like a sack of potatoes, but I'm too exhausted to fight him. He walks me back down my corridor and into my bedroom. He places me ever so gently back in my bed and pulls the covers up. "You need to rest," he tells me firmly. I nod in agreement because I don't have the energy to argue and promptly fall back asleep.

I wake up a little while later and notice that I have curled up against something hard.

"Hey, you're awake. Wanna drink?" Remi asks as he reaches over to my bedside table and hands me a bottle of water. I frown at him as he hands me the bottle, but I take it anyway because my throat feels scratchy. I sit up and unscrew the bottle and take a sip of the cool water.

"Remi, what are you doing in my bed?" I question him.

"Making sure you didn't die in your sleep," he replies with a shoulder shrug as if it's no big deal. I notice my television is on, but he's watching some reality TV show with almost muted volume. He's taken his tuxedo jacket off, his tie, and his shoes. He's rolled his white sleeves up, exposing his tanned, veiny forearms which are my kryptonite. Easy girl, you're sick. There will be no extracurricular activities with Remi tonight.

"Thanks for checking in on me, but you must be late for your event," I tell him, nodding my head in his direction.

"I canceled," he states nonchalantly.

"You canceled?"

"Yeah, it was a boring event, anyway. Looking after you was a great excuse," he explains to me as he flicks through the channels on the television. Am I hallucinating? This truly can't be happening right now.

"You canceled your New Year's Eve plans to look after me?" I ask, perplexed by his motivation.

"Looking after you is a bonus, but honestly I didn't want to go to the event, so win-win," he says, giving me a smirk.

"You know it's creepy to watch people sleep," I tell him, unable to plan any other thought in my brain.

"Normally it would be, but I was doing a public service making sure that you didn't choke because you were snoring rather loudly." I shove him, which makes him laugh at me. "Look, you were going to be alone for New Year's Eve, sick. I also know it's one of your favorite holidays and I thought I couldn't let you be by yourself tonight." Oh. That was sweet and nice of him. I turn and look up at him. He is watching me cautiously. "If me being here is making you uncomfortable, I can go. The last thing I want to do when you're sick is annoy you," he explains wholeheartedly. Now I feel like a moody bitch.

"I guess it wouldn't suck if you stayed, but only if you wanted to."

"Nowhere else I would rather be, babe," he tells me with a wide smile, which makes my stomach flutter, but it could be a symptom of the flu too. "I worked out the microwave, so let me heat the soup for you. You're probably starved," he tells me, jumping off the bed just as my stomach rumbles loudly, which makes us both laugh. Awesome way to break the tension, Nell, I curse myself. I grab my phone and notice it's almost nine. I wonder what the girls are doing at the moment. They must be at the club, probably drinking cocktails, dancing, having fun. I scroll through my feed and see everyone's New Year's Eve party photos, and I'm jealous of the amazing time they are all having.

"Here you go. Be careful, it might be hot," Remi says, walking around the corner with a tray filled with a bowl of soup, some crusty bread, flowers, a mini bottle of champagne and he's wearing a silly party hat on top of his head. Not sure why but tears well in my eyes at his thoughtful gesture. "Oh, babe, did I do something wrong?" he asks frozen in place, confused over why I'm now crying. I shake my head to let him know everything is fine.

"No. You did good, Remi," I say through my sniffles. His face relaxes as he brings the tray closer to me before setting down the legs of the tray on the bed. "Thank you," I wheeze through my snot bubbles. "Are you not going to eat?" I ask when I realize this is a meal for one.

"I ate earlier, all good," he tells me.

I dig in and moan as the first drop of flavor hits my tongue. Rhonda's soup always makes me feel better when I'm sick. I still can't believe he went to Queens to get it for me. Emotion and confusion are swirling around me, but I'm too sick to investigate these stupid feelings. So, what? Remi did a nice thing for me doesn't change the fact he's a player and will never be a one-woman man. Friends, remember, you're just friends. You can't let him have your heart again, even if he is being cute.

"Shall we watch some of the New Year's Eve countdown

shows?" he asks. I nod in agreement as I slowly devour my soup. He changes the channel and settles in beside me and we both sit there in silence, just watching the entertainment, happy in each other's company, not needing to fill the silence. I'm all warm and toasty and place my tray on the floor and snuggle into Remi while we watch whatever is on the TV. It doesn't take long till Remi wraps his arm around me and pulls me closer and not long after that, he's stroking my hair, and everything feels right. I must fall asleep again because I wake to Remi's lips pressed against my temple, wishing me a happy new year.

"Happy new year," I mumble into his chest. I feel his fingers again in my hair as he continues to stroke along my strands. "Thank you for spending it with me."

"There's nowhere else I would rather be, Nell," he confesses, kissing my temple again. I know I shouldn't feel comforted by his words or actions, but I do, and then I promptly fall asleep again.

25

REMI

"Happy new year!" I scream, popping the crackers spraying confetti everywhere when Nell walks down the corridor and into the living room. She screams and ducks at the sound.

"Remi, what the fuck. Are you trying to kill me?" She yells at me, clutching her chest, but all I can do is smile because she looks so beautifully disheveled, and I like that look on Nell. I also enjoyed waking up to her in my arms this morning—what a great way to celebrate the new year with my favorite person wrapped in my arms.

"I was hoping you were feeling better this morning?"

"I do, thank you. Just wasn't prepared for a ticker-tape parade entering the living room," she says, giving me a small smile.

"Thought we could recreate New Year's Eve this morning, seeing as you slept through it all last night. If you're up for it, that is?" I ask her. I watch as her brown eyes widen in surprise. "Look, I've ordered brunch. There are mimosas. I have all your favorite pastries. We have party hats, more confetti cannons, balloons. All you need to do is go have a shower and come back and enjoy." A frown forms on her face as she stares at me.

"You changed?" she asks me, pointing to my gray tracksuit.

"Oh yeah. I asked the hotel's concierge to pack up my room and send my stuff over to here," I explain to her. She stares at me for a couple more moments in silence, shakes her head and turns on her heel, and heads back to her bedroom. Once she's gone, I rush out to the front door and open it to let Rainn and Audrey in, who brought the decorations. They messaged Nell throughout the night and while she slept. I may have used her finger to open the phone so I could text them back because I knew they'd be worried. As tempted as I was, I didn't look any further into her phone.

"You are such a doll for doing all this for her," Audrey tells me as Nell's friends scurry in to help decorate the dining room.

"It's nothing," I tell them, uncomfortable with their compliments as they rarely give me any.

"No, Rem, it is something. You turning up when she needed you the most is something," Rainn adds.

We get to work hanging up streamers and banners all around the dining room until we hear Nell's footsteps down the corridor. The girls quickly hide and wait for the perfect moment to jump out and surprise Nell. When she turns the corner and sees what we've done to the dining room, Nell's face breaks out into an enormous smile and that's the moment Rainn and Audrey jump out and yell "happy new year" to her. Nell's face when she sees her two best friends there has her bursting into tears as she rushes toward them. They all embrace, and I give them all their moment. Until I feel arms wrap around my middle and tits pressed up against my back.

"Thank you, Remi, for making this one of the best New Year's ever," Nell whispers into my back as she squishes me in a tight hug before joining her friends at the dining table. I sit back and listen to them chat about this person and that person, gossiping about who was hooking up with whom and who was drunk, who caused a scene, who cheated, it was rather fascinating, better than those reality TV shows I watched last night while Nell slept. As the girls continue, I pull out my phone and check my messages and DM's until I feel someone watching me.

"She's got nice tits," Rainn whispers beside me as she reaches out and grabs a croissant, her back toward Nell.

"I didn't ask for it, if that is what you're thinking," I explain to her.

"None of my business."

"Feels like you still have more to say though?"

Rainn raises a brow. "Since you asked, I do. Probably not a good idea looking at other women's nudes after spending the night in my friend's bed."

"Noted," I say, placing my phone face down on the table.

"Is everything okay?" Nell asks, looking between Rainn and me.

"Yeah, it's all good. I was telling Rainn that Dom's been asking about her." As soon as the words are out of my mouth, Rainn turns her head and glares at me. I pick up my mimosa and raise it in her direction.

"Why is Dom asking about Rainn?" Nell questions me.

Rainn's eyes widen with panic, and I'm surprised by her reaction, and now feel bad for dropping her in it.

"He said something about going to Bali and knew Rainn lived there or something and wanted to ask her some questions," I explain to Nell.

Rainn nods her thanks in my direction for covering for her. Looks like I might have inadvertently stumbled upon something I shouldn't have.

"Why would Dom want to go to Bali? He hates the sun," Nell queries.

"Probably because some hot model asked him to go, and he wants to impress her or something." Making up more lies, keep digging that hole, Remi.

"Does Dom have a girlfriend?" Nell asks. Oh, man, this is getting out of hand.

"Dom doesn't do girlfriends," I say, which Nell nods in agreement and accepts before turning back to her conversation with Audrey.

"What the fuck, Remi?" Rainn whisper yells at me. I give her an apologetic face, but she just shakes her head at me. Great, just when I thought Nell's friends were warming up to me, I blow it again.

The girls have finished brunch and while I clean up, they've been chatting away in the living room.

"Thanks for looking after Nell last night. She seems a lot better," Audrey says, giving me a warm smile.

"Don't thank me. I think it was Rhonda's chicken soup that fixed her," I explain, placing the last of the pastries in the fridge.

"Or maybe it was a little of both." Audrey winks. "Rainn and I are going to get going, we'll catch up with Nell later, she's looking a little tired. Thanks again for organizing this for her. I know she appreciates it so much. Always knew there was that dependable guy deep down inside. You should show Nell that more often," Audrey tells me.

"I'm not ready for all that yet," I tell.

"That's honest. I can appreciate that. But remember, while you wait to be ready, someone else already is." And with that pearl of wisdom, Audrey leaves me with much to mull over. Rainn gives me a wave from the living room as the girls exit Nell's apartment.

"What are you doing, Rem?" Nell calls out from the living room. I wipe my hands on the towel and head on into the living room where she's seated.

"Was just tidying up," I answer her as I take a seat on the couch beside her.

"Thanks for today, it's exactly what I needed. But I'm so exhausted." She sighs, falling dramatically back against the couch. I grab her feet and put them in my lap, which makes her squeal.

"Relax," I tell her as my fingers massage her feet.

"Oh, wow," she whispers on a moan as she sinks back against the cushions and places her hand over her brow.

"Didn't realize all I needed to do was massage your feet to get you on your back," I joke.

Nell moves her hand away and glares at me, but I can see the corner of her lips twitching with a smile before she covers them again. I keep working my magic on her feet until the light snores from Nell can be heard. I get off the couch and grab the blanket which is hanging over the corner and place it over her. She snuggles into the furry thing and mumbles thanks and promptly falls back asleep again.

I must doze a little because I wake up on the armchair next to Nell who is snoring away happily. I stretch out, and it becomes painfully clear that my dick is standing to attention and doesn't look like he wants to go down soon. I'm going to need to take care of this, especially with Nell curling up against me, he's confused as to the reason he's not inside of her. I head on over to the guest room where I put all my things, but the scent of Nell's body wash calls to me. I peek over my shoulder to double check if Nell is still sleeping soundly. She is. My heart is thundering in my chest, worried about getting caught, but my dick is in control, and he does not care at all. I make my way into Nell's bathroom and quickly strip off my tracksuit and underwear. My dick throbs with excitement now that I have set him free, but he's going to have to enjoy my hand, not Nell's exquisite pussy. I step into the warm shower and lather myself up with her shower gel, and her scent instantly hits my nose and my dick throbs with need. I slide my hand down my body, where I wrap my fingers around my dick and lather it up. I hiss at the contact and before I know it, I'm lost in the sensations and thinking about all the things I want to do to Nell the next time we can get together. I can't wait to savor her lips. Suck on her nipples. Lose myself between her thighs.

"Nell." Her name falls from my lips, but I'm too far gone in my fantasies that I don't know how loud I am. Nell is pretty passed out she won't hear anything. My hands grip myself tighter imagining my hand is her tight little cunt and I'm disappearing inside her, losing myself to the oblivion that is her essence until I can't hold it in anymore, and on a guttural moan, I call out her name as I come in large ribbons all over her shower's tiles. I place my forehead against the tiles and take a moment to catch my breath.

"Impressive."

Nell's voice stills me. Shit. I thought she was asleep. Fuck, what do I do? She probably thinks I'm a creep jerking off about her while she is sick. Maybe she heard nothing. Next thing I know, the glass door to the shower opens and there, standing before me, is Nell, naked. My eyes widen. Taking in her naked form she's literally rendered me speechless.

"Move over," she says, pushing me out of the way so she can step into the shower. "This feels good." She moans as the hot water cascades down her body. "Why are you looking at me like that?" she asks.

"Um, because you're naked in my shower."

"Oh, I'm sorry. I heard you calling my name, so I assumed you wanted me to join you," she replies brightly before taking the shower gel and squeezing it into her palm, then she lathers herself.

"Nell," I say her name with a warning.

"What?" she says, looking over her shoulder at me innocently. My dick is twitching back to life again. She better be careful.

"Are you testing me?"

"Nope. I'm just getting clean," she replies, shrugging her shoulders as if the two of us showering is an everyday normal thing. I watch her rinse the soap off her body. My eyes follow the streams of white foam down her back, over her hips, and down between her ass cheeks. But I'm holding myself back because she's still sick, and she hasn't invited me to do anything to her. So, I'll wait till she is ready for me. "All clean." Nell turns around, giving me a wide grin. Her eyes dip to my lips and then they move further south, over my chest, down my stomach to my now hardened dick. Then she reaches out and scrapes her nail down my chest. "Looks like you're all clean too," she says huskily. This woman is testing me. "But I think I might have missed a spot. It's always hard to get," she explains to me as she reaches out and grabs my wrist, placing my hand between her thighs.

"Nell?" I warn her. She takes one of my fingers and drags it through her folds before inserting it inside of her.

"See, I told you, Remi. I'm still dirty."

I lose my motherfricken mind, that is the hottest action any woman has done to me. My fingers find her wet and ready as they slip between her folds easily. She falls forward at my movement and places her hands on my shoulders. Her nails dig into my skin as she rides my finger.

"You're such a filthy girl, aren't you?"

"Hmmm." Nell moans as my fingers curl deep inside of her. I know I've reached the spot when her nails dig harder into my skin.

"Your greedy little cunt is taking my fingers as if it's starved. Has it missed me?"

"Fuck, Remi," she curses as my hand moves between her thighs.

"No one fills its hunger like I do, do they?"

"Yes!" Nell screams as my thumb connects with her clit. "Yes. Yes. Yes." she screams as her pussy constricts against my hand as she falls forward and rests her head against my shoulder as aftershocks quake through her body. Slowly, I slip my fingers from her and wrap myself around her. I turn the shower off and step out with her wrapped in my arms. I grab a towel and wrap it around her and grab another to wrap around my waist. Then I pick her up and carry her limp body to her bed, where I lay her down and gently dry her off. She's a gooey mess and has never looked more beautiful. I grab a T-shirt from her wardrobe and slide it over her head, there's no need for underwear, then I tuck her back under the covers before drying myself off and jumping in next to her naked. I roll over and pull her against me. She mumbles her thanks and promptly falls asleep and I'm not far behind her.

26

NELL

"Happy Valentine's Day," Jarred says, kissing my cheek as he hands me a dozen red roses. Aw, this is so sweet. I've known Jarred for a while now, he's older than me. I've opened my dating horizons to a new age bracket. We see each other around town at certain hotspots and openings. He's some fancy finance guy on Wall Street. He slid into my DMs, and we've been chatting for a while now, but our schedules have been so out of whack over the holidays that we haven't caught up. But we finally did a couple of weeks ago, and now here we are about to attend Dior's Valentine's party together. This could be the start of something nice for me. Putting Remington Hartford out of my mind again. Yes, we had fun over the new year. We basically never left my bed for a week straight. My friends thought I was crazy, but after the number of orgasms he was delivering, I didn't care. It was nice, just the two of us in our own little bubble, no outside forces like my brother or his many conquests trying to pull us apart. We ate, drank, had sex, and chilled out. It was exactly how I wished things could have been all those years ago, but I guess we are older and wiser now. But as they say, all good things must end,

and our week together did. He had to go back up to my parents
to work, and well, my life is in the city, we are living on two
totally different paths. It's probably for the best our lives are so
interconnected that a relationship would mess it all up, especially for my dad. He loves Remi like a son, and it would kill
him to have to fire Remi for fraternizing with his daughter, but
he would. I could never ask my father to get rid of his best polo
player because he broke my heart again. So, it's for the best that
I concentrate on Jarred and our budding relationship and put
Remi far from my mind.

"Thank you so much for these flowers, they are
gorgeous," I say as I place the vase on the dining table. He
doesn't need to see the other arrangement Remi sent me, which
is in the guest bedroom, hidden away. "I'm excited to introduce
you to my friends. But I will warn you Dior's parties are wild."

"I'm sure it will be fine," Jarred says, pulling me into
his arms and kissing me. Dior's parties are not for the faint of
heart. She is a wild party girl, and she expects the same level of
partying from her guests. We make our way downstairs where
our car is waiting for us. I told Audrey and Rainn to meet us
there. We hop in and head on downtown to where Dior's hipster
loft is.

"How was work?" I ask Jarred.

"Had a big client come in that I had been working on
for the past couple of months and finally signed him on Friday,"
Jarred tells me excitedly.

"Oh wow, that's so amazing. Congrats." I have no
idea what he does. I know he's told me once, but I kind of tuned
out because let's be real, finance can be a little boring.

"Thanks, babe, it's going to be a nice bonus. Maybe I
can get you something nice," he says, giving me a wide smile. I
understand the whole older guy, younger girl dynamics; I've
lived in the city for a long time, but this girl can buy her own
things. But I won't say no to anything from Cartier if he's

wondering. "And how about you, how did your week go with your little business?"

I bristle at his question. I understand people don't think being an influencer is a job, but it is especially if you are a successful one like I am. Just because I have a trust fund that I have access to doesn't mean I don't want to make my own money. I'm just biding my time until I can prove to my mother that I'm good enough to join her business. I understand what my mom is doing is making me stand on my own two feet, learn new skills, build a business from the ground up because those life skills are invaluable, but I hope it won't be for too much longer.

"Actually, I just signed on with a new client, and it was one of my biggest deals yet," I tell him, feeling proud of myself, even Meadow, my manager, was ecstatic.

"Congrats to you too, babe." He leans over and nuzzles my neck. "How does the whole influencer thing work?" he asks. He seems genuinely curious from the arch of his brow he's giving me.

"People pay for posts; they could be daily, weekly, monthly. They could be in my reels or photos. I could do a live demonstration on my socials too. Plus, so much other stuff." It's hard to explain this world to outsiders.

"So, like they pay you what, a thousand dollars a post or something?" he questions me. I don't mean to burst out laughing, but he really doesn't know how much I earn.

"Oh no. My starting rate for one photo is ten grand."

Jarred pales and I can see him doing the math of the number of posts I do. His eyes widen at the figure he thinks I earn, but whatever he has in his head, he should double it or even triple it.

"This new deal is one hundred and fifty for the week," I tell him, trying not to be smug about it.

"Wow. I had no idea. You get paid to just pose and stuff," he asks.

"It's not that simple. I sit down and have a meeting with the marketing team, and they tell me what they want me to tell in my posts. What products they want. I have a schedule of when they want things posted etc. It's a full-time job."

Jarred nods and I can see he is trying hard to be open-minded, but he still thinks what I do is easy. I'm sure playing in the stock market is easy, too. Eventually, after that awkward car ride, we arrive at Dior's loft, exit, and get our names marked off at the door before being let up. Once we exit the elevator, we step into Dior's valentine den of debauchery where we're met with half-naked people swinging from the loft's ceiling dressed as cupids. Near naked staff are handing out food and drink, so I grab a glass of pink champagne while Jarred tries not to stare at the topless server's painted breasts. He fails.

"You made it." Dior greets us before we step any further into her home. She's dressed in a white toga with one enhanced breast hanging out with a red heart pastie covering her nipple. I know she will not be wearing any underwear under that toga that only just covers her ass. Her blonde hair is pulled up into a high pony, and she has a red leather whip by her side. I do not know what she is, but it's slutty and that's all that matters. Because I was coming here with Jarred and I didn't want to spook him so early on, I settled on a gorgeous red sequin evening dress that has a thigh-high split, deep V to show off my cleavage, and my hair is down in old Hollywood waves. I look like a blonde Jessica Rabbit.

"Oh my god, you look so hot, you filthy bitch," Dior says, looking me over. "And who's this, your sugar daddy?" Dior's eyes light up as she takes in Jarred. She has always liked older men, not for their intellect but for their wallets. Jarred introduces himself to her, and she practically loses it over his politeness. "You come look for me when you're done with her." Dior gives him a wink before something new catches her attention and she's off.

I cringe at her overt flirtation with my date. "See, I told you Dior is wild," I say, giggling awkwardly.

"She's certainly different, that's for sure," Jarred says, but not before he turns and looks back in the crowd at where Dior disappeared to. A tiny bubble of jealousy takes flight in my stomach, but I know Dior's flirting means nothing; she does it to everyone male or female so she's probably being friendly and she's drunk. She's even more flirtatious when she's drunk. Usually, I find it funny, but Jarred's reaction has caught me off guard. Maybe I'm overthinking it all and seeing things where there is none.

We continue through the party, saying hello to people as we go until I run into my girls, Rainn and Audrey.

"Happy Valentine's Day," they both greet me.

"Hey guys," I say, giving them both hugs. "Happy Valentine's Day. You remember Jarred, don't you?" I reintroduce the girls to him. They say hello and begin small talk with him.

"Did you ladies want more drinks?" Jarred asks, looking at our empty glasses. I give him a nod, and he walks off in search of champagne.

"How are things going?" Audrey asks.

"I don't know. He's a nice guy but some things he's done tonight have annoyed me," I explain to the girls. Then I tell them about the car ride over, the way he checks out other women, Dior's flirting. "Am I overreacting?" I ask them both.

"No way in the world," Rainn agrees. "Those are legitimate red flags." Great, it's doomed before it's even begun.

"Try to enjoy your night and worry about tomorrow, tomorrow," Audrey tells me.

Maybe she's right, I can't do anything about Jarred now; I'm stuck with him, but I can certainly enjoy myself.

Hours later I've enjoyed myself a little too much, but I don't care I'm having fun, but I can tell my fun is not Jarred's kind of fun.

"Fancy seeing you here," a deep voice whispers into my ear. Oh no. I twirl around rather quickly at the sound of Remi's voice and practically topple over into his arms. He reaches out and grabs me. Electricity runs through my veins at the tiniest of touches from him. "Happy Valentine's Day, Nell." Remi leans in and places a kiss at the corner of my mouth.

"Hey, there." Jarred stands up and pulls me from Remi's arms back into his. He's shooting daggers at Remi as if he is ready to wage war. Remi's glaring back, obviously confused by this dude's claim over me. "That's my girl you are manhandling," Jarred growls at Remi.

"Your girl?" Remi asks, his voice rising to a *what the fuck is this guy talking about* range. He turns to where I am standing, wrapped in Jarred's arms, and raises a brow in my direction, questioning me.

"This is my date, Jarred," I explain to Remi. "And this is Remington Hartford. He works for my father," I explain to Jarred.

"You're the polo player?" Jarred questions him. Remi doesn't even answer. He just glares at me. I shrink under his intensity.

"Nice to see you again, Nell. Guess I'll see you around." And with that, Remi storms off into the party. He has no right to be angry; we aren't together.

"He's a bit of an arrogant jerk, isn't he?" Jarred remarks, bewildered by the exchange.

"You, okay?" Audrey whispers to me. I nod in agreement.

"Don't worry about him. Polo players have the biggest egos," I say, trying to make light of the situation, not wanting to ruin Valentine's night any more than it has. Next year I'm staying single.

"He acted a little too familiar with you," Jarred questions me.

"I dated him when I was sixteen," I answer Jarred with a sneer.

"And you're over it?" Jarred questions me.

"Of course, I am," I tell him, wrapping my arms around him reassuringly. "I have you now." I know pumping up Jarred's ego will make him forget about Remi almost kissing me in front of him.

Once I got Jarred drunk, he was a hell of a lot more fun, but I was ready to go home and wanted to say goodbye to Dior. I walk around the party looking for her, but of course she's MIA. Probably taken someone into her room and is having her wicked way with them. I do not want to see that. But a flash of blonde hair catches my attention as I see her rush past me, pulling someone behind her. She turns around and pulls them into her arms and begins kissing their face off. My stomach sinks as I watch Remi kiss her back.

"Fuck if you kiss like that, I can't wait to see how you fuck," Dior purrs, and I instantly want to be sick.

"Nellie. Oh my god, Nellie, I haven't seen you all night. I'm so sorry," Dior says apologetically. "Nellie is one of my best friends." She directs her comment to Remi before turning her attention back to me. "Babe, I'm about to take this hunk to bed, so check you later," she says with a grin. Remi stands there frozen, just like I am, as we stare at one another. We agreed no friends. He promised me. "Do you two know each other?" Dior eventually asks as she notices the tension between us.

"Not anymore I don't." And with that, I turn on my heel and run back through the party, tears streaming down my face. An overwhelming feeling of suffocation takes over and I run out onto the terrace to catch some fresh air.

"Nell, I did not know you guys were friends," Remi tries to explain to me.

"She's one of my best friends, Remi!" I scream at

him as tears run down my cheeks. "She's all over my socials. How have you not noticed?

"Because I'm not looking at her!" he yells back at me.

"She sure got your attention tonight, didn't she?"

"How's your date going? It seems like it's past his bedtime; don't they have a curfew at the old folks' home." He sneers at me.

"Fuck you, Remi. You don't get a say on who I date."

"And you don't get a say on who I fuck."

We both stand there, each of us vibrating with anger.

"Fuck you. Go on and fuck Dior, I hear she'll let you do anal on the first night!" I yell at him.

Never in my life have I ever been so angry. I'm out of here. I don't need to put up with this from him. I storm off past Remi, but he reaches out and grabs me, pulls me to his chest, and kisses me. Fuck him. How fucking dare he touch me after touching her!

I knee him in the balls, and he falls like a sack of potatoes.

I'm done.

27

NELL

"I think you're being a little harsh on Remi," Audrey suggests to me as we sit getting our make-up done for the annual Davenport Gala that Audrey's mother runs every year raising funds for charities. This year is a little strained as her brother Rhys just found out that his wife and best friend have been sleeping together and it's turned into a major shit show.

"I think she's not being harsh enough," Rainn pipes in.

"Aud, you can't be serious; he kissed Dior!" I exclaim to her.

"Okay, that was shit, but have you ever introduced them to each other?" she asks.

"No. But she is all over my socials."

"To be fair, she looks like a million other blonde influencers," Rainn adds with a chuckle, which makes me frown.

"Have you ever told Dior about you and Remington?" Audrey asks with an accusatory, arched brow.

"No. Because all that happened before I met Dior."

"Then do you think that maybe, just maybe, it was all

one big giant coincidence? A shitty one, but still not premeditated."

"You had a date," Rainn adds.

"I thought you two were my ride or die. I don't see no riding or dying." I groan dramatically, folding my arms across my chest angrily.

"Babe, we are, and that is why we are calling you out on your drama," Rainn adds seriously.

"You think I'm being dramatic?" I ask my friends, a little hurt that they would think that of me.

"Not dramatic. That's not the right word. We think you should at least talk to him," Audrey adds softly.

"What about you?" I ask Rainn. I know she won't sugarcoat things.

"You two have always confused me. You both want each other, but in the same breath, you don't. But you get upset when the other moves on, but you both refuse to move on with each other. Forgive him or don't, either way you're still going to be climbing that fine man every single damn time you see him so all this," she states, waving her hands in the hair, "is all pointless. You are getting stressed and angry for no reason. Who the fuck cares who he is getting it on with because you know that boy's dick is so good you will still climb it and ride it all the way to O-Town?" The make-up artists try to stifle a giggle at Rainn's comments.

"You make me sound weak." I pout, taking in Rainn's thoughts.

"Babe, you're not weak, that is not at all what I am saying," Rainn says, trying to reassure me. "It's just you are killing yourself with jealously. Worry for what? Use that man for the glorious dick creation has provided him with. Have fun, it is what it is with him. Forget everything else, you can't control that and just control what you can, which is him giving you orgasms on your terms on your timeline."

Rainn has a point. I know we have said that it's just sex, but somehow, we keep messing it up, but maybe I'm looking at this all wrong. I have the power, the control, I determine when and where I need an orgasm. I want nothing else from Remi other than his dick, fingers, and mouth. That's all I should be worried about.

"Guessing Rainn has made you see things differently judging by the face you are making?" Audrey asks with a grin.

"She has. But I will reiterate a no hooking up with Dior edict," I tell them both, which has us all laughing.

"And what about Miles?" Rainn questions me.

"What about him?"

"You still have a thing for him?" she asks.

"Of course. He is everything I wish Remi could be."

"So, what you're saying is if Remi was more like Miles, you would want Remi?" Rainn asks, raising her brows at me.

"No. I'm not saying that at all. Miles and Remi are two completely different guys."

"They are two completely different *brothers*," Audrey adds unhelpfully.

"So?"

"You just cut Remi out because he kissed one of your friends by accident, but yet you expect Remi to be okay with you pursuing his brother?" Rainn asks, as her eyes narrow on me. Why the hell are they ganging up on me? I glare back at Rainn as an uneasy tension swirls between us.

"You saying I can't have them both?"

Rainn's eyes widen in surprise at my comment. "Oh, no, not saying that at all. Difference is, when that kind of thing happens, all parties are aware."

"Whatever," I say, pouting, putting an end to the uncomfortable conversation. I don't want to deal with my hypocritical feelings right now. Yes, I know it's not right that I continue to sleep with Remi on the down low while lusting after Miles. I get how messed up that all is. My feelings are confused. Miles is the better person to be in a relationship with. He is dependable, caring, he saves lives, and has his shit together. Then there's Remi, the bad boy player, you know everything about him is bad news, and yet like a moth to a flame, I'm drawn to him. Yeah, I'm fucked up.

Once we have our hair and make-up done, we get dressed and make our way down to the limousine waiting downstairs for us. These charity events are a little more conservative than we're used to and as much as I would love to have worn something ultra-extravagant, I'll save it for the Met Gala instead. I still want to stand out but be elegant, so I chose a stunning fluorescent lime green off the shoulder evening dress that molds to my body like a second skin. There is no way in the world you could not spot me tonight. I wear my blonde hair up in a messy French braid, minimal jewelry, just diamond earrings, bracelet, and an enormous diamond ring, all on loan from a famous jewelry company in partnership for photos on my socials. They are so beautiful. How can I not show them off? Everyone knows with the three of us we are going to be late because of the million and one photos we take, so Audrey's family has left without us. Hey, the three of us are always hustling, you can't deny we don't work for our money. Eventually we are on our way and thankfully traffic isn't bad, and the event isn't too far away. We have done this red carpet many times before, started off hidden behind our parents to now walking alone and working the media's attention to our advantage. As soon as the three of us step out of the limousine, the paparazzi are screaming at us to turn this way, turn that. Reporters are screaming at Audrey for comments on her brother's divorce. Like a pro, she ignores them and continues talking about the charity her family's event is supporting.

"Bitches, I'm here!" Dior screams as she steps out of her car and sees us on the red carpet. Audrey cringes at our friend's cursing on the red carpet. Dior didn't grow up in this life. She doesn't understand the way New York society works. She thinks that because she's famous on the internet, it translates to everywhere else, it doesn't. This is old money and what comes with that sometimes is judgment, and Dior doesn't give a shit, but we do.

"Careful what you say," Rainn explains to Dior as she gives her a couple of air kisses.

"Oops, sorry. I forgot where I was for a moment," she says, fluttering her long lashes at us. Then she hears the paparazzi calling her name, and she's gone, posing, and answering the reporter's questions, getting her time in the lime-light. Can't deny the girl works it. Letting her have a couple of moments before telling her we are going inside. We search the large table list, find the table we are all sitting at, and head on over to it.

I stop in my tracks as I see Remi standing there with his brothers, Miles and Stirling, each one of the Hartford boys looking devilishly handsome in their custom tuxedos. Honestly, it's not fair to the rest of the men here this evening; they really stand out amongst this geriatric crowd. You can see the cougars circle, smelling the young blood, it's rather laughable that they think they are being subtle with their penetrating stares. I guess their husbands don't care because they are too busy flirting with the waitstaff.

"I've got to do my rounds," Audrey tells us before she disappears into the crowd; it's her family's event she must schmooze.

"Oh, well, hello there," Dior purrs, locking her eyes on the Hartford brothers. My stomach sinks. I told her after her party that Remi was my ex and that seeing them together freaked me out. Dior was so apologetic about kissing Remi that I forgave her. And before we can stop her, she is on her way over to where the guys are standing. Shit. Rainn rolls her eyes and shakes her head and follows Dior. How am I supposed to say, I don't want you to hook up with Miles because I have a crush on him, but I'm too chickenshit to do anything about it? Oh, and don't touch Stirling either, because Audrey likes him too. Just because Dior is a flirt doesn't mean she's going to take them to the bathroom and blow them.

"Ladies." Miles greets us, pressing kisses to each of our cheeks. I notice Remi keeps his distance from Dior, which is kind of comforting, but Miles, his eyes seem to be firmly engrossed with her inflated chest. Who can compete with double Ds like hers? Stirling looks uncomfortable, and his face is like stone as he endures Dior's flirtations. Phew, at least he doesn't seem interested. "Nell, my girl. How have you been?" Miles asks happily as he pulls me into a hug. "You going to save me a dance tonight?" Is he flirting with me?

"Sure thing," I say, giving him a wide smile. I look over at Remi, who has a scowl on his face as those green eyes narrow on his brother's hand around my waist. Stirling's eyes narrow on his brother's hand too, and he looks between Miles and Remi. I can see the wheels turning in his mind as he wonders what the hell is going on. How much does Stirling know about Remi and me? Does Miles know too? And if he does, why does he flirt with me still? Then, from the corner of my eye, I see a tiny little blonde and realize it's my sister, Portia. I haven't seen her in ages now that she's in college, so I remove myself from the group and follow my sister.

28

REMI

I've been trying to make amends to Nell since messing up over the whole Dior thing. I honestly, hand on my heart, did not know that the blonde hitting me up was a friend of Nell's, otherwise I would never have gone there. I know it's hypocritical of Nell to demand from me I don't hook up with her friends, all the while crushing on my brother. It's fucked up. But I know deep down inside she's not really interested in him. She thinks he's the good brother, Saint Miles, when in reality he is more of a player than I am. The thing is, I'm honest about it.

I watch Nell excuse herself from Miles's grasp and rush after her sister, who looks like she's arrived at the event.

"You, okay?" Stirling asks, taking in the white knuckles gripping my glass as he stares between Miles and me.

"Yeah. He's just being Miles. He's harmless. Plus, I think he's mesmerized by Dior's tits, anyway," I say, grinning as I take a sip of my whiskey. Let's see if Nell is still interested in Saint Miles after she finds out he's fucked her friend tonight.

"You seriously think he would do that?" Stirling asks.

"Um, yeah. This is Miles we are talking about," I say, taking another sip of my drink, watching Miles flirt with Dior. Don't worry, Nell, I'll be there to pick up the pieces when Saint Miles crushes your idea of him.

We eventually walk on over to our table, and low and behold, Nell and I are at the same table, and look at that, we are sitting beside each other. I take my seat and wait for the fireworks to begin when Nell notices where she is sitting.

"Hey there, stranger." Portia chuckles, taking a seat beside me on the other side.

"There's enough free champagne going around. I don't think I need to steal you any bottles," I tell her, raising a brow in her direction.

"Maybe my sister falls for that grumpy, bad boy act, but I don't," Portia says, glaring at me.

"What happened to you? I remember when you were nice."

This makes her laugh. "I can be nice when I want to be. You just make it so easy to mess with you," she says, fluttering her long lashes at me. I'm fighting a smile, but I can't hold it in any longer. "So, how are things going with my sister?" she asks, looking over where Nell is standing searching for her name tag. We both watch as her eyes land on her name and the person seated beside her. "She doesn't look happy," Portia whispers.

"That's a pretty standard look when she sees me."

"Did you mess up again?" she asks.

"Yeah, I guess. I kissed Dior but didn't know they were friends," I explain to Portia as I play with the cutlery on the table setting.

"Figures, she's a slut."

I choke on my breath at Portia's words. Nell gives me a weird look while Portia tries to hold back a set of giggles. "Portia. Oh my god, you can't say that."

"Yeah, I can. Because she is. She loves coming to these parties looking for a sugar daddy. I bet you fifty dollars she'll be blowing one of these fat, bald guys in the toilets after midnight," Portia comments sharply.

"Fuck. Portia," I warn her again.

"You don't want to take the bet because you'll lose. I thought you made good money being a polo player. Did you lose it all on hookers and cocaine?"

Fucking hell. "What the hell, Portia. You can't say that; if someone heard you, they would report me."

"Only if it's true. Unless it is?" she says, raising a brow at me.

"No. I don't need to pay for sex," I hiss angrily at her.

"If you did, Dior would be up for it."

This girl is driving me nuts. "Stop it," I say, turning my attention to Nell, hoping to shut down this obscene conversation with Portia. "Looks like you're stuck with me again."

"Looks like I am." She fidgets with the menu.

"Have you been getting my flowers?" I ask because I haven't heard from her.

"Yes, Rhonda appreciates them."

I knew that would be the case. "As long as a beautiful woman appreciates them, then that's all that matters." Silence falls between us, but I can see by the subtle twitches across her lips that she is dying to say more.

"Why her?" she asks softly, her eyes lifting to where Dior is seated next to Miles, who she's finding extremely funny by her loud laughter. Miles is not funny.

"I was drunk. She whispered dirty things into my ear. The woman I wanted was there with someone else, so I thought, why not," I tell her honestly. She mulls my words over while turning her champagne glass around in her hand.

"It hurt seeing you and her together," she says, looking up at me through those long black lashes before shaking her head, frowning, looking annoyed with herself that she told me that. "You and I have gotten complicated again."

"Don't think we ever stopped being complicated," I say, agreeing with her.

"Sounds toxic," she says, giving me a sad smile.

"Probably is, but I can't seem to break the cycle. Can you?" I ask her honestly. She sucks in a breath and closes her eyes for the briefest of moments.

"I don't know," she tells me. "It's been going on for so long I don't know how to break whatever this pull is between us."

"You think there's something wrong with us?" I ask her.

"My friends seem to think there is," she answers quickly.

"What do you think?" I push.

"I think we should talk about this later," she says as the staff brings out our first course.

"I'm going to hold you to it, Nell," I tell her. As our eyes meet, she gives me a small nod and turns her attention back to her friends.

The night continues with lots of drinking, talking, and laughing happening at our table. Everyone is having fun and getting along, which is a first with all our complicated relationships. I'm trying to find the right moment to have that chat with Nell, but she's having a good time with her friends, so I leave it. I'm sure we can catch up later.

"You owe me fifty bucks," Portia squeals into my ear as she sits down beside me at the empty table.

"What are you talking about?" I ask, my mind a little foggy after one too many whiskeys.

"Press play," Portia states, handing me her phone.

I do. Oh shit. I quickly shut it off and hand it back to her. The image of Dior blowing some old guy in the toilet is not what I wanted to see tonight.

"What the—Portia. You can't have this on your phone," I tell her angrily.

"Please, it was a proof of life. A bet's a bet, Remi. Now pay up," she asks, holding out her hand. I grab my wallet and hand her a hundred-dollar bill because I don't care enough to ask for change.

"What is wrong with you?" I ask, glaring at her.

"What?" she asks, giving me an innocent look. I just stare at her, perplexed. "Fine. There's something off about Dior. I don't like her, but Nell, for some stupid reason, does."

"And you think showing her this video will make her kick her friend to the curb?"

"That was purely to win the bet. No, Nell will have to work out Dior is shit in her own time," Portia states, shrugging her shoulders. Wow. Okay.

"You should use your skills for good, not evil."

"Yeah, yeah. I know. It's a blessing and a curse to be me," she exclaims with a chuckle before jumping back out of her chair and disappearing into the night. That girl is trouble.

I decide to head on out of the venue, sit in the outside courtyard, and look up at the night sky.

"There you are," Nell says, surprising me as she takes a seat beside me. "Déjà vu, isn't it?"

Huh? Then I realize where we're seated and where we are. Rhys got married in this same venue, and Nell and I disappeared out into the night, not too dissimilar to now. "Seems like a lifetime ago," I muse, stretching out against the chair.

"It certainly does," she agrees with me. "And yet here we are again talking about you and me."

"We don't seem to get it right, do we?" I say, letting out a heavy sigh.

"Nope. Maybe we are gluttons for punishment," she adds.

"Maybe that's our kink," I joke.

"You think what we are doing is a kink?" she asks, amused by my train of thought.

"Well, I'm not an expert on kinks but it feels like it, or maybe we're slow learners."

"Kink sounds better." She chuckles. "What do you think it is, then?" We both sit there for a couple of moments trying to work out what weird ass kink we could have to explain the stupid things we do to each other.

"Not sure if I want to Google it to find out," I say, chuckling. This makes Nell laugh, too. "I miss this, Nell. Us being able to hang out have fun like we used to."

"Before sex complicated it all," she adds. I nod in agreement. "Maybe we need to stop having sex." Silence falls between us at the thought of stopping everything altogether. I dare turn my face to her, and we both end up bursting out laughing. "Remi, I'm being serious."

"I know. I am too," I say, trying to keep a straight face.

"We've tried everything else except no sex," she says more firmly. Oh. Nell's being serious.

"Not sure if I'm down with that," I tell her honestly.

"You're not prepared to repair our friendship?" she questions me.

"That's not what I said nor mean."

"Sex is fucking everything up between us. I don't want us to end up hating each other, Remi."

I understand her concerns and maybe she's right. Sex complicates things between us. If we take the sex away, we may eventually rebuild the friendship we had all those years ago. "I can't believe I'm going to say this, but I think I agree with you."

"You do?" she asks, not quite believing me. I don't quite believe what I'm saying either, but I value our friendship over the sex. Ugh. Just saying that gives me the shivers.

"I want us to be friends again. So, I'm game to try anything. The way we keep going is going to destroy whatever relationship we have. And if it means no sex and you are in my life, I choose that," I tell her honestly.

"That's what I think too." She gives me a small smile.

"Shit, we're maturing. Ew," I add, making us both laugh. Nell stands up, and I do too.

"Fresh start." She holds out her hand for me to shake on it.

"Fresh start," I agree, which makes my dick want to throat punch me for agreeing to something so stupid.

29

NELL

I didn't see Remi for the rest of the summer after agreeing to be just friends with no sex. He flew out to Europe, and I may have compulsively stalked his socials. So many pictures of him surrounded by beautiful, sexy European heiresses, models, actresses, basically you name it, they were after him. Not that I didn't have my fun over the summer with my menagerie of eligible men. We started texting more regularly now that the sexy times were over with, and it's been nice. Since Remi's no longer in a different time zone now that he's back in the states, we've ended up on actual phone calls at least once a week. Not sure how we progressed to that, but here we are. Remi still flirts, I think it's in his DNA to do so, but I find myself not minding because the pressure of sex is off the table, and we can just relax and enjoy each other's company. The seasons changed from fall to winter in a heart-beat then before we know it, it's the holidays. It's Dom's last year in England before he graduates, so the family has decided to do Christmas in the UK this year to celebrate. Audrey and her mom will be in London to have Christmas with Rhys, who's just moved there after his divorce took a turn for the worse. So, seeing as Audrey and I will be in London, we tried to convince Rainn to spend New Year's with us, which was a really hard thing to do because her family were in Bali and hello sun, but we agreed we would fly back with her and spend a couple of weeks exploring Asia with her. It's going to be so much fun.

Dom invited us to one of his friend's country estates for a New Year's weekend, three days in the English countryside. It's freezing, but he reassured us it would be loads of fun.

"How much further. I'm going to pee myself," I moan as Dom drives his Land Rover through the English countryside; the constant bumps are putting pressure on my bladder. I shouldn't have had the tea while we were driving because now, I'm seconds away from bursting if he hits another pothole.

"We are almost there," he says, reassuring us. Okay, maybe I can hang on. Through the white countryside, a tall red-bricked building emerges on the horizon like a castle.

"Is that it?" I ask, pointing at the monumental building.

"Yep. Jasper is royalty. His family has had this estate in his family for like four hundred years or something like that," Dom explains. Oh wow. I can't imagine what that would be like owning something so old. Pretty cool though. We make our way up the long driveway. Large pine trees line the entrance, but everything else is white, a pure white wasteland, but it's beautiful. Eventually we make it to the front of the building and there standing out the front is this tall, well-built guy with blond hair, dressed in what looks to be tweed. I have a chuckle to myself because I thought that was a stereotype but seems like it's not.

"Look, Jasper's cool, so don't be weird," Dom warns us. I turn around and look at my friends over my shoulder, and we all burst out laughing. "I know I shouldn't have said anything." Dom curses.

"Welcome, guys, to Fox Estate," the blond guy greets us. Oh, my goodness, his accent is the cutest and so is he. Hello, country manor guy.

"This is my sister Nell and her friends Audrey and Rainn," Dom says, introducing us reluctantly.

"Come on inside. My staff will look after your bags. You must be freezing. The weather has taken a turn," Jasper exclaims. I could listen to him for hours.

"Sorry, excuse me. Could I use your washroom please?" I ask, hopping up and down on my feet now that we are moving, not sure if I can hold it any longer.

"Of course, so sorry. It's down the hall to the left. You can't miss it," he tells me.

"We're going to go too," Rainn says, following me.

"Girls." Dom huffs, rolling his eyes at us. I flip him off when Jasper turns around and it just makes him shake his head in dismay at us.

"Um, I think we might need a map for this place. Down the hall to your left was a little simplistic when the hallway is a mile long." Rainn moans.

"How many doors do you need in one house?" Audrey asks. It's like we have walked into a museum, everywhere you look there are paintings of people from the olden days, antiques, tapestries hanging on the walls, and oriental rugs on the floors. Eventually, we find the right room. Who the hell has a brass toilet? How rich are these people?

We make our way back to the foyer, where Dom and his friend have hot chocolates waiting for us. Now, this is better than a hotel.

"The estate has over twenty rooms split over three buildings. Dom thought that you girls would like a little more privacy and something aesthetically pleasing for your photos," Jaspers says with a question in his voice.

"We're influencers," I explain to him. His blue eyes widen in surprise, but he nods politely.

"Well, you are going to love the cottage off the main home here, it's a rustic house. My sister is an influencer too, and she's hosted many a photoshoot in there," he explains to us. Oh wow, we need to see this cottage, I'm intrigued.

"Will your sister be here then?" I ask, it would be nice to meet her.

"Oh no, I think she's in Australia; she's traveling around. She's a travel vlogger," Jasper explains, shrugging his shoulders before asking us to follow him down the long corridor again and out the glass door which takes us over a white gravel pathway toward the cutest little cottage, it looks like something right out of Peter Rabbit. It's adorable with its thatched roof covered in snow and tiny windows set against whitewashed walls. The English cottage garden's covered in snow, but I can only imagine what it would be like in summer. Thankfully, there is a fire going when we enter the cottage because it's freezing cold outside. We warm our hands against the flames in the front room. The ceilings are low with their whitewashed walls and exposed wooden beams. There is a large blue, red, and cream striped couch in the living room with a wall of books on either side of the fireplace. It has a luxurious, mismatched antique vibe going on, casual, yet probably expensive.

"There are four bedrooms in this cottage, so you each get to have your own room. There is a fully stocked fridge in the kitchen for food or you can call up to the main house if you want to speak to the kitchen to order food," Jasper explains. This is better than a hotel. "Make yourselves at home. We will have formal welcome drinks and dinner in the main house once everyone arrives at about eight tonight, semi-casual dress. See you, girls, there."

Dom and Jasper give us a wave and head on back to the main house.

"This place is amazing." Audrey squeals.

"Let's explore. Come on," I tell the girls.

After hours of exploring and taking a ridiculous number of photos, we all head off to our bedrooms to rest before meeting up with the rest of the crew for dinner tonight. My bedroom is wall-papered in a green and dusty pink floral with a gorgeous wooden four-posted bed dressed with white linens and pink and green pillows scattered across it. The floor is polished floorboards with oversized mismatched rugs. There is a fireplace on one wall and tiny rustic windows that look out over the snow-covered lawns. All I want to do is curl up in bed, read a book, and never leave my warm cocoon.

As I sink under the layers of blankets my phone beeps, I pick it up and check who messaged me.

Remi: Did you make it okay?

Nell: Yes. It's gorgeous here. I've just gotten into bed.

Remi: Tease. Show me.

My face heats over Remi's flirtation, but I do as he asks and take a photo of me in bed with the blankets pulled up around my chest.

Remi: Looks like there's room for one more.

Nell: Keep dreaming. I'm not sharing this bed with no one. It is divine it's like being on a cloud.

Remi: Wish I was there to test it out.

Nell: Kind of wish you were too. You'd love it here. I'll share some more photos later to make you jealous.

Remi: Why don't you just show me now?

Nell: Pushy. I'm going to have a nap. I'll send them when I'm up.

. . .

The sound of the door opening pulls me from my phone.

"Why don't you just show me now?" Remi says, striding into my bedroom.

What in the actual fuck? I sit up quickly in my bed and stare at Remi physically standing there before me. I thought he was back home on the East Coast, not here in fricken England.

"What the hell are you doing here?" I gasp, stunned that he is in my room.

"Dom invited me over. I had a week free and thought, why not," he says, giving me a wide grin. He closes the door behind him, and I watch as he takes a running leap and jumps on the bed, making me bounce almost out of it. "Wow, this bed feels like a cloud," he gushes, laying back placing his arms behind his head, looking way too comfortable here.

"Get out," I say, playfully shoving him.

"Nope. I wanted to experience this bed that you were raving about, plus I'm jetlagged, so I could really use a nap myself," he states, closing his eyes and ignoring my protests.

"You can't stay in here, someone will see."

"Dom told me I was staying in the cottage next door. And I may have told him I needed a nap after my flight. I also saw Rainn and Audrey leaving the cottage before I arrived. So, we are all alone. Plus, I locked the door," he explains to me as he turns his head and gives me a mischievous grin.

"Nothing is going to happen," I warn him.

"Get your mind out of the gutter, Nell. I just came in for a nap. Jeez," he says jokingly. He's a nut job, but I can't help but smile. Then, before I realize, I reach out and wrap my arms around him because I've missed him and give him a big hug. He returns the hug, and we stay wrapped in each other's arms in silence. Eventually we both must fall asleep because when I wake up, he's gone, but he's left a single rose on the pillow beside me. Aw. I get up and go have a shower and get ready for dinner.

"Hey, you girls look great," I say, walking down the stairs to where they are hanging out by the fire with glasses of champagne and a cheese platter. I settle on a pair of jeans with knee-high boots and a baggy white sweater that slides off one shoulder. I take a seat on the armchair and cut off a slice of cheese.

"Are you going to tell her, or should I?" Audrey asks Rainn.

"Oh no, you can. She won't yell at you," Rainn adds. I look at my two friends with a frown.

"Remi is here staying at the estate," Audrey explains.

"Oh, I know I saw him earlier."

Rainn and Audrey look at each other, their eyes wide, wondering why I wasn't freaking out. "And he brought a date," Audrey adds.

My stomach sinks. What the hell did she say? He brought a date. He was just in my bed hours ago. I don't understand.

"I'm assuming by that face you made he didn't tell you that second part," Audrey states.

"He surprised me in bed," were the only words that could stumble out of my mouth.

"That fucking bastard," Rainn curses.

"Nothing happened, we hugged, and then we fell asleep. He left me a rose on my pillow after he had gone."

"Probably because his date just turned up. Was it a red rose by any chance?" Rainn asks.

"Yeah, why?"

"Because she had a bouquet of red roses in her arms when she arrived," Rainn explains to me. *That bastard.* I suck in a deep breath and try to control the anger that is bubbling to the surface. There have been no photos on his socials. He's been texting me, flirting, and now suddenly, he has a date? I can't believe I let him in again.

"We've got you, boo," Audrey tells me.

"Here, you need this." Rainn hands me the glass of champagne, and I throw it back in one gulp. Audrey and Rainn stare at me, but Rainn refills my glass. Fuck you, Remington Hartford.

We head on into the main house to join all the other guests for cocktails before dinner. Thankfully, Remi and his date are nowhere to be seen, so I can relax for the briefest of moments. Jasper introduces us to his friends, who are an eclectic bunch of people; they all seem rather nice, but my anxiety kicks in the longer I wait for Remi to arrive.

"Remi," Dom yells out, seeing his friend enter the room with a gorgeous brunette on his arm. My stomach sinks as I take in her glossy chocolate hair that falls around her shoulders like she's stepped out of a shampoo commercial. She's dressed in a black sweater with tight jeans that mold to her amazing body, matched with a pair of thigh-high boots. Bright red lipstick shows off her perfect lips, and the bitch has the perfect winged eyeliner going on. Ugh. Remi's eyes capture mine as he hugs my brother, but I look away, turning my back to them. I don't need to see this. I don't know why he didn't tell me. Of course, I would be a little upset, but I'd get over it if he was happy, but to blindside me like this I can't. Remi thankfully doesn't come over and introduce his date to us, and I can forget that they are even here.

It's not long till Jasper calls us to dinner and we all walk in and take our seats, Remi and his date at one end, my girls and I are on the other.

"You, okay?" Audrey asks.

"Sure," I say, throwing back a couple of glasses of champagne one after the other.

After that, the night becomes a blur.

30

NELL

NEW YEAR'S EVE

O h my god, I'm dying as I roll over and scream into my pillow. Why the hell did I drink so much? Oh, that's right. I had to watch Remi and his date all night, smiling and laughing. Remi is not that funny, bitch. My mind tumbles back to this time last year where I was feeling just as shit and was curled up in bed, but Remi was there looking after me, now he's with her. Ugh. I'm such a fool, all these months of us rebuilding our friendship, and he didn't even have the decency to tell me he had a girlfriend. I'm going to stay here all day as I roll back and pull the pillows over my head and promptly fall asleep.

My phone beeping wakes me up and I reach out and grab it.

Remi: We need to talk.

"Fuck off!" I scream at my phone and throw it beside me. No. I pick it up again and viciously start blocking Remi all over my social network and text messages. He can fuck right off.

Audrey and Rainn thankfully have been running block for me. Remi has turned up a handful of times to talk to me, but they have sent him away. I know as soon as we all meet up tonight, I cannot ignore him.

"You ready?" Audrey asks as she pops her head around the corner. I'm still in bed. "Nell, come on, this is crazy. Forget Remi, don't let him ruin tonight for you. You love New Year's Eve."

"Remi's ruined the holiday for me." I pout.

"Fuck him," Audrey curses. "Put on the sexiest outfit you can find. There is an entire estate filled with single guys. Go have fun with them. Forget Remington Hartford." And with that, Audrey slams the door to my bedroom closed.

Right, well, I guess I better get ready then.

In theory, my revenge dress sounded good, but now that I'm in it and walking through the snow to reach the rest of the party I'm second-guessing my choice; not because I don't like it, I love it, but because it's unexpected from me. It's a sheer skin color evening dress with midnight blue sequins over the top part of my dress, but they scatter as they fall down the dress's skirt. I'm wearing nude underwear beneath it, but it still looks like I've been body painted with sequins and just stepped right out dressed like that. It will make people do a double take that's for sure, but hey, it's an evening dress. The theme was black tie sparkle, and I believe I am delivering it. It's couture.

"What the hell are you wearing?" A growl comes from the side as an arm reaches out and grabs me, making me squeal with surprise. Angry green eyes stare back at me.

"Get your hands off me, Remi," I hiss, removing my arm from his touch. "How dare you touch me?" Remi takes a step back at the venom in my voice. "You have no say in what the hell I wear ever, do you hear me?" I raise my voice at him.

"If you are trying to get my attention with this dress, then you have it," he replies as those eyes rake over my skin, making it pebble with goosebumps. I'm disgusted with myself for letting him affect me like that.

"All this is not for you. It won't be your lips that will be on mine at midnight, that's for sure," I tell him angrily.

"Nell."

"No, Remi. You have been flirting with me for months now, lulling me back into your fucking web and stupidly, I had been falling for it. Then you had the audacity to climb into my bed yesterday when your girlfriend was on the way to spend the weekend with you. Fuck you!" I yell, poking my finger into his hard chest.

"Nell, I can explain, just not right now."

Is he fucking serious? Ugh. I shove him with my hands, and he stumbles back a couple of steps, surprised at my action. "Leave me the hell alone!" I scream at him before turning on my heels and storming down the corridor into the New Year's party, where I make an entrance.

Once I put Remi out of my mind, I ended up having a fantastic New Year's. We danced, we sang, we drank way too much, but all in all, it was wonderful. And the best bit was I kissed some hot random with an English accent at midnight and everything was right in the world.

The next morning, Dom told me that Remi and Carla, his date, had left a day early. Thank goodness. Means I can relax and enjoy this amazing estate without Remi jumping out at me at any moment.

It's been months since I've seen Remi. He's still blocked on all my socials but it still doesn't stop me from stalking him, seeing what he and Carla are up to. Honestly, I don't know who Remi is anymore, all these heavily curated posts on his socials since he started dating Carla. I shouldn't be surprised she's a supermodel, and honestly, they look like they've stepped off the pages of a fashion magazine together—so fricken perfect. Pictures of them celebrating Valentine's Day together in practically nothing, photos of all the flowers and gifts Remi showered her with *#blessed*; it was vomit-inducing. Then there were images of her cheering him on at my family's home while he trained. That one really got my goat. I didn't know this about Remi. He never cared about his image like this before. What happened? *He became the number one polo player in the world, that's what happened.* I guess he has everything he's always wanted now. I've been going out with Dior a little more than I used to, much to Audrey and Rainn's annoyance, trying to keep my mind off Remi and Carla. Audrey has a fresh man anyway; a friend of Dior's called David and they are sickeningly sweet. I'm happy for her. She deserves happiness. I'm a grinch at the moment because I can't find my happily ever after.

Audrey: Did you see Remi's posts?

Nell: No. He's blocked.

Audrey: He and Carla broke up.

Rainn: They caught her with some football player.

Nell: Sounds like karma to me.

Rainn: Remi released a statement saying they had broken up months ago, they hadn't announced it publicly. That Carla never cheated.

Nell: He's just saving face.

Rainn: Karma

Audrey: How do you feel?

Nell: Fine. A little hungry, but all good otherwise.

Audrey: About Remi being single again.

Nell: Has no impact on me at all.

I step out of my apartment into the foyer to head out for the day and scream when I see Remi sitting down outside my door.

"Remi, what the fuck?" I question, seeing him there. It's been almost six months since I've seen him last.

"I've been sitting here trying to work up the courage to knock on your door," he explains, standing up dusting himself off.

"You really shouldn't have bothered," I tell him as I press the elevator button.

"Please, Nell, can I have five minutes," he asks, and damn him I waver because my curiosity wins out.

"Fine, you have five minutes," I tell him as I push open the door to my apartment again and he follows in behind me.

"You're looking good," he quips.

"Don't," I warn him, pointing my finger in his direction.

"Right," he starts, placing his hands in his back pockets. "I owe you an explanation about Carla."

"No, you don't."

"I do. It sucked not being able to tell you about us because of an NDA I signed," Remi explains. He has my attention now. "Carla and I weren't really a couple. Our managers set us up because we needed to strengthen our images and they thought together would have been better."

Guess that explains his curated feed.

"We weren't supposed to have started till I got back to America, but Carla was in London, so our managers brought up the timeline of our official picture together. They called me when I was asleep in your bed and explained that she was on the way to meet me. I had no time to tell you. It all happened so quickly. And once she was there, the contract started. If I told anyone about it, I would be in breach of contract," Remi explains as he nervously runs his fingers through his hair, which is longer than it used to be. It looks good. *No. What are you thinking, Nell?* "Then I saw how hurt you were, I didn't care about the contract anymore. I tried to get out of it, but the management company played hardball, as did Carla. They had me by the balls."

"Did you sleep with her?" I ask, but I know the answer.

"Yes, but after you shut me out."

"Right then. Well, thanks for clearing that all up for me. I'm sorry you got yourself into a bit of a pickle. But I'm kind of running late."

"Nell, please."

"There's nothing to say," I tell him.

"I'm sorry that I hurt you. I hated myself for what I did to you just when things were getting back on track between us."

"Remi, it doesn't matter anymore. It's in the past. I wish nothing but the best for you. Truly I do."

"Nell? Please," he pleads, reaching his hand out to stop me from leaving. Seeing his distressed face has me wavering, but I can't be pulled back into his atmosphere again. "I couldn't say anything." I understand contracts, I get NDA's, I know there was no way for him to tell me what was going on without him being sued for everything.

"I know," I answer him softly.

"Nell. I miss you," he says, tugging me closer to him, but I can't look at him because I know as soon as I do it's all over. That magnetism that swirls around us like a spinning orbit bringing us closer together. "Look at me, Nell." I suck in a deep breath and look up at him through my lashes. "I'm sorry," he says as his hands cup my face. "I hate hurting you. And I know I promised I wouldn't do it again, but I did."

"I hate you sometimes, Remi," I answer him softly.

"I know, baby. I know. And I deserve your hate so much." He growls as his fingers tangle in my hair. "I'll never deserve you." He sighs as his forehead meets mine. Damn right he never will.

"I've missed you so much, Nell," he tells me as his lips press against mine ever so softly.

"I hate that no matter what you do to me, I still can't stay away from you." I curse him.

"The feeling is mutual, babe." His lips press against mine, this time with a little more force, and I let him. Betraying all women out there that succumb to a fuck boy. They are just so damn hard to resist, especially when I haven't had sex in months and the last time, I had to finish myself off. I need the good D. *Please, womankind don't hate me.*

"Oh, fuck it," I groan as I open my mouth and let him in. It is the match that lights the tinder box on fire. We just explode against one another. He lifts me up, and I wrap my legs around his waist as he moves me through my apartment with ease, never breaking our kiss until he finds my bedroom and lays me down against my sheets. Thank goodness I'm wearing a dress because Remi is on his knees, lifting the material and burying his head between my thighs. He places my legs over his shoulders, widens my thighs, and before I get a chance, he is pulling my G-string to the side and his tongue is disappearing between my folds.

"Oh, yes!" I scream as my fingers tug on his hair forcibly, holding his expert tongue in place as I hurtle to the edge. Fuck. I can't believe how quickly he is pulling this orgasm from me. Moments later, I am falling over the edge. Holy shit. That was quick. But Remi doesn't give me a moment of reprieve because his fingers are slipping inside of me, begging for more. It doesn't take long till he hits the jackpot again with his fingers and pushes me over the edge for a second time. Dammit, I've missed his magic. Next thing I know, Remi is flipping me over onto my stomach and pulling up the material of my dress, exposing my bare ass to him.

"Fuck I've missed this," he growls as he sinks his teeth into one of my butt cheeks, making me squeal before he is slapping away the bite mark. Oh, that's good. The sound of the metal of his fly lowering and the crinkle of the condom wrapper fill my ears, before I feel the thick head of his dick pressing against my entrance, he coats himself before he sinks inside of me in one swift move filling me so deeply.

"Fuck." He hisses loudly. Then he drags himself out slowly before pushing deeper into me. He does this repeatedly at a blistering pace. My clit is getting pushed against the lace of my G-string and the friction is making me delirious. I don't know if I can hold on for much longer, especially not with the way he is fucking me. I can feel another orgasm rolling through like a freight train, and I don't know if I can stop it.

"Oh, yes!" I scream as I fall over the edge into oblivion and Remi's guttural groan as he comes not far behind me. He pulls himself out of me and falls to the side with a hand lying across his forehead. I push the hem of my dress down and sort out my tangled underwear while Remi cleans himself up.

"Well, thanks for that. It was exactly what I needed," I tell him. He gives me a wide smile, looking pleased with himself as he zips up his jeans.

"Give me five and I'll be ready to go again," he tells me cockily as he tries to reach out for me, but I sidestep his embrace.

"Thanks. But I'm running late for a date. You can let yourself out, can't you?" I ask him. He stares at me open-mouthed as I grab my things and head on out to the living room.

"Nell, what the hell?"

"I told you before you came in I had somewhere else to be. That was the truth."

"You seriously going out on a date after fucking me?" he asks, raising his voice.

"Yeah. I don't sleep with people on the first date so it's all cool," I explain to him, picking my bag up off the living room floor.

"But I thought..."

"What? That your magic dick would cure what you did?" I ask him. He cautiously stays silent. "Three chances and I let you back in past my defenses. Three times you treated them carelessly. So, I give up. You and I have sexual chemistry and no matter what the hell you seem to do to me, I can't say no to sleeping with you. So, I'm not going to anymore. I don't care if you fuck Britney, Taylor, or Candy. Heck, I don't care if you screw the entire polo set. Because all I care about is you giving me mind-blowing orgasms any time you are around. Are you okay with that?"

Remi frowns at me, unsure of how to answer that question.

"It's a pretty simple question, Remi. Do you still want to sleep with me?"

"Yes," he answers hesitantly.

"Great. Well, that's sorted. Go have fun, I'll let you know when I need you again." I place a kiss on his cheek and leave the building with a pep in my step.

31

NELL

O kay, I feel like a bitch for being a fuck girl, but why is it okay for guys to hit it and quit it and girls can't? After the shock of me hitting it and quitting it on Remi and after a disastrous date, I came home to Remi waiting for me. It surprised me he was still there, but he wanted to talk.

"How was your date? See any potential?" Remi asks as I walk into my living room and dump my bag onto the couch beside him.

"Nope, was a disaster. He was a douche, spoke horribly to the staff at the café, and then left a tiny tip. He spoke about himself the entire time. Then told me I had great tits and that we should go somewhere and fuck."

Remi's eyes narrow and I can see my story has made him angry.

"Guess that's why our little arrangement will work," I tell him as I walk over and straddle him on the couch, his brows rise at my forwardness.

"Are you just using me for my dick?"

"Yep," I answer with a pop of my lips. *"You cool with that?"*

He takes a moment to mull the answer to my question over.

But it was for dramatic effects, really. "Guess I'm going to have to be," *he says as his large palms caress my ass.*

"Great, so how about you fuck me then."

No. My memories fade away before I get to the good bits. Stupid phone waking me up. Who the hell is calling me so early? I try to shake the cobwebs of last night's party from my mind to get myself together to pick up the phone. I miss it. Dammit. I look down at the screen and see a heap of missed calls from Rainn. What the hell is going on. Panic races through my veins as I quickly try to call her back.

"Finally!" Rainn screams at me as she picks up.

"Sorry, I just woke up."

"I've called you ten times!" she yells, raising her voice at me. What the hell is wrong with her? "I can't believe that fucking bitch did that to her." Huh, who? What?

"Rainn, you're going to have to back it up for a minute. What the hell is going on?"

"You haven't seen the media. It's all over socials!" Rainn screams at me.

"I just woke up, Rainn, I haven't checked anything."

"There is a video of your girl Dior fucking David in Bora Bora!" Rainn screams at me. Everything stops. No. Dior wouldn't do that to Audrey. No way in the world. This has to be some haters trying to create drama where there is none. My phone beeps with an incoming message. "Check your message," Rainn instructs me. I put my phone down, open Rainn's message, and press play. I watch as one of my friends comes out of the villa of my friend's boyfriend and then precedes to suck face before, oh shit, before she starts fucking him on the sun lounge. What the hell?

Oh, no. No. No. No. This can't be true. Oh, Aud must be devastated seeing this. "Fuck Rainn, this is bad."

"No shit. And I haven't been able to get a hold of Audrey, it's like she's disappeared off the face of the earth. I'm worried," Rainn confesses to me.

"She has to be somewhere in the city. Give me twenty and I'll be ready to pound Fifth Avenue looking for her."

"Great," Rainn says, hanging up on me.

I jump out of bed and type out a message to Aud before quickly jumping in the shower. Once I'm back in the land of the living, I make myself a coffee and scroll through my messages. I see one from Dior.

Dior: Nellie, call me please as soon as you get this.

I can't believe Dior did this. I know she is a flirty girl but that girl in the video; I don't know who she is. I press Dior's number and wait for it to connect through.

"Oh my god, Nellie, you called me. Thank you, thank you so much, babe. I'm like freaking out here. I can't believe some bitch took a private video of me and blasted it all over the internet. Do people not have lives or something?" she whines into my ear.

"Dior, what the fuck? You just got caught sleeping with one of your best friends' boyfriend's and you don't seem remotely sorry about it?" I tell her angrily.

"Some bitch created a sex tape of me and is making money off it. That's not fair, Nell. This tape could do wonders for my career, and I don't even have the license for it. Like, what the fuck?" she answers, completely missing the point of my question.

"Dior, listen, is this real? Did you really sleep with David?"

"Yes," she answers sheepishly. "I've been sleeping with David for years. He and Audrey aren't serious. They are fake news, babe. They have an agreement to be together for the socials to increase their profiles. We didn't cheat," Dior explains to me. I cannot believe what I am hearing. "Is the news like everywhere?"

"I've got to go, Dior. We'll talk later," I tell her, hanging up before she can say anything else to me. I sit down on the couch and stare into the nothingness. I can't believe what just happened. My phone rings and I look down at the screen, and it's a group call between Rainn, Audrey, and me. Thank goodness she's safe.

"Audrey. Are you okay? Where are you?" Rainn asks.

"Aud, your mom said you didn't come home last night. Are you okay? Are you safe?"

"I crashed at Stirling's." We all go quiet.

"Stirling?" Rainn questions.

"Yeah. With Rhys being away, he's the next best thing," Audrey explains.

"Next best thing for what?" Rainn asks.

"Help."

"Did anything happen?" I ask.

"What? No! I crashed in his bed and that's it!" Audrey exclaims.

"His bed?" Rainn's voice raises.

"Yeah. I was sad. It's not weird, is it?" she asks.

"A little, especially if nothing happened," I tell her.

"Of course, nothing would happen. You know he doesn't see me as anything other than family."

"We're so glad you're okay. We were worried. We saw the video. It's fucked up," Rainn explains.

"I spoke to Dior." The call goes quiet upon hearing Dior's name. "She told me it's true. I'm sorry, Aud. That she and David have been hooking up for a long time, she didn't think you and David were serious."

"She didn't think we were serious?" Audrey's voice raises. "She was there the night he asked me to be his girlfriend. She popped champagne with us. That's bullshit, Nell."

"I know it is, babe. I'm telling you what she told me. It's not right what she has done. And I told her that."

"Did you know about them?" Audrey asks me, but I can hear the accusation in her voice.

"No way. If I did, I would have told you, Audrey. I would have let you know before all this."

"Then why did she do it?"

"All Dior told me was they have been a thing for a long time. That David told her you two had an agreement. That you were using each other to increase your followings."

"He said what?" Audrey screams down the phone. "I don't need his shitty followers."

"Fucking convenient excuse," Rainn adds. "Dior knows better. She's been with us when the two of them have been together."

"I don't know. It's a shit situation."

"She's always been jealous of Audrey," Rainn states. "She hates the fact that Audrey and I are close to you, Nell," Rainn drops that little bombshell.

"Wait. Me?" What has any of this got to do with me?

"You and she were tight long before the four of us became friends. I think she got jealous. Especially when Audrey comes in and starts dating her booty call right in front of her. You know what Dior is like. She has to be the center of attention. You've seen the stunts she's pulled before with us. David was a dumb ass for going along with it," Rainn explains. "She's even gloating about the sex tape online," Rainn adds.

"I'm done with her. You girls can be friends with her, but I'm done," Audrey says.

"I'm Team Audrey," Rainn adds.

"I agree what Dior has done is messed up. I'm not sure if I can be friends with her either."

"Are the comments bad?" Audrey asks cautiously.

"Most of them are Team Audrey," I tell her.

"And of course, there is that one percent who are trolls," Rainn adds. "But you know to ignore them."

"Why did they do this to me? Why hurt me like that? I'm a joke now."

"Audrey, no. You are not a joke. You have nothing to be embarrassed about. Nothing," Rainn tries to reassure her.

"But it's bad, isn't it? The entire thing has gone viral, hasn't it? I can't stay here in New York. I just can't," Audrey says, panicked.

"We can go upstate to my family's farm or down to Florida," I suggest.

"What about Bali? We can go to my family's home there. Get massages. Zen out," Rainn adds.

"They all sound great guys, but I think I want to go to London and see my brother."

"Yes. I'm in for London."

"Me too," Rainn agrees.

"You girls sure?"

"Yes," we both say in unison.

"I can't thank you both enough."

"We've got you, babe," Rainn reassures Audrey.

32

REMI

"Morning ladies," Stirling calls out to the girls who are milling around waiting to board the private plane. They all turn and give my brother bright smiles; they all look excited to be jetting off to London. Wonder if Nell is going to be excited to see me. *Probably not.* The dynamic between us has changed, not that I'm complaining, but she is literally using me like I'm a walking, talking live dildo. Again, not that I'm complaining, I'll take Nell any which way she wants me.

"Oh shit." I hear Nell's voice. Watching her reaction to seeing me join her girls' trip makes me smile. Her face falls, her brow crumples, and those doe eyes glare angrily at me. "What the hell is he doing here?" Nell asks through gritted teeth.

"Have no idea," Audrey tells her. A panicked look falls across the blue eyes as she looks between Nell and me.

"What are you doing here?" Nell comes right out and asks me.

"Couldn't miss coming to London with you ladies," I tell them, pulling down my aviator glasses and sending a wink Nell's way, which I know annoys the hell out of her. Gosh, she is so easy to annoy. I love it, it gets my dick hard.

"Remi's got some event to go to in London and asked if he could hitch a ride when he found out we were going," Stirling explains to them. Thanks, bro, for having my back.

"More the merrier," Audrey says, smiling back at Stirling. Aw, it's cute the crush she has on my brother. I know he's not unaffected by her, the girl is gorgeous, he's not blind, but I also know he is loyal to a fault, and his best friend and business partner Rhys is Audrey's older and overprotective brother. Guess he's just going to keep checking her out from afar like he's always done.

"I knew I liked you," I tell Audrey. As I sling my arm around her shoulders, my brother delivers me a scowl and I sure as hell know Nell is sending daggers into my back. I can almost feel them. "Heard what happened with your boyfriend," I tell Audrey as we make our way to the private plane. Was a dick move. Also, I can't believe he did it with Dior too. I had my run in with that girl. Yeah, she's hot but plastic. But to do that to this gorgeous little creature beside me who is such a wonderful soul is disgusting. "You could do so much better," I tell her, honestly. I'm not blowing smoke up her ass.

"Thanks." She sighs softly.

"You know who's a good guy? My brother," I add. She stiffens slightly underneath my touch, but I let her go to bound up the stairs to the plane, being my charming self to the crew before taking my seat.

The girls settle into their flight, taking the mandatory selfies before we take off. Once everyone's settled in, it's time to take off. It's a smooth assent into the air and moments later the crew are handing us refreshments for the journey.

"Don't think Nell was happy to see you?" Stirling states.

"She never is." I chuckle, taking a sip of my whiskey.

Hey, it's five o'clock somewhere. "So, Audrey's single again." I grin, placing that little seed in his head that at least one of us should get the girl.

"I know. What a dickhead. Rhys and I were ready to fly to Bora Bora and kick his ass for what he did to her," my brother answers angrily.

My eyes narrow on him. "Just to help Rhys out? No other reason?"

Stirling looks appalled by my question. "She's like a little sister to me."

"Please, Audrey is a smoke show. There are no little sister vibes there whatsoever. But I get it; you have to tell yourself whatever you need to, to get through hanging out with her."

"It's not like that and you know it," he argues.

I grin. "You've always gotten along. And now Rhys isn't here, you can hang out."

"We're friends, just like you and Nell."

I burst out laughing. "Nell and I are not friends. She tolerates me because of her family."

"And what about you? Do you tolerate her because of her family?" Stirling asks.

"I tolerate her because she's hot."

"You're a dick. No wonder she can't stand you." My brother punches me in the arm. Yeah, I kind of deserved that.

"Look, Nell's upset because I am the one that continues to rock her world and not Miles, the brother she wants." I shrug my shoulders and try to stop the stress tick in my eye. They seem to always bump into each other around town. Manhattan is huge; it's statistically impossible for them to keep accidentally running into each other.

"Are you insane? You know, messing with the boss's daughter is a huge problem. How long has this been going on? What the hell are you thinking? You could lose everything you have worked for if he finds out," Stirling whisper yells at me angrily.

"You don't know anything about us." I point my finger at him, and that's my fault, I don't run to my brothers to tell them every little thing that happens in my life. "There's a long history there. She isn't even interested in me, anyway. Not when Saint Miles is around. I don't understand what she sees in Miles, anyway?"

"Maybe because he's a successful doctor, and you're a polo playing playboy?" my brother answers with a chuckle.

"You're a dick, you know that?" I say, glaring at him. "Miles isn't interested in her."

"Maybe not. But why are you interested in her? And do not say it's because it's just a little fun."

"You wouldn't understand."

"Try me, Rem."

So, I tell him. I tell him about the fucked-up relationship Nell and I have created for each other.

My story must have bored him because not long after it, my brother falls asleep. Dick.

"More shots!" Rainn calls out to the crew.

"And turn the music up," Nell adds.

At what point did the girls go from selfie taking to instant nightclub? I swear I closed my eyes for five minutes and I woke up to girls gone wild. Not that I'm complaining.

"Fuck men!" Audrey screams as she knocks back a shot.

Now I see what's going on. Revenge.

"Yeah, fuck men!" Nell screams, raising her shot glass high in the air, and when she throws it back her brown eyes land on me. Okay, sweetheart, I get the point. But do not put me in the same category as Dior and David; what they did is fucked up. I'm just stupid. I leave the girls to do their thing because they are trying to help their friend get over her heartbreak. I play on my phone and try to ignore the commotion beside me.

Stirling wakes up in a daze and takes a couple of moments to focus on the chaos that is happening. He rubs his eyes again as he stares in confusion at the girls.

"You woke up just in time." I turn to him and grin. "Maybe I should have brought some dollar bills with me." He elbows me for that comment.

"How long have they been going at it?"

"Started off as a couple of glasses of champagne. Then Audrey asked for shots, and now here we are. Do you think I should ask Nell for a lap dance?" I joke.

"Once you put on a parachute because she will push you out of this plane if you do," Stirling tells me. He's not wrong. "Do you think we should stop them?"

"Are you fucking insane?" This is better than porn. "Stirling, they are grown ass adults. If they want to bump and grind on each other, it's their prerogative to do so. They are letting off some steam." My brother just frowns as he looks over at the girls.

"I'm going to go freshen up," Stirling tells me. Probably a good idea; he looks like he might have an aneurism.

"Remi, come join us?" Audrey calls out to me. I look over to where Nell is seated and the fire that is burning in her eyes at me tells me I'm the last person she wants to come sit with them.

"Sure thing," I say, sending a wink in Nell's direction, who shakes her head at me.

"We're playing truth or dare," Audrey adds. Oh, this sounds like fun. "It's your turn," Audrey informs me. "Truth or dare?" she slurs. Wow, okay, we've reached this point of the night it's probably all downhill from here.

"Truth."

Audrey's eyes widen, surprised at my choice. I watch as the wheels begin to turn in her head as she tries to come up with a good question. "Oh, I've got it. Do you still love Nell?"

"Aud," Nell yells at her friend, who's two sheets to the wind, and doesn't notice.

"Yeah, Remi. Do you?" Rainn asks, elbowing me in the side. I look over at Nell, who looks like she wishes the ground would swallow her up.

"She was my first love. That love never dies," I tell them all honestly.

"Aw. Remi, that's sweet. See, you can be sweet, you don't need to be a dick all the time," Audrey mumbles before taking a swig of champagne from the bottle. "Stirling!" Audrey squeals seeing my brother walk back from the bathrooms. "We're playing truth or dare. It's your turn."

"I'm okay. You guys play it amongst yourselves," Stirling tells her. I know my brother is feeling uncomfortable, but he could at least take the stick out of his ass for a couple of minutes. Audrey's face falls at my brother's rejection and today of all days, he needed to give her one little thing.

"Stirling's no fun. But I am," I say, turning their attention back to me. Don't worry, ladies, I can pick up the slack.

"I've got emails to catch up on," Stirling adds, shaking his phone in the air. He's such a moron.

We continue with our games, ignoring my brother and I try to catch up to their level of drunkenness.

"I dare you to give Nell a lap dance," Rainn points at me. Oh, hell yeah, thank you, Rainn. You're my girl.

"Ewww. No," Nell squeals while crinkling up her face.

"She's worried she's going to like it," I tell the girls.

"Doubt it." Nell rolls her eyes at me.

Rainn fiddles with her phone and next thing you know, the *Magic Mike* anthem "Pony" starts blaring throughout the plane. I jump up and gyrate and shake my ass against all three girls, making them squeal and laugh.

"Go Remi, go Remi!" The girls chant. If you insist, I think as I rip open my shirt and swing it in the air above my head. I throw my shirt into Nell's face, which makes her laugh. Audrey and Rainn are clapping and screaming for me to keep going, so I do. I jump into Nell's lap and begin rolling my crotch all over her. That she is laughing and smiling makes me so happy. I turn around and wave my ass in her face and she gives me a couple of slaps across the ass. I know I shouldn't be turned on, but oh boy I am. Unfortunately, the song doesn't last long, but it's long enough for me to bend down and plant a kiss on Nell's lips when she least expects it, which makes her friends holler even louder.

"Now it's his turn." I point in my brother's direction.

"No. No. No," he stammers.

"Audrey, give that man a lap dance!" Rainn screams out. My brother is going to kill me for this. And I can see he is protesting, but Audrey isn't taking no for an answer and gives my brother a lap dance. I can see it on his face, he is loving it but is also freaking out because he is loving it.

"I think that's enough, don't you?" my brother says, shutting Audrey down halfway through the dance. The entire plane falls silent and then Audrey runs to the toilets in tears. The girls follow her.

"You're a real jerk sometimes," I tell him.

"How am I the bad guy here?"

"She was just blowing off some steam, that's all. You're an uptight asshole, aren't you?" I take a seat next to him. Buzzkill.

"Rhys would kill me if he found out."

"Fuck Rhys. This was nothing but a bit of fun. It's not like you're fucking her in front of everyone," I yell at my brother. We both sit there in silence, seething, but I notice a twitch on my brother's face. Oh shit. "Unless you want to fuck her?"

"What? No. And keep your fucking voice down, would you? What the hell is wrong with you?"

"I see the way you look at Audrey."

"I don't look at her in any way."

"Shut up, bullshit. You want her. And it's getting harder for you to hide it. Well, from your brother anyway."

"Nothing will ever happen between Audrey and me. I promised Rhys."

"When you were fucking teenagers," I tell him. I mean, I made the same promise to Dom. Didn't stick to it in the least.

"I have too much to lose. I can't."

"Even if she's worth it?"

"I won't ever find out if she is," my brother tells me sadly.

"Fair enough." I understand so I don't push him anymore and pull out my phone because Stirling will not talk to me anymore about Audrey.

Eventually the girls come out of the toilets, and they ignore Stirling and me. Hey, I'm not the dick here. Audrey is curled up against Rainn, and they are whispering to each other until Audrey falls asleep. I stretch myself out and head back to the bathrooms to relieve myself after one too many champagnes and to freshen up. There's a knock on the bathroom door and I open it, but before I realize what is happening the door slams shut again and the lock clicks. Nell's lips are on mine and she is pushing me up against the plane's sink. There is more room in this bathroom than a commercial plane, but still, it's a little cramped. Who cares? Nell's lips are on mine.

"What do you need, baby?"

"Please, just fuck me."

33

REMI

I've been in London for work, my contract with the Garcia Team is coming up for renewal, and some of the best European teams have been headhunting me. I'm a little unsure as I don't want to jump ship because Nacho Garcia has been a mentor to me all my life, plus there is also the Nell factor. She would probably hate me so much more than she already does.

"Hey, brother, long time." Rhys greets me warmly. It's been a while since I've seen him. Stirling takes a seat beside us at the restaurant in silence. I've called this meeting with the two of them because I trust their business knowledge and I know I can trust them to keep what I'm going to ask them a secret.

"What's with the secretive meeting?" my brother asks me as the server pours water into our glasses.

"Let's order first," I say, looking up uncomfortably at the server lurking around our table. The boys catch my drift and place their orders so we can have some privacy. "Right, so I'm not here in London for a modeling shoot," I tell them both. The guys nod their heads and let me continue. "I'm being headhunted by some of the richest polo teams in the world," I explain to them.

"Wow, that is amazing, brother," Stirling says, slapping me on the back proudly.

"I know. Thanks. It's a dream come true, but..." I let out an exhausted breath. "I feel disloyal even having these meetings behind Nacho's back."

"Nacho has done wonders for your career and has been an amazing mentor for you, Rem. But if you don't think you can progress in your career with his team, then you must consider other options. Nacho will understand this. He has been in this world for a long time," Stirling suggests to me. I know he's right. It's hard.

"Have there been any offers that are tempting you?" Rhys asks.

"They are all amazing, offering me everything and anything I want, but something doesn't feel right," I confess to them both.

"Is it because you're worried about change or something else?" Stirling asks, and I can tell by the way he is looking at me he is asking me if it's because of Nell. Partly, she is a consideration, but not the whole reason for my hesitation.

"With Nacho, he is teaching me about so much more other than polo. He is helping me create a career after the game. And I know if I go to another team, all they want from me is to win and make their team the best. They aren't helping me build connections for after I retire. I mean, I can't do this sport forever."

"That's really smart thinking, Rem," Rhys praises me.

"What do you want after polo?" Stirling questions me.

"Funnily enough, Dom has been asking me if maybe I might be interested in one day partnering with him to run his family's business." He was drunk when he asked me first, but we've had many conversations since. "Dom isn't interested in the polo playing side like his father is, he is more interested in breeding the polo ponies."

"That's an interesting concept," Rhys states.

"Yeah. The conversations started off as a joke, but we have been talking about it more and more. I just don't know how Nacho would feel about it."

"He couldn't say no if you married Nell and became family," Stirling jokes. I turn my head and glare at him. "It's a shame she hates your guts," he says, laughing a little harder. Fuck, he's annoying.

"Okay, so marrying the boss's daughter is off the table. You need to come up with a business plan and present it to Nacho," Rhys explains to me, trying to be helpful.

"You think it's that simple?"

"You can try. The worst he can do is say no, the best he thinks it's great. You won't know unless you try," Rhys advises. Maybe he's right. Could it really be that simple?

"Sounds like you might have already made your decision, then?" Stirling questions, giving me a grin.

The girls are back from traipsing around Europe for the last week. Not that I haven't been stalking their socials or jerked off to the bikini images Nell posted. Damn thirst traps get me every time. Thankfully, Rainn sent me a text inviting me to some party in the city and how could I possibly turn that down.

"Hey, brother," I call out, jumping on him and nearly crash tackling him onto the table. I'm surprised to see him and Rhys here. They are not clubbing guys.

"What the hell are you doing here?" Stirling growls in my direction.

"What's crawled up your butt?"

"Sorry, just have stuff on my mind. Why are you here?" he asks normally this time.

"The girls texted me, and I couldn't say no to a party."

"Remi, come dance with me," Rainn calls from the sideline. She gives me a wink as she prowls over to me. What is going on? I go with it. I trust Rainn, she is definitely not interested in me, but I have a feeling she is trying to prove a point or make a point to her best friend. There they are, the daggers in my back, the ones Nell is mentally throwing at me.

"You better not be messing around with Rainn?" Stirling hits me in the chest with the back of his hand. Ouch. Dick.

"No. We're just friends. Strictly friends," I answer quickly, defending myself. "But it is making a certain someone jealous though."

"Be careful. You're playing with fire, and this could all blow up in your face," he warns me. Whatever, Nell and I have played this game many times before, it's our thing.

"I know what I'm doing, brother. Don't worry about me," I tell him and follow Rainn onto the dancefloor. I see out of the corner of my eyes that Nell gets up from the table looking upset, and Audrey follows her. I feel like a dick now. Dammit.

"She'll be okay. She's upset that I keep pushing her buttons," Rainn assures me as we dance apart from each other.

"Seems like we have that in common."

"How long do you think you two will keep dancing around each other?" Rainn asks.

"Who knows? We've been doing it for so long that it feels normal now," I explain to her, shrugging my shoulders.

"Keep fucking about and you will lose her, Rem," Rainn tells me seriously.

"I already have. She's not interested in me other than my dick. She'd rather Saint Miles over me."

"Your brother is worse than you," Rainn chuckles. Thank you, and here I thought I was the only one that saw it. I knew I liked Rainn the most. "Deep down Nell isn't interested in Miles, he's just the safer option and she knows it annoys you. You are both as bad as each other." Yeah, maybe we are.

Rainn meets some guys on the dancefloor and practically tells me to get lost, so I do. I head on over to the bar area and while I'm waiting, someone pokes me hard in the kidneys. Ouch.

"We agreed no friends, Remi," Nell tells me angrily while still poking me with her sharp nail. "I knew I couldn't trust you." She shoves me hard in the chest. "You keep messing up, Remi. And I stupidly fall for it every single time." Then she turns on her heel and storms off back into the club. Of course, I chase after her because she's really got the wrong idea, not that I blame her because I keep giving her the wrong ideas.

"Nell," I shout after her. "Wait, Nell." I catch up to her before she runs into the women's bathroom. "Nothing is going on with Rainn. I promise. She was trying to annoy you," I explain the stupid plan. Nell stops wriggling, and her mouth falls open in surprise.

"Rainn did it to annoy me?" she asks slowly. I nod, unsure if this is going to turn into a fight between friends. "That bitch." Nell bursts out laughing. Oh, phew. "I can't believe she did that. And then here I am yelling at you like a damn fool. Oh, my gosh, Rem, I'm sorry. I accused you of something you didn't do," Nell says, looking embarrassed over her reaction.

"Hey," I say, reaching out and cupping her face. "No need to apologize it's not like I don't give you enough reasons not to trust me." I let out a heavy sigh.

"You do, do a lot of stupid stuff."

"Yeah, I do." I smile down at her. "It's not on purpose or to hurt you. Just thinking with the wrong head most of the time."

"He seems to get you in trouble often." Nell grins as her hand cups my dick in my pants.

"He's a troublemaker. Most of the time he doesn't listen to me."

Nell bites her bottom lip as she continues to stroke me through my jeans.

"Is he up for a bit of trouble now?" She raises a questioning brow in my direction. Oh, hell yeah. As I grab her hand and pull her somewhere a little less exposed.

"Just what I needed." Nell wraps her arms around my neck and kisses me softly.

"Always at your service." I grin down at her. We hear a commotion and I wrap my hand around her shoulders and pull her to me protectively.

"What the hell is that about?" she asks me. I have no idea but can hear people yelling and screaming and security rushing through the club. Moments later, Nell's phone is ringing, and she picks it up. I can tell by her face it's not good.

"David just turned up to the club trying to win Audrey back. Rhys punched him. And everything's gone to shit. I have to go," she tells me not before she wraps her arms around my neck and kisses me. "I'll see you when we get home, okay. I would like to hook up somewhere that doesn't include a toilet." She chuckles.

"Let me walk you out."

It's time to say farewell to London as I take a seat on the private plane. Thankfully, all my meetings wrapped up in time so I can cruise back with these guys.

"Surprised to see me, brother?" I grin, taking in his expression.

"A little. What are you doing coming back with us? I thought you were staying." He takes the seat beside me.

"My meeting was pushed earlier in the week, so I was free to come home with you all. Wasn't going to say no to the private jet." The flight attendant hands me my whiskey while giving me the come fuck me eyes.

"Thank you, sweetheart."

"Stop flirting with the staff," Stirling grumbles beside me.

It's been a couple of hours since taking off from London and the girls have all fallen asleep.

"You look like you have the weight of the world on your shoulders, brother." I'm noticing the extra tension my brother seems to be carrying.

"It's nothing,"

"I think it's five foot six of nothing."

"What does that mean?" He glares at me.

"It means I know you and I know something is up. Plus, the way you can't stop looking over at Audrey is a dead giveaway." Stirling glares at me. "But in all seriousness. Are you okay?"

"Yeah. I'm all good."

My eyes narrow on him. "So, nothing's happened between Audrey and you since arriving in London?" I know he went into full protective mode after David's surprise visit.

"No. Of course not."

"I can smell your bullshit a mile away." I shake my head.

"I know you and Miles are closer and talk about this kind of shit together." He pauses, mulling over his next words. "Fine. Something happened last night."

"I knew it." I punch the sky with my fist. "Sorry, continue," I say, controlling myself.

"You heard what happened last night at the party?"

Stirling then tells me all about the *intense moments* he's been having with Audrey. I mean, if he's this shook up over kissing her, what the hell is he going to do when he does eventually sleep with her? His mind is going to explode. I explain to him he shouldn't feel guilty about hooking up with Audrey because honestly, she seems way happier leaving London than she did arriving. Then my brother changes the subject and asks about Nell.

"Has something happened with Nell?" he asks.

I'm not in the mood to talk about it. I spoke to Miles last night and he was talking about how he'd been texting back and forth with Nell and telling me he didn't realize she was so funny. Apparently, they ran into each other at a fundraising event before they left for London and exchanged numbers. Nell seemed to forget about that little tidbit.

"Same thing that always happens. I rock her world when she needs me to then when the sun rises, she goes back to hating me and lusting after my brother." Nell has ignored me this entire plane trip. I raise my glass toward the flight attendant and ask for another refill. Stirling doesn't look impressed as I flirt with the flight attendant.

"Does Miles even like her?" Stirling asks.

"He has no idea she wants him."

"Then speak to him. Let him know what's going on between you and Nell."

"Does it matter…" I sigh, "she will only ever see me as the player she thinks I am and the convenient dick ready and willing for her." Damn, these whiskeys are going down nicely. My eyes drift back over to the flight attendant with the come fuck me eyes.

"If you like Nell, then why not fight for her?" He thinks I haven't been. Fuck him. He doesn't understand.

"Who would want me over Saint Miles?"

"I thought you might be hungry." The flight attendant comes back with snacks and places them in front of us.

"How did you know how hungry I was?" I flirt with the flight attendant. I know I have a reputation, but sometimes that reputation can feel like a noose around my neck.

"A big man like you must be hungry," she quips back. A choking cough comes from the other side of the plane from Nell, who I thought was asleep.

"How long do we have till we land?"

"About two hours, sir," she answers me.

"Might be enough time for you to help me with something, don't you think?" The flight attendant's eyes widen in understanding as her cheeks turn bright pink with lust. I'm going to hell, might as well make the ride fun.

"Yes, of course. I'm willing to help. I'll leave your snacks here while I tidy things up down at the back of the plane for you, sir." She gives me a knowing look as she turns on her heel and walks to the back of the plane.

"You're not seriously considering doing something, are you?" Stirling looks at me in disgust.

"Why not? She seems rather helpful." I chuckle, popping a peanut into my mouth.

"What about you know who?"

"I'm the wrong brother, remember?" I remind him as I stand up and stride off into the back of the plane. The flight attendant stills when I come back to where she is working. I can see the excitement on her face that she might go a couple of rounds with the notorious playboy Remington Hartford. Her red lips would look nice wrapped around my dick. But I hesitate. For the first time, I hesitate in front of a beautiful woman. I sway a bit unsteady on my feet and reach out and grab the wall.

"Are you all right, Mr. Hartford?" she asks.

"Yeah. I just need a moment," I tell her. She looks over at me curiously. "Look, I'm sorry about earlier, I shouldn't have led you on like I just did," I tell her, taking a seat in the chair and rubbing my face with my hands. "I'm trying to get over someone and it's not working," I confess. Her brows raise in surprise.

"If you need to talk, I'm all ears," she tells me, taking a seat beside me, no level or flirtation at all. And so I do. I tell her how I've fallen for Nell Garcia, and I don't know what to do about it.

34

NELL

I can't believe Remi did that. With the flight attendant right in front of me. I'm so angry at him, I'm currently knocking on his hotel door. I think he forgot we had arranged to meet up tonight after his little mile high action.

"Remi, I know you're in there. Open up!" I yell at the door.

Eventually the door opens, and Remi is standing there dripping wet with a white towel wrapped around his waist and one drying his hair. Oh shit, did he bring her to the hotel with him? Is he not alone?

"Where is she?" I ask, storming past him as I enter his hotel room.

"What the hell are you talking about?"

"The girl from the plane, is she here?" I'm losing my mind as I storm through his suite, trying to find a naked woman hiding somewhere.

"Nell, what the fuck?" Remi curses behind me. "I'm alone. You've lost your damn mind, woman."

"Because you did this to me." I thump my chest. "You've made me crazy."

"Me." He raises his voice while pointing to himself. "You're the one that's made *me* fucking crazy. So crazy that I turned the advances down of a woman who was prepared to get on her knees for me," I spit back. "Because all I can think about is you, Nell. You. It's always you every damn minute of the damn fucking day!" he yells at me.

Oh. I'm taken aback by his words.

"I can't do this anymore; it's not healthy. I'm exhausted," he tells me, running his hand through his wet hair again. "I think you were right earlier. I should have listened. Sex complicates things. It complicates everything." Hang on, I'm the one that came over upset. How is he turning it around and being the one upset over all this? "I'm done competing with my brother for you, Nell." Those green eyes glare at me seriously. "I know you and Miles have been texting."

Oh. That.

"It's nothing," I tell him.

"Nothing? You have had a crush on my brother for years. I don't call that nothing."

"And yet I'm always in your bed."

"Only because I'm convenient, not because it means anything," he argues with me. "If Miles asked you out on a date, would you say no?" he questions me. I don't know. That isn't even in the realm of possibilities that would ever happen. But he takes my hesitation as my answer. "I've been so fucking stupid. I thought I would sit back and bide my time and maybe, just maybe, you would finally see me and realize I'm the man for you."

Huh? Remi has stunned me with his words. What the hell is he talking about? That's bullshit. He's been dating and hooking up with people. He's hardly been sitting at home pining for me.

"I think you and I need a break," Remi explains softly.

"You can't break up with me, we aren't even dating," I shoot back at him.

"Then you won't notice when I stop answering your calls then."

My jaw hits the floor at his callous words.

"I'm tired. I think it's best you should go."

"You're kicking me out?"

"Guess I am." He shrugs his shoulders.

"Fuck you, Remington Hartford!" I scream at him, shocked, hurt, and confused, as I stomp out of his hotel room.

After spending the next twenty-four hours crying my eyes out over a boy that doesn't deserve it. Remi's pseudo breakup made me reassess my life and what I want in it. I picked myself up and got to work, figuring out what I wanted. And that's how I found myself back home, presenting my mom with my book full of sketches with a business plan. It was a tense time watching my mother look over my creations.

"Sweetheart, I am so proud of you," Mom tells me. "These sketches, this business plan, is everything that I had hoped one day you would bring me." She looks at me with tears in her eyes. "I am so proud of you, sweetheart. So very proud." This is everything I have always wanted to hear from my mom.

"I met up with the designer Yvette Sanchez in Paris, and she wants to work with me on this first collection," I tell my mom, hopeful that she might think it's a good idea.

"Oh, sweetie, that is wonderful. Yvette is the nicest, kindest woman. What a privilege it would be. I trust her. She is a good egg in this business. Of course we will get our lawyers to look over any contracts which is standard practice."

"You'd be okay if I went over there for the summer."

"Let me tell your father because you know what he's like." My mother rolls her eyes. Latin fathers are a little crazy protective of their daughters. "But of course, I want you to do this. It's such a brilliant opportunity, Nell. Yvette wouldn't offer this to just anyone. You are so talented, I just needed you to believe it. And I know I've been hard on you, kiddo, but it's only because I wanted to strengthen you," she explains to me. I stand up and hug my mom. Finally after all these years, she takes me seriously.

Nell: Meet me at Saks tomorrow for champagne. I have news.

"I've missed you, girlies." I squeal when I see them. I haven't told them about the blow-up between Remi and me. I'm not sure why, maybe because I'm embarrassed, maybe I just don't want the Spanish inquisition on my ass, or maybe I'm worried that they might side with Remi on this one. Forget about him. I have more important things to worry about.

"I have some news for you both." I am practically jumping out of my chair.

"Tell us, woman." Audrey huffs.

"I pitched my design ideas to Mom for her equestrian clothing brand, and she loved them." The girls scream. They have been on this journey with my mom for years and they understand how much this means to me. "I explained how I wanted to expand her brand from out of the traditional equestrian scene and move into a more contemporary one—starting with outfits fit for polo parties. We all know when polo season hits, the calendar is jam-packed with events and some events have a strict traditional dress code. Yvette and I will be working on this first line together as a collaboration until I can take over full time."

"We need to celebrate. Let's grab a bottle of champagne," Rainn suggests, as she calls over one of the staff and orders a bottle for the table.

"Does this mean you have to move to Paris?" Audrey asks.

"That's what I wanted to talk to you girls about. Yvette

offered me an internship if I got the green light from my family for the summer. I kind of want to take it."

"You need to take this. This is huge," Audrey states.

"We will pop over and visit you," Rainn adds.

"You girls sure?"

"Yes!" Rainn and Audrey say together.

"Here's to Nell being a boss bitch in Paris." Audrey raises her glass in a toast.

Onwards and upwards!

I think I may have drunk too much champagne because I think I see Miles Hartford standing across the room at the bar with Stirling.

"Miles?" I call out.

"Ladies, it's so nice to see you all again." Miles smiles widely.

"It's been too long."

"Stirling?" Audrey gasps, not noticing him standing there next to his brother.

"You ladies look like you're celebrating something?" Miles flashes his megawatt smile at us all. Damn, he's pretty.

"Nell's been given an opportunity to move to Paris for the summer, so we're celebrating," Rainn tells them.

"Wow, congratulations, Nell. That sounds fantastic," Miles says, giving me a flirtatious wink, which makes my stomach flutter.

"Why don't you join us?" I ask, more the merrier. I'm in the mood to celebrate.

"That sounds great. I think we need to order another bottle of champagne to celebrate your success, don't you think?" Miles asks me as he slides in beside me. I think I might have drunk a little too much because I think Miles is being overtly flirtatious with me.

"I'm going to have to get going, guys. I have to get ready for a date," Rainn tells us. Boo. I'm in the mood to party, but at least

Audrey is still here, and I'm supposed to be meeting up with Portia later and she's always up for partying.

"So, Paris for the summer, hey?" Miles asks, laying his arm across the chair behind me, leaning in closer to me.

"I know, I'm so excited," I tell him.

"Remi is going to be in France for the summer too. What a coincidence?" Miles tells me. I did not know he was going to be there, nor do I care.

"That's nice."

"I thought you were friends?" Miles questions me.

"Nope. Not anymore," I inform him. He seems surprised.

"Did you have a falling out?" he asks, curious. *Yeah, over you*, I want to say, but I don't.

"Ugh. Stanford is such a jerk. He found out I'm here. Thanks, social media. He wants me to meet him downstairs to help pick out a tuxedo for the foundation's ball," Audrey interrupts. My eyes widen in surprise. Audrey's other brother, Stanford, is a dick of massive proportions. Why on earth is she going to meet him? "Stirling, do you mind coming with me? I don't want to be caught in the middle of Sandy and Rhys's fights. You'll make a good buffer."

"Of course. I can handle Sandy," Stirling says confidently, placing his champagne glass down on the table.

"Thank you so much. I owe you," Audrey says to him. What the hell is going on? "Guys, stay, please. There's still some champagne left in the bottle." Audrey turns to Miles and me.

"I'll grab the bill. You guys go deal with Sandy. I'm sure Nell and I can finish what's left," Miles explains. I nod because who's going to say no to free champagne.

We finish another bottle of champagne between us, and we are both feeling the effects.

"Hey, I've got to meet some friends at a bar downtown. Want to come?" I ask Miles because he's been good company. Flirty, but never overstepping the boundaries which I am kind of glad for. As much as I have wanted to have a moment like this with Miles for so long, the butterflies I initially had seem to have scattered and drifted away and all I can picture when I look at him is someone else. Fuck.

We hop in a taxi and head on downtown. Miles seems to get closer and closer to me in the taxi while we chat and I'm thankful when we arrive out the front of the bar. Miles hands the taxi driver the fare plus tip, grabs my hand, and helps me from the car. I thought he would have let go once I was out, but he doesn't, not even when he cuts in line at the bar. The security guard gives him a nod and lets us in, much to the annoyance of the people waiting outside. It's packed in the bar and it's standing room only. Miles orders us cocktails and we find a dark corner to drink them in. Both of us are looking a little worse for wear after an afternoon of champagne, but we're still standing.

"Thanks for asking me to hang out," Miles says, placing a hand beside my face on the wall behind me.

"Thanks for wanting to celebrate with me," I tell him, taking a sip of my cocktail and I try not to focus on his piercing green eyes. Especially not when they dip toward my mouth. Where the hell is my sister, she's supposed to have been meeting us here?

"You're really beautiful, Nell," Miles confesses. Oh no. I should want this confession, but I don't think I do. The hand beside my head moves down and cups my face. "My brother will probably kill me for this, but I don't care," he states before pressing his lips against mine. Oh shit. He's caught me off guard, and my mouth opens in surprise, and he thinks that's an invitation to sweep his tongue against mine. No. No. No. Pushing him away, we are both a little dazed by the kiss. Thank goodness my phone is ringing as I hold it up because I don't know how to get myself out of this mess.

"Where the hell are you, Portia?" I scream down the

phone in a panic. No. No. No. I can't believe I let him kiss me. No. As tears well in my eyes. I'm so fucking stupid.

"Chill. I'm outside. I forgot my ID. Can you lend me yours?" she asks. The older she has become, the more we look like twins.

"Fine. I'll be out in a sec," I tell her, hanging up the phone. "Hey, Miles." I tap him on the shoulder as the music is loud. I lean into his ear, and he wraps his arms around me, pulling me closer. Oh no, sorry, dude, you have the wrong girl, and I'm sorry if I gave you the wrong idea, but it is not happening. "I just have to grab my sister and her friends. I'll be back in five. You good?" I ask him. He nods, but it's floppy because he's so drunk.

"I'll be waiting here for you," he says, giving me a wink. Righto then. I turn on my heel and head back outside to find my sister. Are you fricken serious? We are wearing the same dress. I'm in black and she is in red. Get your own style, girl. But I have too much of a headache to fight with her over us twinning.

"Here." I hand her my ID. "Where are your friends?" I ask, noticing she's alone.

"They're stuck in traffic."

"Right, well, Miles Hartford is inside. He was helping me celebrate my move to Paris," I explain to her. Her brows shoot up high. "He's drunk. Nothing happened." Lie. But as far as I'm concerned, it wasn't a proper kiss. It was sloppy and kind of missed the mark. Probably not his finest hour so it doesn't count. "Make sure you keep an eye on him," I tell her.

"Sure thing. Why aren't you staying?" she asks.

"Champagne headache," I tell her. I give her a kiss on the cheek and leave her at the bar. I hail a cab and jump in. As soon as my head hits the seat, my entire world spins. Please don't throw up. I chant the entire way home.

35

REMI

I promised I'd catch up with Miles before I left for France for the summer. This was his last weekend off before I left, so the only time we could catch up. I walk into his apartment expecting to see him dressed and ready to go, but he's not there.

"Miles!" I call out. He better not have been called into work and forgotten to text me to tell me. Wouldn't be the first time. "Miles, where the fuck are you?" I curse through the empty apartment. I head on over to his bedroom. The bastard rarely sleeps in, but maybe he's indulging today. It is his weekend off, which is few. When I turn the corner there, he is snoring away, naked. I take a couple of moments to take in the room because it's a mess. What the hell happened in here? His room stinks like a brewery, and I chuckle to myself because Miles never goes out and gets trashed. Guess he overindulged last night. Good on him.

"Oi, get up dickhead." I shove him hard, startling him awake. He flips over, and I shield my eyes. I do not need to see another man's morning wood. "Fucking hell, man, put some clothes on!" I yell at my brother.

He pulls the sheet over himself, but he looks a little confused as he searches around the room as if looking for something or someone. Shit, now the messy sheets make sense.

"Looks like you had a good night last night," I tease.

Miles's face turns pale. "Um, yeah, something like that. I might have a shower." He gets up and slams the bathroom door shut. His hangover must be a bitch. My stomach rumbles so I head into his kitchen to see if I can grab something to eat while he sobers up. Miles always has good shit in his fridge, and it doesn't disappoint when I spot a brownie. I grab the chocolatey treat and take a bite, damn it's good. I savor every bite of that perfection until I hear Miles call out my name. Busted. Shit, I drop the plate and it smashes on the floor.

"Shit, sorry, man." I'm looking at the white ceramic mess on the floor.

"Don't worry about it," Miles tells me.

Huh. Did I hear that correctly? Miles is the biggest clean freak known to man. He hates people touching his stuff, let alone breaking it. He must be really hungover to not spin out over the broken plate. "Let me clean up and we can go," I say, opening cupboards trying to find a dustpan. Then I notice an ID on the floor in the kitchen. I pick it up and my stomach sinks. Why the fuck does he have Nell's ID in his kitchen? I stand up and slam the ID on the counter.

Miles frowns at me for a moment, then looks down at the ID. I can see he reads the name because the color drains from his face.

"Look, I can explain, Remi," he says, holding up his hands.

"You can explain?" I repeat his words. My vision is seeing red because he better not be telling me that the reason his bed looks like a tornado has been through it is because he brought Nell home and fucked her. He better not be saying that. No. Fuck no.

"We were both extremely drunk," he explains as if that's an excuse.

"When you say we. You mean, you and Nell?" I question through clenched teeth.

"Remi, please. It just happened."

I see red. "It just happened. It just fucking happened!" I scream at him as I slam my fist through his wall, shocking us both.

"Remi, stop, you're going to break your hand!" Miles screams at me.

"You motherfucking bastard," I say, grabbing him by the collar and pinning him against the wall. "You could have any woman in New York and yet you fucked the woman that I love!" I scream in his face. Miles pales as my words hit him.

"I had no idea you were in love with her." He pushes me away from him. "Fuck, Rem. I thought you were just friends. That's all you've ever told me you were. I did not know you were in fucking love with her. Shit. Fuck!" Miles screams at me. "Fuck, I'm an asshole. I did not know. She said nothing." Miles paces.

"I never want to speak to you again," I tell him.

"Remi, come on. I'm your brother," he pleads.

"Exactly." I turn around and point at his face. "My fucking brother."

"Remi." Miles screams out after me, but I don't care as I slam the door behind me.

I can't wait to get the fuck out of this town.

I should really thank Miles and Nell for sleeping together because I could channel that anger into one of my best summer seasons yet. I'm having the time of my life in France. The parties, the women, the sunshine, I'm living the dream. I heard through the grapevine that Nell had moved to Paris for the summer to work for a designer. Good for her. Not like I care or anything. Thankfully, she hasn't come down to the South of France to any events because I'm not sure what I would do if I saw her again. After I left Miles's apartment, I blocked them both. Stirling is a little confused why Miles and I aren't speaking, and I appreciate Miles not telling him because Stirling is just going to be a mediator and I don't want that. Miles is my brother, and I will eventually talk to him again because I must, we're blood, but he can damn well wait till I'm ready to.

I'm currently in Paris for an exhibition game for polo week, and I'm hoping like hell that Nell is way too busy to come to the event because I don't want to see her again. Ever.

"You, okay?" Callum, one of my teammates, asks me.

"Yeah, all good. Rolly made me try escargot last night and I don't think it agrees with me."

"You know never to listen to Rolly." Callum shakes his head at me.

I wish it was the escargots repeating on me, but I know exactly the reason, stupidly. I checked my socials and saw a photo Nell posted of her in the crowd at the event with friends. Fuck.

"Come on, Hartford, let's go!" Coach screams into the change rooms, hurrying us up. We head on over to the stables and get on our horses, and as we ride out into the area to introduce ourselves to the crowd, I can't help but try to find a particular blonde in a sea of them. Even when we sit through the national anthems, I still can't see her. Not even when I get onto the field, totally distracted trying to see where she is, but nothing. Not until I'm about to take a shot on goal that I see her in the crowd cheering me on, a big smile on her face as she screams my name, and my world stops. And the next thing I know, my horse bucks me off and I fall to the ground in a crumpled heap. The crowd turns eerily silent as I lay there motionless because

I've had the wind knocked out of me. Shit, this is going to hurt in the morning. My team rushes onto the field, someone's grabbed my horse that is bucking wildly. I turn my head to the side, and I spot Nell in the crowd, her hands are crossed over her mouth, and she has tears in her eyes. I can see the concern etched on her face all the way from here. It's like a sucker punch to the stomach. Why is she acting like she cares? When I know she doesn't.

"You, okay, man?" Callum asks.

I push myself up into a sitting position and suck in a couple of deep breaths. "I think so."

"You're off, Remi. Go see the doc!" Coach yells at me. Callum helps me hobble from the field. Once the crowd sees I'm walking off, they give me a round of applause. I give them an appreciative wave and head on over to the medical tent, where they check me over.

"Oh my god, Remi. Are you okay?" Nell rushes over to me.

Everyone stops and stares at her, wondering who this girl is.

"I don't know this person," I tell security, who puts a hand out to stop her. Nell frowns when she sees the man stop her, and she searches for me to tell him to let her through. I don't.

"I'm a family friend of Remi's. Please let me through," she pleads with the security guard, all the while staring at me, wondering what the hell is going on. Security just shakes their head. "I'm Nacho Garcia's daughter." And this gets everyone's attention. The security guard turns to me. Everyone knows Nacho. I shake my head. Nell's jaw falls open at my dismissal and tears well in her eyes. I feel like an ass for making her cry, but she slept with my brother and that is something I can't get over.

"Remi?" she says my name softly. I pick up my phone and start playing on it, effectively dismissing her.

"Dude, that was Nacho Garcia's daughter you just sent away. Isn't he your boss?" Callum asks.

"Yeah. But it's complicated," I tell him.

"Right, well, I guess asking for her number then is off the cards?" he jokes.

"Have at it. There's nothing between us anymore."

36

NELL

I've never seen Remi be so cruel to anyone in my life. He ripped out my heart and smashed it to pieces with one look. It was incredibly embarrassing. He effectively pretended not to know me. What the hell?

I don't know what I ever did to him to deserve that kind of treatment, but I get the message loud and clear from Remi. Don't worry, I will never bother you ever again.

We miss you, Nell!" Rainn and Audrey shout down the phone.

"I miss you too."

"I can't believe you're staying on," Audrey pouts.

"I'm learning so much, guys." And I am in love with Paris. "How are things going back home?"

"Nothing much has changed. I still live at home. We have the ball in the next couple of days, so I've been working hard on that."

"Can't believe I'm missing it. This is the first ball I think I've missed since we were ten."

"Least Rainn came home after the summer," Audrey states, giving me some wicked side-eye. Point taken, Aud.

"I feel invigorated," Rainn muses.

"And tanned. You are so tanned," Audrey grumbles.

"So, how are things going with Stirling?" I ask.

"We're still friends. Nothing more." Like hell they are just friends. She knows Remi, and I used that excuse so many times and we kept sleeping with each other. "No. I haven't strayed from that path, not since Rhys has come home."

"Rhys is such a cock block." I chuckle.

"It's for the best. Stirling is ten years older than me. He has his shit together, and me? I still live at home. I live off a trust fund. I work in the family business. He deserves someone more," Audrey declares sadly.

"Hey, you know I don't allow you to talk about yourself like that," Rainn calls her out. "You are both at different stages of your lives and now isn't the time for the two of you to be together," Rainn explains.

"A man like Stirling isn't waiting around for me to get my shit together." Audrey sighs, and I feel for her because finally she got her man and now her brother is going to pull them apart. I wish Stirling would stand up and tell Rhys to take a hike.

"You realize all of those things on your list are achievable. They aren't barriers," I tell her.

"But my brother is."

"Rhys will come around eventually." Rainn tries to see the positive in the situation.

"Enough about me." Audrey changes the subject. "Have you spoken to Remi since you were away?"

"No. He's ghosted me. I don't know what happened between us. I mean, he was over here playing a couple of exhibition games and I got nothing other than a hello as if I was a stranger. I haven't heard from him at all." I know I just lied to my friends, but I don't want them to worry about me or make things awkward around Remi. Because as much as I hate it, he will still be in my life, especially if Stirling and Audrey get together.

"I'm fine. Think it's weird. But his loss, as I'm having so much fun with all these French guys. Their accents are so sexy. Everything they say drips with sex." Not that I've been dating or anything. I've been focusing on work. "I better go. Love you two," I tell them before hanging up. I lay back down on my bed and cry into my pillow. I've never felt more alone.

My phone ringing pulls me from my sleep, I look down at the screen and it's Portia.

"Hey, babe, how are you?" I say, answering the phone.

"Nell. I fucked up," Portia cries down the phone. I sit up quickly as panic fills my body.

"Portia, are you okay? What's going on?"

"Mom and Dad are going to kill him. Oh my god, Dom is going to kill him too." Portia freaks out all over again and has a panic attack.

"Babe, please, you're scaring me. Tell me what's going on so I can fix it." Big sister protection mode kicks in.

"I'm pregnant," she confesses.

Oh shit. This is bad. This is terrible. I didn't even know she was dating. Why the hell did she not use protection? Calm down, Nell, you do not need to freak her out any more than she is. "I'm here for you. Okay. How far along are you?" I ask her softly, trying not to spook her.

"I just found out I'm like ten weeks," she mumbles. Holy shit.

"And what about the father, does he know?" I ask gently.

"Um. No, not yet. I just took a test a couple of minutes ago."

"I'm glad you called me, Portia. I wish I was closer so I could hug you and tell you everything is going to be okay." I try to comfort her.

"Do you have room in Paris for me?" she asks.

"I would love you to come over, but you need to deal with this first," I explain to her. "You need to book in with an OBGYN and make sure everything is okay with the baby."

"Do you think something is wrong with it?" she asks, panicked.

"No, no, I'm sure everything is fine. It's routine." I think. I don't know, I've never been knocked up before.

"Okay, I can do that."

"I don't mean to pry, but can I ask who the father is? Is he going to support you?" My question is met with silence. I knew I shouldn't have asked her that. "Babe, it's okay. You don't need to tell me."

"I don't want you to hate me," she mumbles, and my stomach sinks. Why would I hate her? "I slept with Miles." Huh.

"Miles who?" And as soon as I finish my question, I realize exactly who she is talking about. Holy shit, this is bad.

"Miles Hartford."

"He's so much older than you." The comment comes out before I can soften it.

"I wasn't thinking about that when I was sleeping with him, was I. All I thought about was he was hot, and he knew how to kiss, and I thought why not," Portia adds. Fuck, my mind is blown.

"When did it happen?" I ask, wondering what the hell has been happening since I left.

"Um, well yeah, okay, this is where it gets weird. I kind of slept with him the night you gave me your ID when you were celebrating going to France. He called me Nell twice, but he was pretty wasted, and I thought he just got us confused because like you were there and then you were gone," she explains.

Fuck. Fuck. Fuck.

Then my stomach sinks again. No. There is no way in the world that Miles thinks he slept with me and not my sister.

"Please don't tell me you lost my ID at his apartment?" I question her. Portia told me she had a crazy night and had lost my ID. She couldn't remember where she left it.

"I may have," she answers sheepishly.

"Fuck." I curse down the phone.

"What. What did I do? Don't tell me someone stole your identity and like murdered a heap of people and now you're a wanted criminal?" Wait, what the hell?

"No. Worse. I think Remi thinks I slept with Miles and that's the reason he has iced me out."

"Oh. Is that all? I thought it was something bad." She sighs.

"Portia, it is. I love him, and he thinks I slept with his brother. No wonder he hates me!" I scream at her.

"Oh shit. Yeah, that's bad," she says. No shit. Fuck. No wonder he thinks I'm the worst human in the world.

"You need to tell Miles so we can sort all this out," I tell her angrily.

"What. No. I can't do that. Everyone is going to hate me," she whines.

"Miles needs to know he's going to be a dad. And you both need to decide together whether or not you are going to keep it."

"I'm keeping it. I'm not getting rid of my baby. No way in the world. And if Miles wants me to, he can go get fucked."

"Well then, seeing as you're going to be a mommy soon, you better pull up your big girl pants and break the news to Miles that he's going to be a dad."

"Fuck," she grumbles. "You're right. I promise I'll sort it all out. And for the record, I'm sorry I messed everything up with Remi for you."

"Don't worry about me. I'll be fine. You look after yourself and my niece or nephew," I tell her.

"Oh shit. That just got real." She cries before hanging up.

I fall back onto the bed, exhausted as I try to process the bombshell Portia dropped on me.

Will Remi ever speak to me again when he finds out? Or has too much damage been done?

37

REMI

My phone rings and I see that it's Mom calling me.

"Hey, Mom," I answer.

"Please don't hang up, Remi," Miles says quickly. My hand curls around my phone and I swear I hear the screen crack. "It's important, Remi. Please."

I pinch the bridge of my nose, contemplating hanging up or not, but he's calling from Mom's phone so it might be serious.

"I'm listening."

"Thank God." He sighs into the phone. "I found out I'm going to be a dad today." Oh shit. No way. That's awesome news. "Not sure how to say this because I'm confused myself, but I knocked up Portia Garcia."

"You fucking did what?" I scream down the phone. "She's like young. Really young."

"She's legal. She's twenty-one," he answers, annoyed at my accusation. I don't understand how this happened. Well, I know how it happened. Was he not content sleeping with Nell that he had to sleep with her sister too? Fuck, Miles, you're a real asshole.

"I don't understand."

"Here's the bit you're going to find funny," he adds sarcastically. "Apparently it wasn't Nell I brought home that night, it was Portia," he confesses. I drop my phone as I take in his words. He slept with Portia, not Nell. "Rem? Remi, are you there?" Miles calls out from the floor. "Did you hear what I said?" I pick up the phone and put it back to my ear.

"Yeah, I heard. Congrats I guess, buddy."

"Thanks," he answers awkwardly. "But are you understanding what I'm saying? I never slept with Nell."

"I understand," I tell him, my voice void of emotions because I honestly don't know how to take in this information. My brain doesn't seem to process it.

"Remi, I am so sorry I fucked things up between you and Nell. But if you still want her, then you need to tell her how you feel," Miles exclaims.

"Yeah. I don't think she's interested in anything I have to say," I tell my brother.

"What did you do?" he questions me.

"Does it matter? Congrats, man, and I'm glad I'm on the other side of the world when you two break the news to Nacho. Next time I see you, you might be in a casket." I chuckle darkly.

"Fuck," he curses before hanging up.

I sit on the edge of my bed and hang my head in my hands. My brother just blew my life up a second time. There is no way in hell Nell is ever going to talk to me. Then the idea strikes me, and I pick up my phone and text my brother after unblocking him, of course.

Remi: I need you to ask Portia for Nell's address in Paris.

Miles: Fuck, you're not asking for much.

Remi: This is all your fault. You owe me.

Miles: Fine. Consider it done.

Now I must work out how the hell I'm going to convince Nell to speak to me again.

It took Miles a couple of days, but eventually he was able to get Nell's address. In those days, I obsessively stalked her socials like a damn creeper to see where she was going so that I might run into her. I also checked that she wasn't dating some French guy. Thankfully, she's not, as per her sister. Portia, God love her, once she found out I was trying to win Nell back, she was all for it. I think she felt guilty over her pregnancy and that I thought it was her sister that was with Miles that night when it was her. But tonight, there is no way in the world I want there to be any miscommunication between Nell and me. I'm done with it all. I want us to start fresh from this moment forward. I'm hoping she feels the same.

Somehow Portia got Nell's boss involved, who asked Nell to meet her at the penthouse at the famous George V hotel. She wanted to check it out for a photoshoot.

I feel like I'm going to be sick while I wait for Nell to come up to the room. I've tried to keep it a little simple because I don't know if Nell will appreciate an over-the-top grand gesture, this feels like a good middle ground. Now I wait and pray that everything is going to work out.

38

NELL

I'm so excited that Yvette has asked me to check out the penthouse at the George V for a photoshoot. She told me to dress nicely, which I have in a black jumper dress with red heels. I make my way through the opulent surroundings of the hotel and give my name at reception. The receptionist nods and hands me the key to the room and gives me instructions on how to get there. I head over to the elevators where a man in a suit holds the doors open for me; I swipe the button for the penthouse and head on up. I step out of the elevator into a long corridor, I see the penthouse door clearly marked and swipe my key across the switch, and it opens for me. I take a couple of steps into the opulent room and freeze. There spelled out in red rose petals is the word *sorry*. What on earth? I'm so confused. Then movement from the side catches my attention and I see Remi dressed in a tuxedo, looking as handsome as ever. Emotion wells in my eyes, seeing him as it's been so long, and I don't notice that I'm crying until I feel the first couple of drops on my cheeks. I swipe them away quickly.

"Remi, what the hell are you doing here?" I ask, shaking my head.

"I don't think there are enough words in any language to express how sorry I am that I hurt you, Nell," he explains to me. "A couple of months ago, I went to my brother's home and saw your ID on the floor after finding out he brought someone home. My heart shattered into a million pieces thinking that my brother got to experience you. I was so angry that you chose him I couldn't think straight. I hated you, Nell. I hated you didn't understand how much I loved you. That you didn't understand that you were buried so deep in my soul that there was never ever going to be anyone else for me. I'm sorry that I hid my true feelings, but I was so scared that you would pick him over me. How could I compete with Saint Miles? And knowing that you did. It killed me."

I can see the anguish on Remi's face as he relives the betrayal he thought I had inflicted, and I can't take it anymore. I'm done. I'm his. All his. For as long as he wants me. I'm done running because all it has done is give the two of us a shit ton of baggage when we could have been together with just carry on.

Fuck it.

I rush over to Remi and wrap my arms around his neck and kiss his lips. He hesitates for a couple of moments, unsure if this is really happening, but then I feel his arms wrap around me tightly and his lips open for me in a searing kiss. We eventually pull away from each other and I will never understand why I kept running from this man.

"I love you, Remi," I tell him through my tears of joy.

"You do?" he asks cautiously. Then the first tear rolls down his cheek as he pulls me to him again. "I love you so much, Nell. I can't believe how stupid I have been for running away from you."

"We both have been," I tell him as I look up into his eyes. "But never again."

"You're stuck with me for life, Nell. I mean it. I'm all in.

Marriage. Kids. Domestic bliss. The whole hog. You and me. Can you deal with that?" he asks me sternly.

"Yep. I think I can handle that." I grin, feeling like the luckiest girl in the world.

"But can you handle all this?" he asks, placing my hand on his hardening dick which makes me giggle as I shake my head at him.

"Not sure if I remember how. You might have to jog my memory," I tease.

"Woman." He growls before picking me up and throwing me onto the bed and jumping on top of me. Now everything feels right in the world as I wrap my legs around his waist and pull him close to me.

"No need to be nervous," I say to Remi as we drive up to my parents' farm. "You've been here a million times before. You know them.

"Yeah, but this time I'm going to be telling your family that I'm in love with you. Your dad has a shotgun by the mantle. Is it loaded? I've never checked over the years," Remi asks.

I don't mean to laugh, but it's adorable how freaked out he is over telling my parents about us. "Look, things could be worse. You could be Miles."

This makes Remi chuckle as he looks in the review mirror at the car behind us carrying Miles and Portia's little bombshell.

Miles and Portia decided we would go first to see how the family would react to us coming out as a couple, and if they were fine, then they would hit them with their news.

"Miles should definitely be worried if the shotgun on the mantle is loaded." We both have a laugh at our siblings' expense.

Mom and Dad are waiting for us as we drive up. We called a

family meeting and I know they must be concerned about the reasons.

"I've missed you, sweetheart," Mom says, pulling me into a hug. We only got back from France a couple of days ago, and honestly, I want to go back. Weeks of us being together with no outside influences was amazing. Reconnecting in the city of love.

"Remi, good to see you." Dad greets Remi with a firm handshake as his eyes flick suspiciously between us.

"Good to see you again, sir," Remi says.

"What's going on? You and your sister are freaking out the entire family." Dom steps out of the front door and greets us. But as soon as he sees Remi and I together, standing side by side, he groans. "You fucker. You promised." Dom storms out over to Remi and pushes him up against the car which makes the entire family yell at him.

"I love her," is all Remi says to him before my mom starts hyperventilating with delight. "And I'm sick of hiding it from you all."

"Oh my god, Nacho. They are in love. I told you it would happen one day. Oh my god, this is a blessing." Mom carries on. "Dom, take your hands off Remi. He's part of the family now."

Dom gives Remi one last brotherly glare before pulling him into a bro hug. "You break her heart, you're dead," he warns and walks away from Remi and up the front stairs.

"Welcome to the family, son," my dad says, giving Remi a smile and a nod. I can see the relief on Remi's face. Don't think he needs to worry about the shotgun anymore. He just got Dad's seal of approval. I take Remi's hand in mine and bring it to my lips.

"You're stuck with me, now," I say, grinning wildly.

"Wouldn't have it any other way," he says, staring at me hungrily.

"Later," I say, biting my lip.

"Gee, that went well," Portia says, following us inside. "Hope Mom and Dad are that happy when I tell them they are about to be grandparents."

I want to say that when we all sat down to finish our family meeting that everything worked out.

But that's my sister's story to tell.

THE END

ACKNOWLEDGMENTS

Thanks for finishing this book.
Really hope you enjoyed it.
Why not check out my other books.
Have a fantastic day !
Don't forget to leave a review.
Xoxo

SEDUCING THE DOCTOR

He wasn't supposed to be forever.
One night of passion with Miles Hartford was all it took to turn
my world upside down and change it forever. He was supposed
to be nothing more than a good time and a great memory.
Except those two pink lines say otherwise.

She wasn't who I thought she was.
That night she lied to me. She pretended to be someone else.
The thing is, I can't get her out of my head. I know it's wrong. I
know I shouldn't. I'm too old for her but now that I know the
truth all I can think about is rewriting that night.
Until she turns my life upside.

ABOUT THE AUTHOR

JA Low lives in the Australian Outback. When she's not writing steamy scenes and admiring hot cowboy's, she's tending to her husband and two sons, and dreaming up the next epic romance.

Come follow her

Facebook: www.facebook.com/jalowbooks
TikTok: www.tiktok.com/@jalowbooks
Instagram: www.instagram.com/jalowbooks
Pinterest: www.pinterest.com/jalowbooks
Website: www.jalowbooks.com
Goodreads: https://www.goodreads.com/author/show/ 14918059.J_A_Low
BookBub: https://www.bookbub.com/authors/ja-low

ABOUT THE AUTHOR

Come join JA Low's Block
www.facebook.com/groups/1682783088643205/

www.jalowbooks.com
jalowbooks@gmail.com

INTERCONNECTING SERIES

Reading order for interconnected characters.

Dirty Texas Series

Suddenly Dirty
Suddenly Together
Suddenly Bound
Suddenly Trouble
Suddenly Broken

Paradise Club Series
Paradise

Playboys of New York
Off Limits
Strictly Forbidden
The Merger
Without Warning

The Hartford Brother's Series
Tempting the Billionaire

ALSO BY JA LOW

The Dirty Texas Box Set

Five full length novels and Five Novellas included in the set.

One band. Five dirty talking rock stars and the women that bring them to their knees.

Suddenly Dirty

A workplace romance with your celebrity hall pass.

Suddenly Together

A best friend to lover's romance with the one man who's off limits.

Suddenly Bound

An opposites attract romance with family loyalty tested to its limits.

Suddenly Trouble

A brother's best friend romance with a twist.

Suddenly Broken

A friend's with benefits romance that takes a wild ride.

One little taste can't hurt; can it?

If you like your rock stars dirty talking, alpha's with hearts of gold this series is for you.

ALSO BY JA LOW

The Paradise Club Series

Book 1 - Paradise

Spin off from the Dirty Texas Series

My name's Nate Lewis, owner of The Paradise Club.

I can bring every little dirty fantasy you have ever dreamed of to reality.

My business is your pleasure. I'm good at it.

So good it's made me a wealthy and powerful man.

I have one rule—never mix business and pleasure, and I've lived by it from day one.

Until her.

** WARNING: If you do not like your books with a lot of heat then do not read this book. **

ALSO BY JA LOW

International Bad Boys Set

Standalone Books

Book 1 - The Sexy Stranger (Italian)

Book 2 - The Arrogant Artist (French)

Book 3 - The Hotshot Chef (Spanish)

INTERCONNECTING SERIES

Reading order for Interconnecting Series

Bratva Jewels Series

The Sexy Stranger

ALSO BY JA LOW

Bratva Jewels Duet Box Set

SAPPHIRE - BOOK 1

An unconventional love is tested to its limits.

Mateo is used to being in the spotlight, he craves it in everything he does . . . except when it comes to his love life - that is firmly in the closet.

Tomas shuns the spotlight, the one he was born into, he wants nothing to do with it or his high-flying family who now reject him for his choices in love.

But Tomas' and Mateo's carefully constructed lives are turned inside out when they discover a beautiful, battered woman on their doorstep. The woman with the sapphire eyes has no memory of who she is or how she got there. She doesn't know about the Bratva Jewels - the Russian mafia's most desired escorts - or how her story intersects with theirs. Can Tomas and Mateo help her remember before the men who are after her find her first?

DIAMOND - BOOK 2

Round 2 with the Devil begins.

Grace thought she had left the nightmare of the Bratva Jewels behind her. Her days spent as one of the Russian Mafia's most desired escorts were some of the darkest of her life, but she was safe now. Or so she thought.

When Russian mobster Dmitri seeks revenge, he gets it, and Grace knows she must call on every ounce of inner strength she has to withstand what he has in store for her. What she didn't expect was to meet someone like Maxim . . .

Maxim is one of the Bratva's most skilled, and most feared, assassins. But his relationship to the Bratva is a complicated one. And when he meets Grace, suddenly everything becomes clear.

Printed in Great Britain
by Amazon

21916511R00152